"A page-turning mystery and a deft exploration of the thorny intersection of marriage and parenthood and the complex, often fraught reality of new motherhood."
—Kimberly McCreight, author of *Friends Like These*

"Engagingly multifaceted—clearly Janie and Max are keeping bombshells from one another, but this is also a woman's cry for help, saying *You Should Have Told Me* how difficult motherhood would be."
—*Paste Magazine*

"There's so much to unpack in this taut, compelling thriller: new motherhood, a missing husband, a ton of secrets, all brilliantly written and plotted."
—Samantha Downing, author of *My Lovely Wife*

"An urgent, read-in-one-sitting story that asks when we should believe the worst about someone we love."
—Katie Gutierrez, author of *More Than You'll Ever Know*

"This gut-wrenching and breathlessly tense thriller perfectly captures the vulnerability, desperation, and helplessness of a new mother trapped in a nightmare scenario. Raw, unflinchingly honest, and emotionally compelling."
—Allie Reynolds, author of *Shiver*

"With breathless suspense and cliffhangers in nearly every chapter, Leah Konen has written a pitch-perfect thriller with a plot so propulsive the pages practically turn themselves."
—Megan Collins, author of *The Family Plot*

"Raw, brave, and gripping . . . Every chapter is more addictive than the last, leading to a stunning ending that you won't see coming."

—Samantha M. Bailey, author of
Watch Out for Her

PRAISE FOR *THE PERFECT ESCAPE*

"Konen knows how to write great dialogue and keep readers surprised. . . . Will make you wonder who your friends really are."
—*Albany Times Union*

"This page-turner will appeal. . . . Chilling."
—*Publishers Weekly*

"This twisty and increasingly disturbing story has a delicious, unhinged energy, hinting at all manner of suspects as the women's motives are gradually revealed to be even deeper—and perhaps darker—than they first seemed."
—*BookPage*

"With its eerie setting, unsettling plot, and shocking reveals, this book had me completely captivated from the first page to the very last."
—Megan Miranda, author of *Such a Quiet Place*

"Nobody writes twists like Leah Konen—this woman puts Hitchcock to shame. Thriller lovers: You need this book."
—Andrea Bartz, author of *We Were Never Here*

"A clever, locked-room mystery that is compulsively readable and impossible to put down!"

—Wendy Walker, author of *Don't Look for Me*

"*The Perfect Escape* is the type of captivating, masterfully constructed thriller you'll consume in a breathless rush— and then flip right back to the beginning to figure out how the author pulled it all off."

—Layne Fargo, author of *They Never Learn*

"Fans of Ruth Ware should run, not walk, to grab this twisty, shocking thriller about a girls' weekend from hell!"

—Halley Sutton, author of *The Lady Upstairs*

PRAISE FOR *ALL THE BROKEN PEOPLE*

"Skillfully captures the unnerving tensions that come with building your chosen family while never knowing quite who to trust."   —*Marie Claire*

"Even the biggest thriller fan will struggle to guess the ending of this twisty, gorgeously written debut."   —*Rolling Stone*

"Remarkably insidious. Extremely readable."

—Caroline Kepnes, author of *You*

"An assured and astonishing debut from an author destined to become a big name in thriller fiction."

—Sarah Pinborough, author of *Behind Her Eyes*

"A fast-paced, unputdownable roller-coaster of a read sure to appeal to fans of Gillian Flynn or Paula Hawkins."

—*Library Journal*

"A steady narrative draws the reader into Lucy's anxiety, and what might seem an implausible story is made believable by intricate plotting, culminating in a didn't-see-that-coming conclusion."

—*Booklist*

"Konen proves herself a master of weaving webs that slowly contract, strangling characters in the threads."

—*Kirkus Reviews*

"It's rare that a novel keeps me guessing until the very last page—but *All the Broken People* delivers in a big way."

—Sarah Pekkanen, coauthor of *The Wife Between Us*

"Leah Konen hits it out of the park. A sly, up-all-night thriller that ends with a surprising bang."

—Kimberly Belle, author of *Dear Wife*

KEEP YOUR FRIENDS CLOSE

LEAH KONEN

G. P. PUTNAM'S SONS
New York

PUTNAM
— EST. 1838 —

G. P. PUTNAM'S SONS
Publishers Since 1838
An imprint of Penguin Random House LLC
penguinrandomhouse.com

Library of Congress Cataloging-in-Publication Data

Names: Konen, Leah, author.
Title: Keep your friends close / Leah Konen.
Description: New York: G. P. Putnam's Sons, 2024.
Identifiers: LCCN 2023044743 (print) | LCCN 2023044744 (ebook) |
ISBN 9780593544723 (trade paperback) | ISBN 9780593544730 (ebook)
Subjects: LCGFT: Thrillers (Fiction). | Novels.
Classification: LCC PS3611.O58468 K44 2024 (print) |
LCC PS3611.O58468 (ebook) | DDC 813/.6—dc23/eng/20231013
LC record available at https://lccn.loc.gov/2023044743
LC ebook record available at https://lccn.loc.gov/2023044744

Printed in the United States of America
1st Printing

For all the friends who see us—
and love us—exactly as we are

KEEP
YOUR
FRIENDS
CLOSE

PROLOGUE

Red. All I could see was red.

On instinct, I tried the door, found it unlocked. I threw it open, stepped across the threshold.

Red was everywhere. Raked across the off-white walls. Caking onto all that original wood—an elaborate chair rail, an exposed-beam ceiling. Dripping, even, onto a tufted ottoman, a sheepskin throw. Droplets on an antique mirror. Splashed across all the décor added to make this place look cozy. A mounted Gibson guitar. Antique snowshoes. A topographical map of Esopus Creek. Red, destroying what would have been a picture-perfect image, something you could pin up in the windows of the real estate office in town. I stepped forward, pulse pounding in my ears.

What the hell is going on? What happened here?

My eyes focused, and I spotted the open paint can in the corner, the brush dipped inside.

It wasn't blood; it was paint.

And before me, scrawled in huge letters across the wall:

DIE RICH PIG

A break-in, of course. Another break-in. But what happened?

Was . . . was he here when it happened?

Oh god, oh god, oh god.

I turned to my right, but as I did, my toe caught on something soft and heavy, weighty and, and . . .

I fell forward, reaching out and scrambling to catch myself, my knees smashing against the hardwood floor, my hands barely breaking my fall. I struggled to push myself up, but once I did, I screamed.

Because there it was, red again.

But not paint this time. Blood. Spatters and splatters and splotches and pools.

And in the midst of the blood, a body.

PART ONE

PART ONE

1

NOW
SATURDAY, AUGUST 14
WOODSTOCK, NEW YORK

**If you came back now, you'd never have to worry
about losing him.**

Would you?

My soon-to-be-ex-husband's texts sent a tickle up my
spine, crawling like a spider, vertebra by vertebra,
until the feeling exploded down my shoulders,
making goose bumps rise in spite of the warm mountain air
breezing through the open window. Why was George talking like this now, after he and I had *finally* reached our tenta-
tive verbal agreement regarding custody of our two-year-old?

I flipped the notifications away and checked my latest
text from George's mom, Ruth, instead. There was little
Alex, happy and sandy, on the Haywoods' massive porch in
Montauk. Immediately, I felt that typical mother pull—the
desire for a little space from your kid at war with your primal

instinct to be hugging on them, wiping their boogers, and popping Cheerios into their tiny little mouths at all times. It was strange to be so far away from Alex for a whole week, like my left limb had been abandoned hundreds of miles away, but I knew it was necessary. I needed this time to get everything together.

I sent a heart-eyes emoji back to Ruth and set my phone on the rough-hewn wooden countertop, just as the bartender, a twenty-something woman with blunt-cut bangs, a septum piercing, and a wreath of ivy inked across her shoulder, put my plate before me.

"It's hot," she said as she pushed it an inch or so toward me. "Watch your fingers. Refill?" She pointed to my glass, empty apart from sudsy foam crawling up the side.

"Why not?" I smiled, and she traded one glass for another, which she filled from a tap behind her, then set another draught of amber-yellow liquid in front of me. The beer in question was a locally sourced Saison, hinted with citrus and low on alcohol content, my preference in the two years since I'd had Alex. My Sunday night margaritas with my former best friend, Willa—extra salt, no kids—had been my only real exception.

I took a sip, and the bartender ran a rag over each tap, then turned back to me. "You up here just for the weekend?"

"Oh," I said, setting my drink down. To this day, I still got nerves striking up a conversation with someone new, especially someone who seemed as cool and self-assured as this girl did, unless it was for a story and I had a notepad or a tape recorder in hand. "Er, the week, actually, but I just got in. I came straight here."

"Good choice," she said. She glanced around the place, a

bar-slash-café that was caught between the lunch and dinner rushes and empty apart from a guy reading the paper in the corner. "From the city?"

"Technically, yes," I said. "Brooklyn. But I'm actually originally from the Adirondacks area. Old Forge."

"Cool," she said. "I'm from around here, but I have a cousin up there. Bit of a different vibe, isn't it?"

"That's an understatement," I said with a laugh. "Feels like it's nothing but city people up here now."

"Right?" the girl said. "But hey, good for business, at least."

I smiled politely, then took a bite of my burger, topped with a fried egg. Yellow ooze ran down the side of the bun, and I wiped my finger with a napkin, just as the girl pushed an extra stack my way. Through the window, I took in the view of downtown Woodstock, a crunchy-chic mountain town smack-dab between the city and my hometown of Old Forge. Clear blue skies on top. A stretch of shops, selling everything from crystals to comfort shoes, on the bottom; the outline of the Catskill Mountains sandwiched in between. Most people saw something charming, a storybook—after all, even the name of Woodstock's main downtown strip was quaint—Tinker Street—as if a child with a set of wooden blocks and interlocking train tracks had made it up after their lunchtime nap. But for me, between the hippies and hipsters, tarot card readers and twee dog breeds, it was hard to see anything but the city, spreading its tendrils wide.

Even after years living there, I always felt like I had to be *on* in Brooklyn, and I feared Woodstock would be no different, but I didn't really have a choice—George would *never* let me take Alex back up to Old Forge, but he had finally agreed to let our son split his time between Brooklyn and here.

"You still have family up in the Adirondacks?" the bartender asked.

I chewed quickly, surprised she wanted to keep talking, but not unhappy about it. "My mom and sister," I said, picturing Mom in the lounge chair she'd reupholstered three times, her leg propped on a floral ottoman—she was homebound for the next six weeks with a severely broken ankle. I felt awful not being there to help her, but Rachel, my sister, was staying with her, at least. They were probably eating Craisins and watching bad reality TV right now, and my heart swelled. God, I missed them. My life with George had been so very different than theirs, and it had made it hard, sometimes, to truly connect. But all that was changing now.

"So what brought you down, then?" the bartender prompted. "Tired of peanut-shell-covered dive bars?"

"No," I said with a laugh. "I mean, don't get me wrong, the beer *is* better here and in the city, but I never really minded. I wanted to be a journalist. And at the time, to do that, you really had to move to the city."

"And did you do it? Become a journalist?" she asked, using a rag to work at a single errant stain on an otherwise immaculate bar top.

"I did," I said.

Her eyebrows shot up. "Have I read anything of yours?"

"Maybe," I said. "My biggest bylines were *The Atlantic*, *Forbes*. *Glamour*, when it used to be in print. But that was a while ago now . . . I got married, had a baby. It's been years since I wrote anything of substance, but I'm trying to get back to it."

The girl nodded. "So where's the fam now?"

"Oh," I said, caught off guard. "Well, I'm actually planning on moving here . . . er, with my son. That's why I'm up. My hus—" I paused, took a quick breath. "My soon-to-be-ex-husband, he's staying in the city, and my family, like I said, is up in Old Forge, but that's too far for me to take my son. Woodstock is close enough between the two places so our toddler can split time between both. So I'm here to see about securing a rental, getting a daycare spot, while my kid is with my in-laws for the week. It's tricky, working everything out like this, but I don't really have a choice."

I stopped talking, felt my face redden. I didn't want to overshare. Not again.

The girl only scratched at her ivy tattoo, apparently unalarmed by my info dump. "Soon-to-be-ex-husband," she said. "I've got one of those, too. Pain in my ass."

"Oh, you do?" She looked far too young to be married, much less have an ex. "But no kids, right?"

"No," she said. "Thank *god*." She bit her lip. "Sorry. It just seems messier. At least all we really had to fight about was the brand-new Xbox."

"It *is* messier," I said, skin prickling at the thought of George's texts. After my leaving in February and a spring spent dealing with George's threats to take Alex away from me, my ex had finally cooled down over the summer, agreeing to this Woodstock plan. The texts were nothing more than a last-ditch attempt to throw me. They *had* to be.

I looked down at my plate, popped a fry into my mouth. It still surprised me that I was up here at all. The downfall of my marriage had been slow, like a house that badly needs an update—cracks in the foundation, popped floorboards—but then fast, like said house had been struck by a hurricane, flooded beyond repair. And I'd been dealing with it all on my own. I felt awful complaining about my problems to my mom and Rachel, when they were always struggling with money and I was practically rolling in it; and my beloved sister-in-law, Cassandra, was no longer speaking to me. Only Willa had heard the whole of it, her warm demeanor, casual intimacy, and relative newness in my life like a port in the storm. I'd trusted her, told her all, and look how that had turned out. Hell, I probably should have just gotten a therapist.

From the outside, you'd never have guessed anything was wrong with George and me. We'd been *that* couple, always holding hands, always doing everything together. Morning oat-milk lattes, lunch at the French sandwich shop on Seventh, long walks around Prospect Park, meandering through the mossy-lush Vale of Cashmere on the north side. Retreating back into the brownstone on Prospect Park West, flicking on a thousand-dollar pendant lamp and sinking into an Eames Lounge Chair, the same one I'd seen once in the MoMA, when I'd used an expired student ID to get a discounted ticket. Heading to one function or another with his family, the Haywoods; his brother, Henry, and Henry's wife, Cassandra, by our side. Dressed to the nines, while the servers and bartenders and other have-nots did their best to blend into the scenery like pieces of silverware.

The sheen of glamour, of ease, to our entire relationship was the kind of sheen that only comes when money is absolutely no object at all. George was no finance guy bringing in low six figures or a landlord pushing people out of their apartments for a few hundred extra bucks in rent. He was from the kind of money that didn't have to think about it one bit. George headed up the Haywood family's nonprofit, providing micro loans to women from developing nations, leaving the less altruistic elements of the family business to Henry and his dad.

I'd been so lucky, I'd thought once. I had found the dream. A smart, generous man who could give me the world. Who could remove money completely from the equation of our lives. For a struggling journalist from Old Forge, for someone who was balancing state school loans with my share of rent in a modest apartment, even into my thirties, it was more than I could have *ever* hoped for. I'd fallen for all the glitz and glamour, oblivious then to the darker side of what that money can buy.

"So how old's your little guy?" the bartender asked.

I smiled. "His name's Alex. And he turned two in July. A total handful, but a sweet one." I pictured him with George's parents now, building his block towers and getting irrationally angry if anyone tried to offer him help. Anyone but George, that is. Alex used to build his blocks chaotically, shapes tilted every which way, like a miniature village spreading out, but now he only built straight up, like a tower, because George had insisted, over and over and over again, that that was the only proper way to do it.

"I have nieces and nephews," the bartender went on. "They're *definitely* a handful. The good thing is, he's young. My sister split with her first husband when her daughter was three, and the girl's super well-adjusted now. Loves her mom, loves her dad. Loves the stepmom and stepdad, too. My sister swears coparenting is better. You actually get some time off," she said with a laugh.

I forced a laugh, too, but even though George had finally agreed to something, this picture of coparenting still felt unattainable for us. Would he try to control us, even when he wasn't there? Would I relent when he made one demand or another about how to raise our son? Was little Alex bound to repeat our patterns? Either ruling with an iron fist, like George, or, even worse, becoming a pushover like me?

I didn't have an answer, but I had to at least try to break the cycle—for both of us.

"I'm Blaire, by the way," the bartender said, bringing me back to the present. "If you're soon to be a local, might as well know my name. I'm at this place just about always and, I know I'm biased, but it's the best food and beer in town."

"Mary," I said. "Nice to meet you."

For a moment, I felt that familiar thrill of meeting someone new, someone kind, someone who wanted to listen, a potential friend I could open up to. I let myself imagine it. Moving up here, coming to this café every weekend, when I didn't have Alex, drinking low-ABV beer while sunshine spilled through a window, making this new friend.

Then I pictured Willa the last time I'd seen her, back in June, at the spot that had become our go-to, the fairy lights casting a warm yellow glow across her icy-blond hair, a bit of salt on her bottom lip, sticking to the Yves Saint Laurent lipstick in classic red she always wore. Making me feel secure, comforted, like I mattered. Willa was my first genuine new friend since I'd become a mom, and that last night together, she'd been so earnest, insisting that she cared for me, that I could tell her anything.

But she didn't, and I couldn't. Her actions had proven as much.

I took another bite of my burger, and the bartender started wiping down the back counter, and I tried to focus on my goals for the week. In addition to setting everything up for Alex and me, I had an interview scheduled for Tuesday, a profile for *Forbes*, a female CEO who was working entirely out of a mountain house in the Catskills after spending two decades pounding the pavement every day in the city. It was part of a larger package on "the new face of the corporate world," and it was my first print piece since I'd stopped taking assignments to have Alex. It paid two dollars a word, and even though there were plenty more well-connected and well-bylined writers to assign it to, a former editor of mine—a bridge that hadn't been burned—had given it to me as a chance to "get back in the game."

I looked out the huge windows, watching Woodstock's residents and visitors walk by, mentally beginning to run through a list of topics to chat about with the "girl boss" of the moment . . .

I heard myself gasp before I felt it.

Willa was walking by. Right here in Woodstock. Her hair—shorter now, and brown—shining in the midday sun, a black leather tote slung over one shoulder, an extra-long, extra-yellow lace sundress kissing the stone sidewalk: my friend, my drinking buddy, my companion in bitching about how terrible the terrible twos were while our kids slid down the slides.

The woman who'd been my lifeline, who'd been there for me when I needed someone the most, who I'd thought, for a time, was my best friend.

How could I have been so wrong?

2

THEN
TUESDAY, APRIL 13
BROOKLYN, NEW YORK

The sodium won't kill him. Not for several decades, at least."

Young, gorgeous, and impeccably put together in a royal-blue jumpsuit and stick-straight platinum shoulder-length hair, the mother sitting next to me held a shiny bag of Lay's potato chips out like an offering.

Across the oversized sandbox of Prospect Park's Harmony Playground, another mother, this one dressed like she was about to go to yoga class, raised an eyebrow at us before handing her daughter a baggie full of cucumbers cut into the shapes of stars.

"Thank you, but I can't take your food," I said to the beautiful woman—god, imagine looking like that with a toddler running around. It was mid-April, two rocky months since I'd left George, since the bad had outweighed the good; the sky was overcast and gray, and I was more than a little depressed. I'd finally heard back from my sister-in-law, Cassandra, after I'd tried to reopen the lines of communication between us, given our new common ground. Her response had cut hard: *Fuck off, Mary. You had your chance and you blew it.* Alex had been begging all morning to go to the park, and I'd completely forgotten to bring snacks.

Now my son, oblivious to anything but the lure of salt, pawed at the bag in the woman's hand, making the cellophane crinkle.

"Alex," I said firmly, pushing his hand away. "Not ours."

"I hungry," he said pathetically, his cherub lips falling to a pout that could melt even the coldest of hearts. "Want puffies."

"Please." The mother smiled, showing off sparkling teeth that looked extra-white against bold red lipstick and high, prominent cheekbones. Around her neck hung a stone that looked like a real sapphire. "As long as you don't care, I don't, either. I mean, I *usually* bring something a bit more respectable like Veggie Straws, but it's salted carbs pretty much however you look at it. The kids can't get a coronary from one little bag, can they?"

I laughed out loud as Alex continued to paw. "I hungry," he said again. "I hungry."

"Well, thank you," I said, taking the bag from her and opening it quickly, pulling out a chip so greasy it was practically transparent. Alex snatched it before I had a chance to wipe the sand from his hand and plopped it into his mouth. "I really appreciate it."

"A true connoisseur," the mother said, looking lovingly at Alex. "You know, sand is one of Jack Junior's favorite condiments, as well."

Again, laughter. In two years, I don't think I'd ever laughed this hard with another mom. Typically it was just discussions of screen-time limits and which preschool would set them up on the right track for life.

The three of us adults—Gorgeous Potato Chip Mom, Healthy Snack Yoga Mom, and me—were the only people at the playground, apart from a group of older kids on the jungle gym across the way and a nanny talking on AirPods.

Across the sandbox, the little girl, tiny ankles crossed as if she were at high tea, finished the last of her star-shaped cucumbers and moved on to baby carrots.

"Really," I said again as Alex shoved chips into his mouth. "Thank you."

"Oh, please!" the woman said. "You'd do the same for me, wouldn't you? You seem like you would."

"I would," I said, because she was totally right. I was a people-pleaser through and through, a blessing and a curse. "And I usually am more prepared. Until a couple of months ago, we lived right across the street," I said, gesturing at the mammoth brownstones where George might be right now. I grabbed a baby wipe and did my best work on Alex's sandy hands. "We used to pop back home whenever he was hungry. But now we're in a place on the other side of the expressway, and I forgot I have to actually pack a snack. Bad mom alert."

"Oh, you're just the *worst*," the woman replied mischievously. "And if you're the worst, then I'm the *mega*-worst. I mean, I just gave your toddler potato chips. May the crusaders against childhood obesity strike me dead on the spot."

Once more I laughed hard, like an earnest college kid

watching their first improv show, and the yoga mom across from us raised a well-groomed eyebrow. "Childhood obesity really *is* an epidemic, you know," she said. "Come on, Mabel." She packed up her carrots and reached for her daughter's hand. "Let's get home for your nap."

I stared, slack-jawed, as she and her perfect toddler walked away.

Gorgeous Potato Chip Mom burst into guffawing laughter before the other lady was even out of earshot, her thick, chunky bangs practically dancing along her forehead. I joined her—and then Alex and the other boy did, too, his mess of blond curls shaking, the four of us laughing until our cheeks ached.

"Who shoved the baby carrot up her bony ass?" she asked.

"Right?" I said. "I mean, I try to give the benefit of the doubt, but that was legitimate mommy shaming, wasn't it?"

"The very definition!" the woman said. "And seriously, spare me. Jack, don't ever let someone tell you to stop eating chips. They're one of life's great delights, and I won't have you thinking otherwise."

The little boy grinned. I swiped Alex's hands again, getting off the last of the sand, and handed him another chip.

"I'm Willa," she said, flashing her smile again.

"Willa! Willa!" the little boy echoed.

She grinned. "I swear to god, that's all he'll call me these days."

"Mary," I said.

"Oh, I just *love* that name," Willa said.

"Really?" I asked. "It's pretty, you know, run-of-the-mill."

"Are you kidding?" she asked. "It's regal and powerful

and romantic and—" She lowered her voice. "Even a little *fucked up*; you know, did you ever watch that movie about Mary, Queen of Scots? Her life was just *wild*."

My eyes widened. She'd said it quietly, but still, she'd said it. *Fuck*. At the playground. Who was this person? And why was she so incredibly refreshing?

"And Alex is—" Willa went on. "Okay, let me guess—two?"

"In July," I said.

"Awesome," she said. "Jack's about to be three. Two is the best age, you know. So many emotions, so much intensity, but so much fun. I mean, who's cuter than you?" she asked, leaning toward Alex. "No one's cuter than you! Well," she went on, glancing to her own. "You and Jack can be tied, at least."

"Hi, Jack," I said, but the boy didn't look up, only worked at a bit of sand in his dump truck.

"Oh, you're nothing to him when a truck is in his hand." Willa rubbed at her bare arms, then slunk into a puffy jacket with *MONCLER* printed along one side, the exact sort of flashy thing that Cassandra would wear and George would abhor. "And you'll excuse my chattiness, but it can be hard to talk to other moms at the playground. I mean, *hello*, Ms. Lululemon and her perfect, veggie-munching daughter prove as much. It's refreshing, you know? To find someone who doesn't take it all so seriously."

I smiled, feeling a blush creeping to my cheeks. "'Refreshing' is exactly the word I would use, too."

A beat, and then Willa smiled. "You want to exchange numbers? Just because it's kind of hard to find a real connection at the playground. We can do a playdate or something?"

I didn't hesitate. "I'd love to."

. . .

That Saturday night, just four days after first meeting Willa, I was standing in front of the hall mirror, reapplying a coral lipstick and spritzing my wavy hair with the sea spray that was supposed to make it look like I'd emerged from the shores of Montauk. I glanced over my black Phillip Lim dress, one of the few designer wares that I hadn't yet sold on Facebook Marketplace or Poshmark for my lawyer fund. I heard a honk from down below, and I jumped, then rushed to the window to see a black town car approaching. Lord, I was nervous. I hadn't had a night out, not a real one, since I'd left George. Hell, I hadn't even gotten dressed up. I checked my reflection once again, slunk into a wool coat, and headed down the stairs as fast as my kitten heels would let me.

I opened the door to see Willa in the back, absolutely resplendent in a dress of head-to-toe sequins, a leather bomber jacket, and a tiny little crocodile-embossed Balenciaga purse, her sapphire necklace glimmering between her clavicles. "Mary, my dear!" she said. "Get in, get in. I'm so glad you could join me!"

"You look incredible," I said as I pulled the door shut behind me and the driver jerked forward, headed to the expressway that would take us toward the city.

"And so do you. Amazing what we look like when there's no sand or crumbs on us, right?"

I laughed. "Right."

"Anyway," Willa said as the driver made a sharp right turn. "You're the best for accepting my invite. I swear to god none of my other friends in the neighborhood can ever get a sitter. It's a Park Slope plague. And no, I will not give you the name of ours. I hoard her to myself like someone snatching toilet paper during the pandemic."

"Not a problem," I said with another laugh. I had known this woman less than a week, and I'd laughed with her more than I had with *anyone* since Cassandra. Then I took a deep breath, steadying myself. If we were going to be friends, it was bound to come out. "See, my husband, well, we're separated. He has Alex on the weekends. I don't get him until Monday afternoon."

To my surprise, Willa didn't go all serious, her eyebrows didn't knit up with pity, and she didn't look remotely shocked. "The benefits of separation!" she said with a laugh instead. "No sitters required!"

The glistening skyline of Manhattan, just across the East River, came into view, and the car cruised past brownstones and bodegas, construction scaffolding and stray cats. Willa's text had come just the day before, shortly after Alex's nanny arrived to pick him up and cart him back to the world of wealth for the weekend. I'd expected Willa to be asking to set up a playdate, but instead, she'd told me that Jack Senior had bailed on her for the opera, and she knew this was a bit crazy since we'd just met, but none of her other friends could join her and did I want to be her plus-one? I'd forced myself to wait a full five minutes before replying yes, not wanting to seem too eager, and now my face went hot just thinking about how long I'd spent digging through the closet of my temporary apartment for the right outfit, trying on different lipsticks and eyeliners to get a glamorous-but-not-trying-too-hard look.

Soon enough, we were in front of Lincoln Center. Strutting

past the fountain and under the building's fabulous archways. Across the red carpets, up the staircase, spiraling around like a seashell brought to life. Underneath the starburst chandeliers, ones I had always thought looked like mini solar systems. Sipping on oversized plastic glasses of pinot gris, ones Willa had insisted we stop to grab. And then the lights were dimming, and Willa was lifting a ridiculous pair of black-and-gold opera glasses to her eyes, and the first notes of Puccini's *La Bohème* were piercing the air. Through it all, I marveled at my good fortune. Wondered how in the world I'd gotten so lucky to meet this woman, whose energy filled the space as much as or more than the music did—and at the playground, no less. How quickly our worlds can turn, I thought. How strange that magic is waiting for you, tucked away in the most unexpected of places.

My heart was swelling and my veins were warm from the wine when the curtain closed for intermission. We were sitting stage left, and I glanced furtively toward the box seats up on the right, before I stood quickly, needing the bathroom, and made my way through the tightly packed seats and to the lobby before the rush hit. On the way back, I stopped at the concession stand, grabbed a pair of waters that cost as much as a full meal in Old Forge.

Slipping back into my seat, I handed Willa a water. "For you," I said. "A few sips here and there will prevent a headache in the morning."

"Mary, my dear," she said, the second time she'd said my name that way. "That's so sweet." She looked genuinely touched. "You're so thoughtful. Such a *mom*."

"I know," I laughed. "Guilty as charged. And old enough to get the most bitter hangovers. You'll see in a few years."

Willa smiled sweetly, and I was high on it all—the glamour, the pinot gris, the music that was about to return, and most of all, Willa and a sort of energy I found myself wanting so badly to be around . . .

But then I saw him, just as the lights were beginning to dim for the next act.

Henry, my brother-in-law, his silky black hair slicked back, a single lock askew on his forehead, a blonde who looked barely more than twenty-two hanging on his arm and giggling insufferably. The Haywoods had a box here. I knew that; I'd been a few times with George. But the fact hadn't been enough to sway me against Willa's invitation. Half the time they didn't use the seats anyway, gave them to friends or colleagues or people they wanted to impress.

Henry's steel-blue eyes caught mine, staring intently, disdainfully, just before the lights went fully dark, and my heart clenched, and I could see it all playing out: Henry calling George tonight, between pounding vodka or ranting on Twitter about his rental properties perpetually being vandalized. *Don't buy any of Mary's sob stories about being tight on cash; she was living it up at the opera tonight.* Even more than that, I wished I could talk to Cassandra about everything, knew I couldn't.

The Haywoods' box was empty again by the time the opera ended, and I was tipsy from the jumbo serving of wine. I stumbled into a cab alongside Willa, and we made our way back to the Slope, me wishing desperately that the night wouldn't end, Willa texting on her phone. It was only once we were back in the neighborhood that Willa looked up at me, pressing her ruby-red lips together: "Should we get a drink or something? It's not even that late, you know."

"Oh," I said, trying not to show my delight. "Yes. I mean, that sounds nice."

Like that, the car was stopping, and we were pouring into the Mexican-fusion place on Seventh Avenue. The back-yard was open, and fairy lights were twinkling, and soon a pair of mezcal margaritas—as well as waters, per my request—were before us, even the waiter seeming to be taken by Willa's beauty, her charm, the way her eyes lit up with wonder, almost like a child's.

Willa lifted her drink to mine, and she clinked it, loudly, salt rim to salt rim, then smiled conspiratorially. "I know it's got to be weird, I mean, accepting an invite from someone you've only met once, but I'm really glad we did this."

"Not weird at all," I said. "Nice to get out. Thank you so much for the tickets."

"Oh, please," Willa said. "To Jack Senior, they're noth-ing." She took a sip then, and her head bent forward. "But was everything okay tonight? You seemed a little bit ner-vous. Especially after intermission."

"Oh," I said. "Sorry. I didn't realize I was that obvious."

"Don't be sorry for having a feeling, Mary. I mean, that's what we tell our toddlers, right?"

"Right," I said, and I realized it then, just what was so special, so unique, about Willa. She didn't apologize for her existence. For taking up space in the world. For packing the wrong sorts of kid snacks. For having feelings. Hell, for say-ing *fuck* in front of my toddler. Maybe it put some people off, I'm sure it would many a woman—after all, Willa had said herself it was hard to connect with other moms—but to me, it was like a drink of water on a hot July day. Or that sensa-tion you get when your toddler finally goes to sleep and you

have two hours of freedom before crashing into bed and doing it all again in the morning. Relief.

I'd spent so many years feeling like I was never enough,
it was intoxicating to be around someone who seemed to
believe, beyond a doubt, that she was.

"But what was it?" Willa pressed. "I hope it's not something I did. When our friendship is off to such a fun start."

"Oh no," I said quickly. "Nothing to do with you at all.
Please, don't think that." I set my drink down, pushed it an
inch forward on the table. "I probably should have said
something when you invited me, but I thought it might not
even come up. See, my in-laws, well, my hopefully *ex*-in-laws,
they have a box at the Met. A lot of times they don't even use
it, so I was hoping no one would be there."

"Don't tell me," she said, fingering her necklace. "Your
estranged hubby was there?"

"No," I said. "But his brother was, Henry. He's a bit of a
dick, for one thing, and I know he's going to run back to
George, tell him I was living large when I've been complaining about money being tight. Seeing him sent me into a bit of
a tailspin."

"Yikes," Willa said. "I'm guessing he's taking George's
side in the separation, then?"

"Oh, that's more than a given," I said. "But it goes beyond
that. His wife, Cassandra, she was one of my best friends.
But last fall, she left Henry. And—" I hesitated, my eyes
moist. "And then she and I had a falling-out, too. Seeing
him, it brings all of that back."

Willa hesitated, then reached a hand across the table and
linked hers through mine. "That sounds so hard. I'm sorry."

I felt the warmth of her hand, the balminess in the air, the tequila already coursing through my veins. "Losing my best friend—and then having my marriage fall apart so quickly after, it was too much." I pulled my hand back, swiped at tears with a cocktail napkin. "Sorry," I said. "We just met, and I didn't mean to get all weepy. Must be the alcohol."

"No, it's okay," Willa said. "But have you reconnected with her? Now that you've left, too?"

"No, I've tried, but . . . the damage is done, I guess."

"That really sucks," Willa said, matter-of-fact. "And I get it, believe me. I had this roommate, when I first moved to the city. She meant everything to me, but she got in a relationship with a guy I didn't really care for, and it all came undone. I still miss her," Willa said, her lips pressing into a thin, tight line. "I still wish I could fix it all. See, I'm the kind of person who would do *anything* for my friends."

For a second, it almost looked like Willa was about to cry, too, but then she quickly lifted her drink. "Point is, it hurts, losing a girlfriend. It hurts in a way that no one really appreciates. I mean, like I said at the playground, it can be hard to connect with other women—for me, at least. But—" She shrugged. "Then a connection comes around, and it surprises you."

Willa took a quick sip. "Right, Mary, my dear?"

"Right," I said. "*Exactly* right."

3

NOW
SATURDAY, AUGUST 14
WOODSTOCK, NEW YORK

Willa walked quickly, purposefully—like a true New Yorker—across Woodstock's main drag.

I sat there, nearly frozen in place. Should I run out, call her name, beg her for answers? Or pretend like I never saw her, try to keep an ounce of my self-respect?

She kept walking, my butt still glued to the stool in indecision, and then she disappeared from view, the moment gone, my chance slipping through my fingers. I pushed my plate forward, asked for the check.

The bartender raised an eyebrow. "Food okay?"

"Yes," I said. "I'll take a box for the rest, please."

By the time I was outside, Willa was nowhere to be seen, but I turned right anyway, heading in her direction, my brain running in familiar circles. What if Willa hadn't meant to ditch me at all? What if she'd lost her phone, lost any way to contact me? What if there were reasons she'd stopped responding, and they had nothing to do with the secrets I'd shared? What if she, Jack Senior, and Jack Junior had needed to move, spur of the moment, for some reason? Well-off people were always doing things like that, especially this time of year. Jetting off to Mexico. Summering in Sweden. And we'd only really been friends for two months when she ghosted me. She was saved in my phone as Willa Playground.

Face it. The logical side of me fought back. *She ditched you. She had your name, your number, she could have found you on one social network or another. Hell, she could have pulled up the contact form on your journalism website. She heard what you had to say and decided she was done with you. She made that abundantly clear.*

I wandered down the stone sidewalk, past a candle boutique and a bakery, a mom-and-pop hardware store, and a toy shop that looked like it hadn't changed much in the last fifty years or so. At the corner, I paused in front of a sign that said *Flea Market Every Saturday, Noon to Four*, debating whether label-loving Willa would ever wander a flea market.

My phone buzzed, and I pulled it from my purse, naively hoping it was Willa. An email instead—from my lawyer's paralegal.

Dear Mrs. Haywood,

Apologies for the delay, but Ron and I were both out of the office yesterday. The firm has received initial paperwork from Mr. Haywood's team. Please review it in the client portal. Ron would like to set up a call to confer at your convenience early next week. Please send me your availability Monday or Tuesday.

Immediately, I tapped out of my email and into a web browser, cueing up the firm's portal. I was met with a spinning wheel; the page wouldn't load. I glanced at the top of my phone. My service was shit. Fine for checking email, but the lawyer's site had always been a bit finicky. I needed Wi-Fi. I wasn't able to check in to my rental until four p.m., which gave me another thirty minutes to kill. Reluctantly, I flagged the email as important and slipped my phone back into my purse, making for the flea market instead. The paperwork should reflect what George and I had agreed: I'd have Alex Monday through Friday in Woodstock, take the train across the river in Rhinebeck down on Fridays and meet the nanny or George in Grand Central. Do the same on Monday mornings. The prenup ensured I wouldn't get any real money, but between alimony and child support—and hopefully, more and more two-dollars-a-word assignments— I'd have enough to get us a nice place, maybe even with a third bedroom for my mom or Rachel to stay in once my mom was mobile again. After all the drama, I couldn't believe that something might actually work out.

I was approaching a table of cast-iron molds when my heart leapt at the sight of her. Willa, emerging from around the corner, walking toward a stand of framed old posters, only a few yards ahead. This was my chance. I walked forward, my heart still in my throat, until I was a couple of feet behind her, then cleared my throat. "Willa."

Nothing.

"Willa," I said, louder this time, but she still didn't move. I reached out then, touched her shoulder. "Willa."

She finally turned, but her face was blank and cold— stoic. "Can I help you?"

"What are you talking about?" I asked. "I'm saying hello."

"I'm sorry," Willa said. She took a quick, sharp breath. "But I don't know who you are."

I stared at her, dumbfounded. "You're going to pretend you don't even know me?" I asked. "Is this about what I . . . well, you know. What I texted?"

"I can see you're upset," she said, her voice thin and calm. "But I think you have me confused with someone else."

My jaw dropped. It actually did. "Really? How can you pretend you don't—"

My words were swallowed by the squeal of a little girl, running from behind the next table, tugging on Willa's bright yellow sundress. "Carry me, Annie, carry me."

"Come here, sweetie," Willa said, lifting the girl.

"Where's Jack?" I asked, looking around, my heart beating fast. "Where's your son? Willa, it's *me*. I get it, you don't want to be friends with me anymore, but please. Stop the charade."

Willa pulled the girl closer to her, stroked the back of her head familiarly. "I really am sorry for any confusion, but my name is not Willa."

"It's Annie!" the girl proclaimed cheerfully.

"But—"

"Can we go get ice cream?" the girl asked. "You promised ice cream."

Willa's head whipped back and forth, as if looking for someone, before settling on the child. "Yes, baby, we'll go right now."

She started to turn, but I reached out and grabbed her arm, desperate now. "Why are you doing this?"

She shook me off, and she pulled the girl closer. "Please,"

she said. "Please just leave us alone. I've already told you. You must have me confused with someone else."

I stepped back. I felt like either I was crazy or she was. Her voice, even her posture; it was Willa's, had to be. But as I stared at her, taking her in, I wondered. The resemblance was uncanny, even down to her thin, graceful hands, but then again, this woman *did* have shorter hair than Willa, she did have *darker* hair than Willa—brunette rather than blond. And her clothes were wrong, too. I looked closer— her lacy sundress wasn't designer at all, more like something you'd pick up at H&M.

The Willa I knew wouldn't be caught dead in something so cheap.

Was it really possible that it wasn't her?

"I'm . . . I'm sorry," I stammered, taking another step back. "I'm sorry to bother you."

"It's okay, really," the woman said. "It's fine."

As she turned, the Catskill light caught her profile just so.

There, beneath the lace, I could see it, shimmering like only a real stone could—a glint of brilliant royal blue.

Willa's sapphire necklace.

4

Willa fingered the necklace, her nail tracing the edges of the cushion-cut sapphire, while Jack and Alex chased each other up the steps and pathways that led to the double slide, both of them delighting in the lovely late-May weather. The two had taken to going down together, hand in hand.

It was six weeks since we'd met, but the opera night had cemented our friendship. The intervening weeks had been filled with frequent playground playdates and near-weekly margarita nights. Willa and I had talked about anything and everything—our favorite TV shows; the best bars and restaurants in the neighborhood, most of which I hadn't even been to since leaving George; my career as a journalist; how Willa really wanted to write something, some day. I'd complained about the way Alex always tried to push back bedtime, and she'd shared Jack Junior's hesitance to eat any dinner food besides mac and cheese and chicken nuggets. I'd bitched about my apartment situation, a unit that the Haywoods owned and George was letting me stay in for free, but that was so temporary it felt like anything but home. She complained, as all well-off people do at some point, that her home was full of contractors installing some state-of-the-art security system, which Willa thought was overdone and I'd agreed, telling her that one of the few things George and I had seen eye to eye on was that there was little better than a strong deadbolt and a good old-fashioned chain lock.

In all those meetups, I'd never once inquired about the quite-large rock around her neck, which she was never without. "Family heirloom?" I asked now, nodding to the necklace. "It's beautiful."

Willa's hand left the gem, as if it had suddenly turned hot. "This? God, I wish! My family could never afford anything like it. The height of our heirlooms were knitted afghans in awful beige and mauve—you know, the kind that do nothing but attract cat hair and lint. My mom was honest-to-God *horrified* when I told her I didn't want to learn to knit."

I laughed. "My mom never knitted, but she's really into quilting and embroidery. She has this old Singer. George even insisted we buy her a new one a couple Christmases ago, this top-of-the-line machine he found from Japan. She was really gracious about it, of course, but I know she never uses it. The Singer prevails."

"Of course it does," Willa said. "Boomers don't like to change their routines, you know. You ever take up the art of sewing?"

"No," I said. "I mean, I tried, but I was never as good as my mom. She made us all sorts of things. And she got rid of nothing. She still has half my baby things." I hesitated, then forged ahead. "When Alex was born, she took my old baby blanket, restored it, rehemmed the edges, and embroidered his initials onto it." I sighed. "He loved that thing."

"I'm sure," Willa said. "Does he still sleep with it?"

"No," I said, the memory cutting deep. "He's moved on to something newer, more expensive."

Willa guffawed. "A New York City child, of course he has!"

I leaned back, stretching my legs into the triangle of sun on the edge of our shady benches, then sat up straighter as I saw Alex rushing across one of the playground's bridges. "Slow down, Al," I said as Alex bounded after Jack.

"Jack-Jack, make sure you keep Alex's pace. He's smaller than you, you know, and younger," Willa said. "When is Alex's birthday again?"

"July fifteenth," I said.

"Coming up," she said. "How exciting."

"Hardly," I said. "George's family is going to do this big thing, and it's been made clear to me that I am absolutely not welcome so long as we remain separated."

"Yikes," Willa said. "So much for coparenting loyalty."

"I wish," I said. "George's loyalty begins and ends with the Haywoods."

"We should do something together, then," Willa said casually, breaking my train of thought. "Just us and the boys. I'll raid the dollar store for the most vile and garish *Paw Patrol* decorations. And bubble wands that will spill sticky stuff all over us. Add Doritos, and you've got a party—right?" She called up ahead. "Seriously, Jack, ease up."

The two slowed down briefly, as my heart warmed at the thought of spending Alex's birthday just like this, covered in Dorito dust and holding doggie balloons. I stretched my legs farther into the sun, and the sapphire caught the light again.

"Okay, back to the necklace," I said. "I hate to obsess, but I really am curious. Was it a gift from Jack Senior? George has the money, but he never got me anything eye-catching like that. He thought even the plain Cartier Love bracelet, which my sister-in-law had in droves, was too flashy."

"Jewelry doesn't only come from men, Mary," Willa said, faux-chastising me. "No, this one I got on my own, like a bona fide *independent woman*." She launched into a quick, off-key rendition of Destiny's Child. "Seriously, though. I had a tricky time leaving my hometown, and my ex back there, and I wanted to commemorate my freedom. I mean, it was either that or dye my hair, right, and you know blondes have more fun. I bought the damn thing on a credit card, and it nearly maxed it out, but I'm glad I did," Willa said with a smirk. "The thing about coming into money, marrying or dating into it, is that, end of the day, you're always at someone else's mercy. You're never fully in charge of your own path. And especially if you're a woman—most of our contributions go unpaid, after all. Anyway, I'm glad I have something, something I can wear every day, that reminds me that I can make my own luck, too. And maybe my little pot will never be as big and full as Jack Senior's, but it's mine."

She was right. I married into money and didn't protect myself. I didn't outright quit my job, like Cassandra, but I pitched and took on fewer and fewer writing assignments, and then I all but stopped when Alex was born. It left George holding the reins—always. He managed the joint bank account, he had eyes, at least, on my personal account, and he was in charge of all the real wealth, as well. Stuff that was tied up in trusts, accounts I never even saw. Which had been all well and fine when I was in his good graces, when I was being exactly who he wanted me to be.

Not so much now that I wasn't.

"I wish I had that sort of confidence," I said. "I wish I'd planned everything out a bit better."

Willa looked at me, eyes serious now. "Don't beat yourself up, Mary," she said. "It's not like a damn necklace can pay the rent anyway. Well, not one of this caliber, at least. Hell, if things blew up with me and Jack Senior, I'd be in the exact same spot as you. Probably having to take a bus back to—" She stopped.

"To where?" I asked.

"My awful hometown," she said with a laugh. "You know, Bumfuck, USA."

"Oh," I said, but I didn't press her for anything more. The thing about Willa was that she didn't often volunteer details about her past. You had to lure them out of her, like an asphalt-breaking excavator, the ones Alex adored spotting in the street so much. There was something nice, almost enchanting, in the mystery of Willa. It made me feel like there would always be more to learn, like the drinks nights and playdates would never, ever end, like I didn't have to worry about losing her—at least, not yet.

It all felt like promise, like possibility, and when it was

like this with her, the sun on our bare legs and our children playing together so happily . . .

It almost felt like falling in love.

We stayed in the playground for nearly three hours, until Willa insisted she get Jack back for a nap. At the park entrance, she wrapped me in a hug and play-kissed me on each cheek, as was her way. "See you around, Mary, my dear."

I watched until she was out of sight, and then, with Alex asleep in the stroller, I took a sharp right, straight up Prospect Park West. George should be at work now, and there were a pair of dresses and a blazer that I'd noticed were missing from my temporary apartment's closet. Willa had looked fabulous at our last drinks night, and I wanted to step it up the next time we met up.

In a few blocks, I was back in front of the brownstone. It was as classic as they come, complete with that sumptuous cafe-au-lait coloring, curved windows, and a stoop that was made for sitting. The front steps were packed with pots of flowers, ornate millwork surrounded a circular window in the center, and an Art Deco relief cut a pattern in the first story.

But the best part, the only one that was truly all mine, was the door, painted a brilliant candy-colored coral red— Farrow & Ball Lake Red, to be precise. I'd spent a month mulling it over and another month convincing George to let me go for it, since all decisions—decorating, parenting, shopping, socializing and otherwise—had to be approved by him. Eventually, he'd come around, after I'd shown him a stunning row house in Georgetown I'd found featured in the *Wall Street Journal*, sporting the exact color door I wanted. George had said we could hire the job out, but I'd painted it myself instead. My mom was a DIY queen when we were growing up, and even though I'd never gotten too much into it, I wanted to send her a photo, show her that the well-off Brooklyn girl could still get her hands dirty. The sticky latex paint had even gotten in my hair, took two full weeks to fully come out, my sister telling me to put on something to protect my locks next time, but I'd worn the red striations proudly, a job well done.

I glanced up and down the street, then made a quick decision. Carefully as I could, I pulled Alex's stroller backward up the brownstone steps, past the lockbox that the nanny used to get in, fished in my purse for my key ring, and slipped the key in the lock. It turned easily—George hadn't changed the locks—and I backed through the front door and into the vestibule. Out of habit, I slipped off my sandals and left them in the front, then parked the stroller in the middle of the expansive living room, Alex mercifully still asleep.

Everything was just as I'd left it. Immaculately cleaned and organized, as George required. Family portraits—all of us in crisp white linen—still adorning the original mantel. The shaggy woolen rug I'd loved so much cozy beneath my toes.

I headed up the stairs, glancing at Alex's room. The room was a darling seafoam green, surrounded by shelves of books and wooden Montessori toys, a gauzy canopy for reading and cuddling in one corner, one where I'd sung Alex "Twinkle, Twinkle, Little Star" more times than I could count. I'd put my heart and soul into making this room with the Haywood-approved family decorator, and I missed it so. The second bedroom of my current apartment, the one George was letting me stay in gratis since he claimed we would soon find a way to "work all this drama out," was little more than an eight-by-eight-foot box, barely holding more than a crib. This, on the other hand, was the place I used to spend hours with Alex. A dream spot, for a child, for a mother.

I perused the bookshelves and grabbed a few I knew Alex loved. George hardly read to him—if anyone would notice one missing, it was Genevieve, the nanny, who loved to read to Alex in a range of adorable voices. Then I grabbed a fox stuffie my mom had sent him and a puzzle that had come from Rachel.

At the door, I turned back, thinking of the text I'd gotten from George only yesterday.

Come on, Mary. Enough with the theatrics. Just come back, and we can be a family again.

My heart ached for how much a part of me wanted to. But then my eyes caught the crib, saw the expensive blanket where the one my mother had so lovingly crafted should have been, and I knew there was nothing to come back to.

What I'd thought I'd had with George had been little more than an illusion. I, a Stepford robot that George could control. One he could punish if need be. And Alex, taking this dynamic in. I'll never forget the way my toddler looked at me one morning and said, "Enough, Mary." The words came out in a garbled toddler mess—"ee-nuh may-ree"—but the tone was somehow pitch-perfect, and I knew their meaning, believe me. They were the same words George said to me anytime I pushed back. *Enough! Enough! Enough!* Like I was a child, a dog, a ward to be taught how to act properly.

God damn it if I was going to let my son grow up to think that all of this was okay.

I moved on, making my way to our bedroom. From the looks of it, nothing was amiss. No condom wrappers on the nightstand, no evidence that the place had been converted into some sort of seedy bachelor pad. I moved to the closet, found my side mostly empty, spotted the two dresses and the sought-after blazer in dry cleaner bags. I grabbed the trio, then walked back to the main room.

The bed stared at me, one where George and I had shared so many moments. Where we'd conceived Alex. Where we'd slept in late on Sunday mornings. Where I'd jotted early memories of my son into the journal I kept just for him. Where George and I had argued about Cassandra and Henry, terse and quiet so as not to wake Alex.

Cassandra. Shame shot through me, and then I had to check, to see if George still had it all. I chucked the clothes and books in the middle of the bed and went around to his side. I slid the painting aside and keyed in the code to the wall safe's combination. It worked.

The door of the safe opened quietly, and in the front I found a single stack of bills and George's passport. Mine and Alex's were with me, I'd made sure of that when I left. I pushed aside papers—life insurance policies, bonds—and reached all the way back, until my hands hit a velvet bag. Carefully, I pulled it out, slowly opened the drawstring. There it was, just as I'd seen it months before. Gold and platinum, diamonds and pearls, glitz and glamour and so, so much money. Willa had joked that a necklace couldn't pay the rent, but these pieces could—and then some.

I fingered one of the bracelets on top, ran my hand along the pure yellow gold, the inset diamonds . . .

What if I just . . . took it all? What if I did the right thing?

Then I thought of the second text George had sent me yesterday.

You seem to think that joint custody is a given here, but if you don't come back, believe me, it's not. There are ways around these things.

If the jewelry disappeared, George would know it was me.

Then he'd take Alex. He'd take him just to spite me. He'd sic his lawyers on me, take away the one person I loved most, if only to show me he could.

I heard a cry then—Alex must be waking up—and quick as I could, I pulled the drawstring of the bag, shoved it back to where I'd found it, slammed the safe shut, righted the painting, and grabbed the clothes and books and toys.

Alex was my first priority. He had to be.

Besides, a child couldn't ever compare to a bracelet, no matter how much money it could bring her if she sold it. Sorry, Cassandra.

I got off Prospect Park West as quickly as I could, placating Alex with a pack of Veggie Straws that Willa had given him as we headed home. I walked quickly past building after building, and then I froze, because there she was, walking toward me.

"Cassandra," I said, the word practically spilling from my mouth. I stopped the stroller on instinct, and in spite of everything I felt a warmth swimming through my veins, because it had been so many months since I'd seen her, and she had been my best friend, and I missed her terribly. Half of me wanted to hug her, and I let go of the stroller, almost thought I would, but her cinched-up shoulders, the firm line of her mouth, immediately made it clear: that was nothing more than a fantasy.

"Mary," she said, disdain in her voice. She looked down to Alex, and a softness entered her eyes, if only for a moment. "Hey, bud."

Alex ignored her, reaching only for more crunchies.

"I . . . I thought you were back in Pennsylvania," I stammered. Her wavy dark brown hair was brassy at the top, where I knew she covered her gray, and her ends looked overgrown and split, her hair nearly down to her elbows. No more three-hundred-dollar haircuts from Étoile, the Haywoods' stylist, that much was evident. She had a pimple beneath her chin, and I guessed she didn't get facials anymore, either. Still, she looked so very beautiful, as she always did, with her pouty lips, her wide, curious eyes, and her long, graceful limbs.

"I am," Cassandra said. "I'm just visiting. My lawyer is nearby."

"Is the divorce . . . is it getting finalized?"

"Only if I let the Haywoods royally fuck me over, which I'm trying my best not to."

"I'm sorry," I said, my words falling flat, half-absorbed by a garbage truck speeding down the avenue.

Cassandra tucked a bit of hair behind her ear, and suddenly, I saw her, at that party at Cipriani's downtown, in a gold dress perfectly tailored, making the same gesture before reaching out for a dirty martini—extra dirty, extra olives—just like she loved it. Leaning toward me: *I may be wearing a two-thousand-dollar dress but I'm still the Pennsylvania girl who likes it dirty.* The way I'd struggled not to spit out my own drink I was cackling so much. Cassandra and I were always laughing at those things, with everyone so formal and buttoned up around us.

Now, she let her hand fall back down to her side, her wrist empty. It wasn't even like she wanted the jewelry to *wear* it. She needed money, and desperately, because Henry was taking it all. She'd given up her career for him. Her parents had nothing. She was screwed—no safety net—she'd explained it to me so many times.

"Are you?" Cassandra asked finally.

"What?"

"Are you sorry?" Cassandra clarified, crossing her arms in front of her. "Because if you were, you would help me."

My face went hot, and I didn't know what to say. Alex dropped his snack bag on the ground, and I knelt to pick it up, return it to his hands, the distraction welcome.

"I don't even know . . ." I was going to say I didn't even know if George had her jewelry, like I'd told her before, but my voice trailed off, because the lie felt even more horrible now that I'd seen it all, only moments ago.

Cassandra raised an eyebrow. "I can see that things haven't changed, then, even now that you've left him."

"No, I—" I started, but how could I explain it? That I had argued her side, over and over and over, that all that had gone down between her and Henry had turned into the wedge that dug into my marriage, exposing—widening— the cracks that were already there? That I wanted nothing more than to help her but I was too scared to go up against the Haywoods and all their power.

"I have more to lose than money," I said. It was harsh, because I knew Cassandra had wanted kids, too, and if Henry could only have gotten his drunken, cheating act together, maybe she would have had them. "I can't risk pissing off the Haywoods any more than I already have. I love you," I said. "I miss you, and I know it's shitty, and I know it's not right, but George could take Alex from me."

Cassandra took a step away from me. "There's always a reason to let them win," she said.

She walked past, but after a few more steps, my old best friend turned back, the afternoon light catching her hazel eyes, making them shine with a look that was almost manic. "Maybe you'll be lucky," Cassandra said. "Maybe they'll be kinder to you than they're being to me. Maybe they'll actually give you something to start your new life with."

Then she shook her head, and her eyes looked awfully, unbearably sad.

"But who am I kidding? We know they won't."

5

NOW
SATURDAY, AUGUST 14
WOODSTOCK, NEW YORK

I pulled up to the rental just after four p.m., found a spot on the street, and grabbed my purse, leaving the rest of my bags in the trunk, Willa's sparkling sapphire flashing in my mind like a strobe light. It *had* been her, hadn't it? It looked just like her, and the necklace confirmed it, so why had she acted so strangely? And who was that little girl? Where was Jack?

I approached my home for the week, a yellow clapboard-siding bungalow, only a few blocks off Tinker Street, and situated at the end of a lush, sidewalked road with overgrown trees. I reached for the gate, lifted a rusty latch, and walked down the stone pathway, trimmed with flowers. I stepped onto the porch, creaky and squeaky in a way that Alex would love, then knelt in front of the lockbox. I tapped into my email and opened the message from the rental agency, scanning it quickly for the code. I punched it in, pulled the tab down to find a single key, and opened the door.

I dropped my bags and was about to return to the car, when I was hit with two texts from George.

We're a good match, Mary. And Alex deserves to grow up with his family intact.

I love you. I always will.

My stomach clenched as I swiped the notifications away. Why was George doing this, now? When things were finally starting to settle between us, after so much intensity, after so many threats, after my own mind went places I never, ever thought it would?

Sometimes I wish . . .

Was he changing his mind about our agreement? Would he, really? But then why not just tell me? George had never had problems being direct.

No, I thought. This is finally about to work out.

I walked through, giving the rooms a quick once-over. The place was small, with a cozy living space, overstuffed chairs and a sofa surrounding a cast-iron woodstove, an eat-in kitchen, where I glimpsed lacquer-red cabinets and checkerboard floor tiles; and a bedroom that looked out on the overgrown front yard. It would do just fine for the week. The place even smelled pleasant, sweet and floral and somehow almost . . . familiar.

I headed back out to the front—I still had two bags in the car—and was tapping the button to unlock the trunk when I saw a man in a crisp navy linen blazer walking quickly down the street, toward my rental. Something about him looked familiar, from the cut of the blazer to his impressive height to his steel-blue eyes—

"Henry?"

My brother-in-law jumped, his face reddening, as if somehow caught out. I hadn't seen him in the flesh since that night at the opera with Willa, back in April.

"What are you doing in Woodstock?" I asked.

His shoulders relaxed, and the color drained slightly from his face. The cool, collected Henry—the one you saw when he wasn't on a drinking bender—seemed to come back. "I've got a place here. Just up the block and around the corner. Doing renovations."

"You do?" I asked. "George never said."

"Well, it's not George's," he said. "It's *mine*." The Haywoods had places seemingly everywhere, and Henry's portfolio was especially deep. He loved to flip and rent for unmentionable sums, like it was all just a game. A game I'd always felt queasy about.

Now the thought chilled me a bit, that even here, I wouldn't be away from the Haywoods' power, their pull. Worse, it felt like something George should have mentioned the moment I told him I was planning on moving here.

"Got some vandalism to clean up here?" I asked, trying to gain back a firm footing. Over the past six months, there'd been a streak of break-ins at Haywood properties in the tristate area, all complete with what I thought was hilarious graffiti—*EAT THE RICH, FUCK THE ONE PERCENT,* and *WORKERS UNITE.* Henry was so much more shameless about money than George had ever been, would argue with socialist-leaning politicians and organizers on Twitter and fully embrace his capitalist-bro personality, to the horror of his parents, who made substantial donations to Democrats up and down the ballot and had a photo with Obama framed on their carved-marble mantel. We all blamed the spate of recent break-ins on Henry's antics, the graffiti so pointed, as if only there to troll him.

Henry's face reddened and he briefly bit his lip. He raised an eyebrow in slight disdain. "No, actually. But you know local contractors. Seems they can't do much of anything without supervision."

Henry was always saying shitty stuff like that. I hardly knew how Cassandra stood it for as long as she did.

"What are *you* doing here?" he asked, then immediately smirked. "Oh, right. George told me. Your little *week on your own*."

Anger boiled in my insides, and I wanted to barb right back, but telling Henry what I really thought of him wouldn't help one lick in getting George to continue to play nice. The two had always had a bit of a sibling rivalry, but when push came to shove, they stuck together—what they'd done to Cassandra proved as much. I nodded to the car instead. "I have to get the rest of my bags."

"You need some help?"

"No," I said firmly. "I'm fine."

Henry stared at me a moment. "George won't let you go this easy, you know."

The truth, the history, all that had transpired between Henry and Cassandra hung between us. I hated Henry. I really did.

"That's between me and George. Now, if you'll excuse me." I pushed past him and walked toward the trunk.

"I'll be seeing you, Mary," Henry said. "Do take care."

He headed down the road, and I didn't say another word, just opened the trunk and stared at my bags, my heart pounding against my ribs. I sang "Twinkle, Twinkle, Little Star" three times in my head before I let myself look up to make sure Henry was out of sight.

Street clear, I pulled the bags out and shut the trunk so hard I thought it might dent it, then lugged them up the walk, slamming the front door behind me and locking it tight.

I headed to the kitchen, suddenly desperate for a glass of water, and stopped short in front of a small round table tucked into the corner, nestled between two windows.

Freesia. So *that* was the smell that had seemed so familiar.

It was my favorite flower, purple and white with hints of yellow. Fruity and sweet, like fresh strawberries, a summer day. We'd had bunches and bunches of them, tucked in among hydrangeas and orchids, at our wedding at the New York Public Library. And George, no matter what sort of bouquet he got me, always managed to procure a few sprigs of freesia as well, even if they weren't the easiest to find. He even teased me that they were a silly flower to love, the sort that gets used to make mall fragrances for middle school girls.

The flowers were perched, rather perfectly, in a simple gray vase.

My heart beat a bit quicker. Could he—would he—have sent Henry in here to do his bidding? Tasked his brother with arranging these flowers, as what, some sort of . . . plea . . . or promise . . .

Then why would Henry have walked down this block, giving himself away?

Still, the thought nagged at me. George believed he could

buy anything, always said that there was a price, you just had to find it. Was he trying to find mine now, see if I would sell myself—change my mind—just because my favorite flowers were in the kitchen? As if that could even begin to make everything else right.

In front of the flowers was a notecard, in loopy writing that looked like a woman's.

Welcome to our home, have a wonderful stay!

My heartbeats slowed down. It was just a friendly welcome. It had nothing to do with Henry or George.

And then, as if he could somehow hear me thinking of him, miles and miles away, my phone buzzed again with more texts from George.

You know we'll find our way back to each other, in the end.

We always do.

6

Georgia thinks that everything in the world has a price," I said. "And you just have to find it."

Willa and I were walking the loop that circled the park, and Alex was comfy in his stroller, eyelids heavy, finger twirling the hair at the nape of his neck like he did when he was about to drift off, while little Jack zoomed ahead on his scooter, Willa's eyes trained on him. It was a sunny day in early June, and we'd spent the last hour at the playground, watching the kids battle dump trucks in the sandbox. The place had been hopping, in that way Brooklyn playgrounds are when the weather's nice. It was a microcosm of the world we moved in: working moms and dads on their phones, surrounded by bubble machines, scooters, and sidewalk chalk. The stay-at-homes—all friends—with their wooden toys, organic blueberries, and yoga wear. The nannies doing their own thing, camped out in a corner with the toddler potties set out, Caribbean accents thick, and the kids with them much better-behaved than the ones with their parents.

"Why am I not surprised?" Willa said matter-of-factly. She glanced behind us, then tugged her designer trench tighter and called up ahead at Jack to slow down, a peloton of cyclists zooming by us.

I spotted a bit of dog poop right in Willa's path, and I grabbed her elbow, pulling her quickly out of the way.

"You're the best, Mary," she said. "*Really*. Miss Eagle Eyes. These shoes are new, too." She gestured to her pristine white Reeboks. "And I never look where I'm going, do I?"

Willa was always beelining straight for a pothole or a piece of errant trash. It wasn't the first time I'd redirected her path. "No, you don't," I laughed. "Not unless it's a safety thing, like helping Jack cross the street."

"Well, that's why I have you." Willa picked up the pace then, and I pushed the stroller faster to match her. "How old is George, by the way?" she asked.

"Forty-two," I said. "Why?"

"I think that mindset is always there for rich kids, but it really sets in when they hit their forties."

"Probably," I said. Willa had a way of cutting straight to the point, something I'd come to love about her. "It certainly hasn't gotten better these last couple years."

It had gotten much worse, in fact, because now he thought I was someone he could buy, too. The price? Alex.

You think I'm going to let you raise my son in some shit-box apartment? George had texted, only the day before. **Unless you come back, you lose him.**

I wondered if George really could do what he'd threatened,

if there could be a world where I'd only see my son a couple times a month, where George and his family raised him fully in their world, a mini little Haywood boy, with everything that brings.

"It's not just George. Jack Senior thinks the same, you know," Willa said now. "Anyone who grew up that way does. It's how they're taught. Make an offer, counter, go round and round—eventually anyone will sell you anything, right? It's all one big transaction."

"How do you deal with it?" I asked, maybe a bit earnestly.

Willa's eyes sparkled with mischief. "Well, you see, Mary, I can't be bought. Can you?"

I looked down at Alex, whose eyes were wide open now, gazing up at the gray sky, the limbs of trees that arced over this loop like canopies. His own eyes were gray, like George's, not mine. I briefly wondered whether there was any chance, however small, that Alex would remember this conversation, his almost-two-year-old mind somehow logging the trauma, trotting it out on a therapist's couch one day.

"I don't want to be bought," I said, looking briefly at Willa, whose hair was freshly trimmed and whose skin looked clear and glowing, whereas mine was shiny and sticky from the heat. I wished I could have her confidence, a natural spring in my step, could go through the world not worried about potholes or dog shit in my path—just *go*. But that had never been me. And I think George had known that; manipulated it, even.

"You never told me what exactly he did that made you leave," Willa said. "I mean, besides being a rich, entitled dude. But that comes with benefits, of course." She adjusted her trench with bravado.

I looked up at the road in front of us, which was winding along one of the park's prettiest meadows, towering old turn-of-the-century co-op buildings standing proud and graceful on the other side. "It wasn't one thing, it was . . . it was a lot of things . . ."

"Jack," Willa called ahead. "Still too fast. Wait for us. No more speed demon."

Jack stomped his foot, but after a bit more prodding from Willa, he let us catch up to him, resigned. He always listened to her in the end; a marvel, really. She placed a hand on the handle of his scooter, preventing him from barreling ahead.

Beneath me, Alex's lids fully closed. He would be asleep for as long as I kept the stroller moving.

Willa turned to me, picking up right where she'd left off. "What things, then? Affairs?"

"No," I said. "I don't think so."

"Then what?" she asked. "You can tell me, you know."

My lips parted, and so badly I wanted to unburden myself, but the kids were right there, and around us, people were having such normal conversations.

"It might even feel better to get it off your chest," Willa went on. "There's no shame in it, whatever it is."

"I know," I said. "Just not here."

"Gotta buy you a drink first," Willa said, one eyebrow raised.

"Definitely," I said with a laugh. "Maybe even two."

"Sunday again?" Willa asked. "I'll liquor you up and extract every last juicy detail?"

"Yes to drinks," I said with a smirk. "But we'll see whether I spill."

I was about to say something else when Jack pushed

Willa's hand away and plowed forward on his scooter, a bat out of hell.

"Daddy, Daddy, Daddy!"

It took me a moment to see who Jack was talking to; you can't call "Daddy" in the park without at least a few men turning their heads.

Then there he was, eyes lit up, running our way, sweat creating beads against the sort of tanned, almost-leathery skin you so often see among white men on the other side of forty. His hair—all silver—was short, close-cropped, but thick and full, and his eyes were large, dark brown. So this was the man who had won Willa's heart. He was gorgeous, with a raw, powerful energy. Someone who was bound to turn more than one woman's head.

"Baby," he said, slowing his run to a walk and taking a few strides to the side of the loop, so we wouldn't block others. He pulled out an earbud as Jack Junior ran into his arms. I dodged more oncoming joggers to park my stroller near the three of them.

"Look at all your daddy's lovely sweat," Willa said, laughter in her words. "Jack-Jack, you're going to need two baths today."

Jack Senior set his son down and leaned toward Willa. "Hi, other baby."

He was tall, had to be more than six feet, and he had to stoop down to meet Willa's petite frame. He was clad in runner's shorts, showing off toned, tan legs, a 5K T-shirt, and an armband that held his phone. He leaned in for a kiss, one that lingered, right there, in front of his son, in front of the runners and cyclists and mundanity of Prospect Park.

I found myself actually counting—three full seconds until they broke apart—and gut-aching with bitter, ugly jealousy, I wondered when I'd ever be kissed like that again, now that I'd made up my mind to leave George. For a brief wild second, I imagined Jack kissing me instead.

When he pulled back, he tucked his earbud in his pocket and extended a hand toward me. "Jack," he said. He took my hand, sending a little shock wave up my arm, his handshake strong and firm, his hand clean and dry in spite of the sweat on the rest of his body.

"Mary."

Willa jumped in as soon as he let go of my hand. "Don't let us interrupt your run. Besides, we're deep into girl talk."

"And a nap, I see," he said, nodding to Alex.

"Jack here wore him out."

He raised an eyebrow. "He wears everyone out." Then he smiled, reached toward Willa again, squeezed her bare arm. "Except Willa here."

I laughed. "I guess us mothers are used to it."

He opened his mouth to speak, but Willa gave him a playful shove.

"Baby," she said. "You better get back to your run. It really is girl time for us, and you know how seriously I take that. You're encroaching."

"Point taken," he said, breaking into a smile. Then he looked straight at me. "Wouldn't want to make Willa mad."

He kicked up his feet and kept on running, Jack Junior calling "Bye, Daddy" until we couldn't see him anymore.

7

I unpacked my laptop, hooked it up to the rental's Wi-Fi, and briefly checked my email. I was confirmed for the visit with the preschool on Monday and the *Forbes* interview on Tuesday morning, and the real estate agent had sent a bunch of rental properties for our meeting on Tuesday afternoon. I hopped out of my email and headed for the lawyer's portal. The site loaded this time, and I typed in my username, tabbed down. Usually the password autopopulated, but it didn't this time. I ran through my list of go-tos until a red pop-up appeared, telling me I'd been locked out. Christ. I grabbed my phone, dialed the firm's number, but it went to voicemail. I left a rambling message, trying to explain the situation, then ended the call.

I forced myself to take a deep breath. There was no point in obsessing over it now. George and I had been so clear, so detailed, in our recent communications with each other. This was only a formality.

Still, Henry's words rang in my head.

George won't let you go this easy, you know.

Did Henry really have a place here, or was it all a convenient excuse? I navigated over to the search bar, typed "Henry Haywood Woodstock New York." A few links appeared, and I clicked the first one, to see a photo of Cassandra, with Henry at the Woodstock Film Festival, so tall and glamorous, on his arm, the Cartier Panthère bracelet—her pride and joy—shimmering on her wrist.

I clicked back, found another article.

City Investors Set Sights on the Hudson Valley

It was from the real estate blog of one of the local papers, and it went on for several paragraphs about how the landscape of this part of the Hudson Valley was changing. I read more of the article, unsurprised by the focus on my brother-in-law. This area, in all its progressive crunchiness, would hate someone like him swooping in and buying a bunch of properties, and the blog listed three that were now his—one in Rhinebeck, another in Kerhonkson, the final in Woodstock: 12 Waterfall Way.

I pulled it up on Google Maps. True to Henry's word, it wasn't far, just about a block away. You could get there by returning to Tinker Street and heading around the corner or cutting down a side street down the block. Maybe my running into him was nothing more than a coincidence.

I checked the time, then FaceTimed George's mom, intent on talking to Alex while he was still in a good mood. The two hours leading up to bedtime could be chaotic at best, hell-raising at worst.

It rang three times, and then the call went through. Immediately, I saw my son's beautiful face, Ruth just behind him. Alex's cheeks were chubby as a chipmunk's, and his crooked smile was wide and open. He was delighted to see me.

My heart swelled, and I felt a longing so strong, so powerful, and I knew that what I was doing, coming here, making a good, simple life for him and me, was the absolute right thing.

"Hi, baby," I said, grinning wide back at him. "Mommy misses you so much."

Just after seven, I shut the front door behind me, key tucked into the interior of my purse. I'd spent the last two hours, after saying bye-bye to Alex and reminding Ruth that the boy demanded we adapt the lyrics of "Twinkle, Twinkle, Little Star" from "like a diamond in the sky" to "like a *dinosaur* in the sky," researching my *Forbes* subject and outlining my interview questions. The sun wasn't anywhere close to setting on Woodstock, the light, yellow and hazy, still dancing among the leaves and azalea bushes, climbing ivy and wild lilies, the kind that grow on the sides of the roads like cheerful weeds up in Old Forge. The asphalt road was cast in an intricate pattern of shadows, and there was a coolness in the air, sweeping down from the proud mountains in front.

I hovered at the crosswalk, waiting, a bit impatiently, for the parade of Subarus and Volvos to step on the brakes, then crossed and headed toward a gravel-and-grass lot with a hut in the back that sold bagels in the morning and wood-fired pizza in the evening, landscaped to welcome families and young couples up from the city for the weekend. There were picnic tables on one side, stone seats on another, and firepits in the middle, the whole place sprinkled with Instagrammable spare tires and rusted farm machinery.

The menu was absurd, especially for a place that was all to-go—twenty-six dollars for a smallish pizza covered in "locally foraged" mushrooms—but I put it on my credit card anyway, as well as a glass of wine. When they called my name, I grabbed a cardboard box that was steaming out the top and already soaking with grease on the bottom and a generous pour in a plastic cup. I situated myself at a lone table close to one of the firepits, as far removed from the families and couples as I could get. The resolve I'd felt only hours ago, hopping off the phone with Alex, detailing interview questions, faltered as I realized that this would be my life now. On the weekends, when Alex was with George— or, at least, with the nanny—I wouldn't even have my son as a social buffer. I would have to make new friends. I would maybe even have to date, if I ever wanted to have a partner— or hell, a sex life—again.

It was then that I saw a mom from the baby group I'd joined when I was pregnant with Alex, a little girl with a pixie cut sitting on her lap. They were about twenty feet away, at the edge of one of the firepits, and my shoulders tensed, because I didn't want to see anyone I knew, didn't want to explain why I was up here, on my own. My fears, I realized, had been quite real. There was no escaping Brooklyn life, not even here. I would always have to be *on*, would always be running into people from the city, in a way I never would if I could go all the way back up to Old Forge.

I took a rather large gulp of wine, cool and crisp, and

turned my chair to be sure the woman couldn't see me. For a second, I imagined giving up this entire plan, going back to George, putting all that had happened out of my mind, enjoying all the comfort money brings. I could get Alex into the best elementary school, I could join the PTA, I could do the sorts of things that rich women were supposed to do—become Pilates-instructor certified, join the board of the Brooklyn Museum. I could really work on George, get him to buy me my *own* Cartier bracelet, the simple Love one in warm rose gold, the only one of Cassandra's I'd ever coveted.

I could make friends in Brooklyn, friends who weren't Willa. That were *nothing* like Willa, or Annie, or whoever she was. Then I would never have to explain to perfect women like the one across the way that my whole life had fallen apart. I wouldn't have to be up here, halfway between my life in Brooklyn and my family in Old Forge, completely untethered, without anyone to rely on.

I opened the pizza box and took a first bite. I was about to start the book I'd been meaning to read when my phone buzzed.

It was my sister, Rachel.

Hope you're enjoying your week in Woodstock. Mom is doing well, though mostly still armchair-bound. Can't wait for you to be back in nature and to have you and little nephew-kins oh so much closer xx

Between bites of pizza, I wrote Rachel back.

Thanks so much for taking care of her. Can't wait to be closer to you and Mom. Love you.

I tapped out of my messages, but with the phone in my hand, wine on my tongue, I found myself losing my earlier resolve to put Willa out of my mind. I took another sip and opened Google instead. What if she *lived* here now? What if, among the Brooklyn moms up all the time from the city, I was destined to run into her, too?

I started a new search and keyed in my best guess at Willa's full name, "Willa Walton."

I'd done it before, so I skipped past the hits I knew had nothing to do with her. An obituary for an older woman in Kansas. A lady with a custom hat business on Etsy. A grandmother who'd set up a GoFundMe for her grandson's medical bills—Jesus. Records from OfficialLocator.com that promised to provide me with an address and phone number in Half Moon Bay, California, if I only signed up for the affordable price of $19.95 a month. None of these people were my Willa.

I finished my first slice and dug into another. The real problem here was that I didn't even know if Willa Walton was right. We'd never used last names with each other, had been on a first-name basis from the start, but I'd seen the last name Walton on the credit card that last night we'd had margaritas, and that was all I had to go on. I had no idea whether she'd actually taken her husband's name; I didn't even know if she and Jack were properly married, since I'd never seen a ring on her finger, but that alone didn't mean much. So many women I knew in Brooklyn had these massive rocks that they left home for things like the playground. The whole *I don't take off my ring, not even for a minute* felt passé, like something our moms would do.

Still, with nothing else to go on, I poked around a bit

more, looking for Willas on Facebook, Instagram, and even Park Slope Parents, a behemoth of a message board that Brooklyn parents relied on. But there were no matches, of course, and so I sighed, finished the last of the wine, and tapped into my texts instead, began to type Willa a message.

> **I know you obviously don't want to talk to me, but I wish you hadn't lied to me. I know that was you this afternoon.**

The text delivered instantly, and I set my phone down, knowing she probably wouldn't respond, but leaving it open to that screen in case she did.

I gobbled down more pizza and convinced myself I didn't need any more wine.

And then, only moments after I'd sent the text, three dots appeared. Willa was typing.

I waited like that, five seconds, ten seconds, fifteen . . .

The dots went away, almost like they had never appeared at all.

I was finishing up my last slice of pizza, and the mom from my baby group was finally gone, when I looked up from my book, and there was Willa.

She pushed a stroller along on the road, maybe a hundred feet up and to my left, walking next to a man who was tall and skinny, with shaggy hair, a thick brown beard, and a faded T-shirt, the words *MEDICARE FOR ALL* emblazoned across the front. A crunchy socialist, really? The guy couldn't be further from Jack Senior if you tried. I looked down at my dinner, at the pages of my book, and when I looked back up I saw the two of them stop to grab something from the bottom of the stroller.

Should I attempt another encounter? Tell her I knew it was her, that I knew she'd seen my text, insist she be straight with me?

Willa and the man started walking again, and making a split-second decision, I dropped the crust of my pizza, shut the cardboard box, flicked my book closed, and abandoned my seat before I could stop myself. I scrambled around a fire-pit, up a dirt path, and onto the sidewalk.

With Willa only twenty feet or so ahead, I considered running to catch her, but then two little arms stretched lazily from the top of the stroller, and I lost my nerve. I was a mother, for Christ sake. Was I really going to go accost Willa when this little girl—whoever she was—was probably trying to sleep? But that didn't mean I couldn't see where she was going, did it? After all, the sun still hadn't fully set, the air cool and crisp, the mountains standing proudly to my right; I was nothing more than a woman on a walk through town.

Who was this man? Where was Jack Senior? More important, where was Willa's son? What was really going on here?

I followed them past the old shut-down gas station, one that looked like it could be a setting for *Twin Peaks*, a vintage Corvette and an eighties Dodge Caravan parked in front of the nonworking pumps like toy cars left behind by a toddler when playtime is over. Past the art and framing shop, nestled in a beautiful white Victorian building. Past the colorful sculpture that looked like a bunch of oversized crayons and a bookstore-slash-crystal-shop that probably had at least ten different tomes on tarot.

We were getting farther from my rental, and a blister was forming on the back of my right foot, but I had to follow, had to learn as much as I could, for my own sanity, if nothing else. Maybe they were going to duck into the parking lot, drive back to a rental—hell, even the city; maybe after today, I would never have to run into Willa, and all her mysteries, again.

She and the man didn't turn into the parking lot, walking on toward the mountains. We passed a cemetery, headstones lined up neatly, so many souls potentially watching what I was doing, and with every step the feeling got stronger: Willa lived here now, and if she did, what did that mean for me? How could I start anew in a small town where the woman who'd broken my heart was walking around, pretending to be someone else completely?

A few more blocks up, Willa and the man turned, rumbling the stroller over a stone path that led to a lovely home. Navy blue and enormous for a house this close to town. With twin dormers that mimicked the mountain's peaks and a sweeping front porch that stood bold and boastful, a *NO MORE NUKES* sign hanging proudly in the window.

The man walked around the front of the stroller to grab it.

I ducked behind a tree, only a handful of yards from the front porch.

Together, they lifted the stroller carefully up the steps, the little girl most definitely asleep within. When they got to the top, the man set it down, then leaned in toward Willa and kissed her.

When he pulled back, he dug into his pocket, pulled out a set of keys, unlocked the door.

The man walked inside, and I knew I would lose her then.

Before I could stop myself, I pulled out my phone, lifted it up between the foliage, took a photo of Willa ushering the stroller inside. Then I tapped into my texts, uploaded the photo, added five imploring words below.

Tell me this isn't you.

I was exhausted by the time I approached my rental, and the sun had finally set back behind the mountains; the streets were dark now, the nocturnal animals beginning to come out. I heard rustling trash cans when I was a couple of houses away, looked to my right to see a shadow among the bins. I feared it was a bear, something that had been common in Old Forge but was entirely foreign to me now, but was relieved to see it was a raccoon instead, its white stripes catching the moonlight like reflectors.

I stepped into the house, tossed my bag onto the side table, and shut the door behind me, then paused. I scanned my surroundings, my breaths coming faster as I realized something wasn't right.

There was a light coming from the kitchen—had I left it that way? The sun had still been out when I'd departed for dinner, and no matter how long I'd lived with George and all his gobs of money, I'd never gotten out of the habit of turning the lights off when I left a room, my mom always reminding me and my sister that electricity is expensive and "every penny adds up."

I stilled myself, listening for movement, and I again scanned the room, seeing if anything else was out of place. Nothing.

I must have left it on, I thought. That was the only explanation.

I took a step forward, then another.

One more step, and I saw it. A flicker of light, but not from a lamp, something different, something like . . . candles.

Oh my god, I thought. Oh my god.

There were two flickering taper candles on the table, surrounding a silver ice bucket with a foil-tipped bottle of Krug bobbing within.

I looked up to see a shadow in the corner, and for a terrifying moment, I thought of Henry, the way he always got so drunk, how Cassandra had once told me he could be mean when he was angry.

The figure moved toward me, and I froze, too scared to scream, my veins pulsing, sweat prickling the back of my neck.

Then he stepped into the light, and it wasn't Henry. It was George. Before I could say a word, his hands were on my shoulders, and he was leaning in, and I could smell the subtle hints of his aftershave and the salty scent of his skin.

"It's okay," George said, rubbing the sides of my shoulders. "It's okay, baby. Don't be scared. It's just me."

I looked up to my husband, so handsome and self-assured, who looked so much like Henry but whose features had always been softer, kinder somehow, his hair slightly more curly, his eyes gray instead of blue.

My stomach roiled with fear, with confusion, with shock. "What are . . . what are you doing here?"

He leaned in for a kiss, and I didn't return it, but I didn't push him away either, I was so very thrown.

Then he plastered on his George smile, the one that had won him so very many things, myself included.

"I hope you liked the flowers."

8

Was George ever into tequila?" Willa asked, perusing the menu at our Mexican spot. "Jack always has us going to these ridiculous tastings where worms made full McMansions in the bottoms of the bottles and everything, and shoots me side-eye when I order a regular margarita, but I mean, make it strong, make it salty, and you can't really go wrong, right?"

"I'm with you," I said. "But no, George wasn't a tequila man. He liked wine and champagne, but I can never taste the difference past a certain price point. Half the time, I don't think he can, either."

"Same!" Willa said. "They want us to think they have these super refined palates, but they're really just getting sloshed in a way that makes them feel okay about it. What's George's sign?" she asked.

"Libra," I said.

"No way," Willa said. "Jack's, too. What's his birthday?"

"October twenty-third," I said, without thinking about it too much.

"That's it, then," Willa said. "Jack's is October twenty-second. Libras are all well-bred and polite. If someone tells them about a fine liquor or wine, they can't help themselves. You're Sagittarius, right?"

"No," I said. "February eighteenth. Aquarius."

"Oh," Willa said, eyes lighting up. "I must have just assumed. I always vibe with Sagittarians," she said, then raised an eyebrow mischievously. "You might be my first Aquarius bestie."

My heart leapt, in spite of myself, at Willa's choice of words, but if she saw the pleasure in my eyes, she pretended not to notice, at least. The waiter came over, and Willa beamed up at her instead. "We'll start with two mezcal margaritas, extra salt, please. And an order of guac. Spicy."

I took a sip of water and looked around the back patio of this tiny little restaurant. Park Slope was like a different world at night, especially now, as summer approached. When the strollers and the scooters and the kids, kids, kids, finally went indoors, to their cribs and their toddler beds, to their bunks and their burrowed nests with their parents who co-slept. At night, we shed, or at least attempted to shed, the skin we wore all day. To peel back a layer and attempt to become a closer version of the people we were before. Date nights. Drinks with friends. Discussions about politics and poetry, contemporary art and Kendrick Lamar. It was a magical world, this place, when our tiny little wards were tucked away. When we could finally be ourselves again.

The waiter returned with our drinks, salt like ice crystals

on the rim, and Willa said thank you and lifted hers straight-away. "To being free of the little monsters," she said, like she had the last couple of times.

"To being free," I echoed, taking a sip, then licking the salt off my lips.

Willa set her drink down, traced her well-manicured fingers against the crystal's condensation. "And not to be weird or anything, but I wanted to tell you I'm sorry about the other day. You know, in the park, prodding you about George. Jack Senior is always on me about being so pushy. You don't have to tell me anything you don't want to. About your marriage, about your past, about anything. I just . . . I get this way, sometimes, with people I care about, people I love . . . like I want to tear down every single boundary between us. God, you should have seen me when I met Jack. But I know not everyone is that way. And I know maybe it's not even the healthiest, demanding that people unburden themselves to me. So I wanted to say there's no pressure to tell me anything. I hope you know that."

Already my cheeks were reddening, my face hot, and it wasn't from the drink in my hand or the humid almost-summer air, the hint of what Brooklyn would be in just a month or so more. It was from what she said. *People I love.* Couple that with the word "bestie" and I felt practically on cloud nine.

"You don't have to apologize," I said.

Willa reached a hand across the table, then linked her fingers through mine. "I just want you to know I've come to care about you so much, and that's the only reason I was pressing."

"I know," I said. "You mean a lot to me, too." My hand

stayed in hers, and I could feel the warmth of her fingers in mine, the electricity pulsing between us. Two opposing charges, coming together. Positive and negative. Magnetic. An enthralled wanting that I felt deeply when I was with her and when I was away, too. A romance of sorts, even if it wasn't sexual. A feeling of some sort of communion, understanding, one that swelled and ballooned within me, as if it could fill me up, then pop me right open.

I knew then I was going to tell her everything. Someone had to hear it, after all.

I pulled my hand away, wanting to break the spell, take a little bit of control back before I let her in completely. "I always thought he was a good man," I said hesitantly, as if dipping a toe in the water. I looked around, as if one of the family's many employees could be watching me even now. "George, I mean."

Willa nodded me along. "But he isn't?"

I pursed my lips. "It's strange, like if you look at him, if you take stock of every part of him, you would say he is. His work helps women all over the world. He votes for the right people, supports the right causes. He certainly thinks he's good . . ."

Willa took another sip of her drink, all patience, and I liked that she didn't push.

"I don't think he ever really loved me. I think he just wanted to control me."

Willa raised an eyebrow. "One of those types, huh?"

"Yes," I said. "I mean, he was always super confident and self-assured, and I think that's a lot of what drew me to him, but at some point, I guess shortly after we got married, the confidence turned into . . . something else. He dictated

everything. What we watched on TV, what music we listened to, what decorators we hired, where we went out to
eat, what vacations we took." I shrugged. "It took me a long
time to see it, because he was giving me all this amazing
stuff I'd never have otherwise. I mean, was I really going to
complain about a fully planned vacation to the Seychelles or
a brand-new dress, even if it wasn't exactly my taste, or a
rule that we couldn't watch reality TV—reality TV is stupid
anyway."

"Hey now," Willa said playfully, taking a quick sip of
water. "Let's not say things we might later regret."

"Right," I said. "I forgot that *The Bachelor* is the closest
thing to religion you have."

"Will you accept this rose?" Willa asked as she made the
sign of the cross.

"You know what I mean, though. George was the sophis-
ticated one, I was the one from the small town with student
loans. I didn't always mind that he was teaching me how to
be a bit . . . classier. But then I had Alex—"

"Let me guess. Now he had someone else to control, too."

"Exactly," I said. "It was like he was molding me into this
super submissive person, and he was trying to mold Alex
into—well—into *him*."

Willa licked the salt off her lips. "Big yikes."

"Yes," I said. "And part of me thought it was all in my
head, that I was being too sensitive. Some people were a bit
headstrong—did it really matter if we were all happy together? I needed to find a way to go against George, to test it
out. I needed to prove to myself that if there was something
that I really wanted to change, that if I really spoke up, he
would support me."

"So did you?" Willa asked.

"I thought we'd probably go head-to-head over something with Alex, but then . . . a different opportunity to challenge my husband came up. Remember how I mentioned Cassandra, my sister-in-law?"

"The one who you had a falling-out with?" Willa prompted.

"Yes," I said. "And no. See, I only actually fell out with her because of George."

Anger, so familiar, surged within me once again.

"Because of what George did to her."

9

George reached for my elbow, but I pulled it back and away, close to my body, as Alex used to do when he was so very little. As if he—or I—could curl up in a fetal little ball, seek protection from the ills of the world.

"What's going on? What are you doing here? How did you even get inside?"

"Don't act *so* surprised," George said. "You sent me all the information. The email had the lockbox code in it. It can't be completely out of the blue that I took it and went with it."

I reared back, horrified. "I sent you that because I thought you and your parents should know where I was when I wasn't with Alex," I said. "Not so you—so you could—" It clicked for me, so powerfully obvious, so . . . creepy. "So you *did* send Henry, then. To set up the flowers? To . . . what . . .

scope it out? I saw him, walking down this street, right after I got in."

George's smile faltered only for a second. "Henry was up for a contractor meeting this morning anyway. I thought you'd like the freesia. The rest I brought when I got in."

"I still don't understand *how* you got in," I said. "I have the only key."

"Henry left the back door unlocked so I could slip in. If he hadn't, I guess you'd have found me waiting on the porch with the champagne, but I thought this was better. And don't worry. I'm not forcing myself upon you entirely. I can stay at Henry's if you really insist."

He turned away then, grabbing the bottle of Krug, twisting the wire off in two economical turns. He thumbed at the cork, letting it out with a satisfying pop, grabbed a pair of flutes and poured us each a glass.

"You always loved a grand gesture," George said, matter-of-factly, as he pressed the drink into my hand. I found myself curling my fingers around the stem, knowing, somehow, that he would let it fall if I didn't. "To us," George said, clinking his glass against mine.

That was when I saw it, streaked against his hand. *Red.*

"Jesus, George, what happened to your hand?"

It took him a moment to clock my surprise, and then his eyes found the side of his thumb. "Oh," he laughed. "It's not blood. It's Farrow and Ball Lake Red."

"What?"

"The paint," he said. "From the front door. The brownstone. The paint you campaigned so hard for." He examined his hand. "I guess it does look a little like blood when it dries on skin."

My eyebrows knitted up, trying to make sense of it. "But what is—"

"I told Henry it was a good color. Showed him that *Wall Street Journal* story and everything. He's doing a full revamp, too, and he wanted his contractor to redo the door. You had half-a-gallon left in the basement. I brought it up so Henry could see it."

"You painted a door?"

"Not all the way, no. But a little test area, to see what Henry thought. And it looks good, too." He raised his glass, waiting for me, eyebrows raised.

"George," I said again.

"Come on, Mary, you have to say our phrase, or else it's bad luck. To us," he said again, leaving it all hanging in the air. And then, more firmly. Almost like a threat. "To *us*."

After a moment, I found my voice, to get past this point, if nothing else. "To us and the many adventures we'll have together."

He'd said it on one of our early dates, and we had said it together countless times since, for luck. Or maybe because George always insisted.

George took a drink, then eyed me.

The champagne was good, fizzy and cool and warming, somehow, too, like a hug from within. George reached his hand out, linking it into mine. "This is all my fault, you know." He squeezed, rubbing the skin between my thumb and forefinger like I always loved so much. "I helped you get the apartment. I sent Genevieve over to help you out. Yes, I was *saying* I wanted you back, I was arguing with you about custody of Alex, but I wasn't showing it, was I?"

"George, I—"

"Please," he said. "Let me finish. I know I haven't talked about getting back together as much, not in these last couple months, but that doesn't mean my feelings went away. We *belong together*, Mary. You have to see it like I do. Do you really want to go through with all this?" He gestured around the rental. "Live up in Woodstock? When we could keep on building a life together, a life we always loved?"

I pulled my hand away, back toward my body, but George stepped closer, so I could almost taste the champagne on his breath. I closed my eyes, fingers still cradling my own glass, and imagined, for a moment, stepping back into our old life. So easy, so simple. No lawyers. No move. No researching schools up here. No finding new friends. No agonizing that I didn't have the geographical closeness of my mom or my sister or the safety net of George and all the people the Haywoods employed. Alex would have two parents living with him, always. And I wouldn't *ever* have to worry about money. It was so tempting, for a moment. Like stepping off the spin bike before your workout is through. You know it's not good for you. You know it won't make you happier in the end. But wouldn't it be nice to just stop spinning, to unclip and catch your breath and suddenly feel the ground beneath you?

"Mare," George said, his voice close now, right in my ear. I opened my eyes. Slowly, he pulled the glass from my hand, set it on the table, put his own down, too. "Mare, we could have another child, you know. Just like we always wanted."

I looked up at him, and his eyes showed he meant it. We had always intended to have two, maybe even three, because when you have the sort of money that George does, those dreams are open to you, your life like a candy store where you can simply take, take, take. I'd known, with every step I was taking away from George, that I was also taking a step away from that dream. And there had been grief in that knowledge, grief that was impossible to feel fully with my life all but imploding. Because I had always wanted children, plural. And I longed for the experience, not only for myself, but for Alex, too. To see him gently touching the downy hairs of a baby's head. To give him the chance to grow into the fiercely loving big brother I knew he would be. George, with all his flaws, was the only way I'd ever get that. I was nearly thirty-nine, and the thought of dating again, of throwing myself toward all that and with a biological timeline, too, was impossible.

Leaving George was leaving that life behind. I knew that, and I'd been okay with it, because how could I live with myself if I chose to stay with someone who controlled every move I made, who punished me if I went against him, just for the hope of another child?

How could I let Alex turn into his father—"*ee-nuh may-ree*"—just for the chance of a sibling?

George lifted a hand to my cheek then, and for a moment, it felt so good, because I hadn't been touched in months now. Alex's hugs, his kisses, his cuddles during "Twinkle, Twinkle, Little Star," and his gentle pats that weren't so gentle at all: they'd been the beginning and end of all my physical affection, and it wasn't enough. I missed having someone in my bed, having someone to kiss hello and goodbye. I missed George, or what I'd thought he once was.

Maybe everything I'd felt for Willa, all the intensity of our friendship, the hurt at being left behind by her, maybe it all stemmed from that. Maybe I was simply rebounding—after George, after Cassandra—and like anyone who rebounds, I'd made a terrible choice. I'd fallen for the affections of a liar, of someone who wasn't who she said she was.

"I want this," George said. "And I know, somewhere inside, you do, too. You want to grow our family. You want to put all of this behind us."

I felt moisture in my eyes, because I did want that, I really did. The problem was, I didn't think I could have it with him.

"Come on, Mare," George said, letting his thumb trail down the side of my cheek, resting beneath my chin, lifting my face to his. I had no choice but to look in his eyes. Gray, colorless eyes. Ones I'd loved so dearly, once. "You're still my wife, you know. Don't let all this petty stuff—this truly meaningless drama—destroy us."

He kissed me then, and I didn't stop him. I didn't fight, even though I knew I should. Knew that after all George had done to me, I *should* have the self-respect to say no. I let it happen, like a drink you shouldn't have being pushed into your hand. Like closing your eyes when you were so very tired, letting sleep snatch you at last.

I let him kiss me, and I let George dictate our next move. Like I always did.

10

Willa stared at me, a cool margarita in her hand, willing me to explain what I'd said:
Because of what George did to her.

"George was the one who encouraged me to befriend Cassandra, in the beginning," I said. "I can't believe that was already seven years ago."

"Seven years," Willa said. "That's a good chunk of time."

I nodded. "Our dating anniversary would have been this week, if you can believe it."

Willa's eyes narrowed. "Not June fifteenth, is it? That's the day I met Jack."

"The seventeenth, actually. George always insisted we re-create our first date. Did it every year, even once Alex was born." It had been yet another way that my husband had controlled everything, but I'd enjoyed it, I really had. "Any-

way, Cassandra was like me. She was from Pennsylvania—
Pennsyltucky, she always said. She didn't belong with the
family at all. But she was gorgeous, and Henry fell for her
hard when her PR firm organized one of the family benefits. Just a junior PR assistant from nowhere who hooks the
eldest son of one of the most well-to-do families in Brooklyn.
A fairy tale. And even though she wasn't raised with money,
she was one of those people who could fit in anywhere."

"A bit opportunistic, then," Willa said, her mouth set
firm. "A social climber."

"I guess you could say that, but I understood where she
was coming from. She was a few years younger than me, and
she met Henry much earlier than I met George. I mean, she
was living in this shitty apartment in Queens—rats, roaches,
the works. She was barely scraping by with her meager sal-
ary and she didn't have a safety net to fall back on. When
Henry plucked her from that world, she didn't want to look
back. It was different for me. I met George in my thirties. I
had a network, and even if I lost touch with a lot of them,
still, it was something."

Willa nodded me on.

"Cassandra would always get done up, these gorgeous
dresses, incredible jewelry, and she looked like she'd been
raised that way. We spent so much time together, at the
beginning—it always felt like we were two kids who'd hit
the jackpot. Two country girls who got to play in the castle,
you know? She might have been decked out in Harry Winston, but she still knew how wild all this money really was."

"So how did Miss Couture lose her footing?" Willa asked.
"Obviously things went south."

I nodded, lifting the margarita to my lips.

"I always thought Henry was a bit of a dick, super entitled, much more classic rich guy than George ever was. He drank too much, he was always planning these stupid 'boys' trips' to Vegas or Ibiza. And I know he cheated on Cassandra—I don't know if there were ever real relationships or affairs, but I'm sure there were plenty of high-priced hookers and hangers-on. It's how she got so much expensive jewelry."

Willa raised an eyebrow. "Maybe that was the trade-off, what she agreed to. She'd look the other way in return for all the spoils."

"Maybe," I said. "But I do think it hurt her. Cassandra loved Henry, as unlovable as he could be. But his alcoholism got worse, and I think the cheating did, too. I know she wanted kids with him, but she didn't feel like she could do it unless things stabilized. I think when she realized they never would, it got to be too much. When you look the other way that many times, you kind of run out of places to look. She decided she'd had enough, and she left."

"Let me guess," Willa said. "They took it all. They always do."

"They haven't even finished working it out yet," I said. "It's not just the prenup, which is bad enough. Henry is trying to get everything. And I mean *everything*." I took a last watery sip. "The second Henry found out she was going to leave him, he cleared out all her closets, gave all her stuff to charity. He took her jewelry, too. Some seriously valuable stuff. And it's not like she wanted to run around town wearing Cartier. She knew that part of her life was over. She was desperate for cash. All she was even going to do was sell it so she could build a new life without him. He made sure she couldn't."

"Wow," Willa said. "I mean, I know rich people can get away with literal murder, but is that even legal? The clothes, fine, but the jewelry. Jewelry is valuable. Shared assets, right?"

I hated to admit the truth, but I had to. "Henry told her she must have misplaced it, which was obviously a horrible, unbelievable bit of gaslighting. Cassandra checked everything they shared—joint deposit boxes, all that—but she couldn't find it. Then about a month after she left him, she came to me."

Willa raised an eyebrow.

I bit my lip, forced myself to go on. "She thought Henry had it hidden away somewhere. And she thought maybe George had helped him. She asked me to look for it."

"Uh-oh," Willa said, leaning forward now.

"Right. I told her that she shouldn't make assumptions like that. Yes, George was particular, yes, you could even say controlling, but I really didn't think he'd stoop so low. Honestly, I walked out on our lunch, I was so pissed."

Willa nodded me on.

"So I went straight to George, and he acted all shocked and appalled—'How dare she? Don't you see what kind of a person she is? Trying to get you and me involved? Making these accusations? It's way out of line.'" I pressed my hands into the table, forcing myself on. "So a couple of days passed, and I called Cassandra. I apologized for running out on her in the café, but told her that she really hurt me, the way she assumed George would do that. I told her I talked to him, and that he swore up and down he wouldn't do that. And she—" My stomach roiled, reliving the memory. "She said, 'If you're so sure, just look. Check. Wherever he keeps valuable things. Just do that for me. Please.'"

"So did you?" Willa asked.

"There's this safe in our bedroom, where we keep our passports and extra cash and stuff. I never really used it much, but I knew the code." I shrugged. "I really didn't think it would be there . . ."

"It was, wasn't it?"

"I couldn't believe it. It was tucked in the back. I'd spent so long letting him get his way, but I knew I had to confront him now. I went straight to George's office, waving the jewelry around in his face. He told me it was none of my business. That we shouldn't get involved."

"Kind of rich," Willa said. "Coming from a man actively hiding assets during his brother's contentious divorce."

"I know," I said. "Believe me. I told him all of that. I said that I trusted him with a lot of things—our money, our plans, hiring nannies, the works—but this was too much. That he couldn't get his way this time."

"What did George do?" Willa asked.

"He said what he always said—'*Enough*, Mary. Just leave it'—like I was a dog, not his partner. But I didn't leave it, not this time. I kept bringing it up, and that's when . . ."

"That's when *what*?"

I caught Willa's eyes, willing her to understand.

"That's when the punishments started."

11

NOW
SUNDAY, AUGUST 15
WOODSTOCK, NEW YORK

I stared at George, lying in this bed in Woodstock. I'd barely slept all night, even though he'd been conked out, at peace, it seemed, with the fact that he'd won me back, with the effortless well of confidence George always managed to draw from, dip his cup in and drink, drink, drink.

My limbs were heavy, my bones tired from lack of sleep, and my skin, naked, was damp with sweat, my chest burning with acid from the pizza, the sips of champagne, from the anxiety of all these months—who even knew.

Shame filled me up as last night's images flickered through my mind. George kissing me, harder and harder, as I let him. George's hands all over me. The smell of his skin. The way our bodies knew what to do even though I didn't really want it, was tired of fighting, exhausted from these last months and all that would follow. It was like I shut down, just let it happen, because I didn't really have the energy for anything else. And then, my body completely taking over, contracting, convulsing, because in that moment, I *did* want it, because George knew what to do—he'd always known what to do with me—and that in and of itself was something, after so many months lost on my own. And maybe for a few moments afterward, as we shared a glass of champagne; as George flicked through his phone, showing me photos of Alex that his parents had sent him; as we made our way, sleepily, into bed, George's fantasy—because that was *all* it was—had seemed tempting. Another child; an easy, financially secure life. All the comfort that security brings. Letting inertia take over.

Now, in the bright daylight, I knew I'd made an enormous mistake. I couldn't—wouldn't—go back to him, not after what he'd done, not after he'd proven to me that my fears had been right, that he'd never let me have my own voice, that he'd call the shots, or else.

I grabbed my phone now, checked the time—nearly nine. Alex would already be up, digging his hands into a bowl of Cheerios and moving his trucks back and forth along an imaginary track on the rug. Lord, what would Ruth and Frank Haywood be telling my little boy, that Mommy and Daddy were on vacation together in Woodstock, that Daddy was going to make sure Mommy came home for good? My stomach churned.

I wiggled a bit, so the mattress would shake. George took only a moment before his eyes fluttered open. He smiled instantly, the corners of his mouth turning up, almost to a smirk, one that had always got me going before. His teeth were white, shiny, and perfectly straight.

He pushed himself up, then leaned in, planted a kiss on my lips. "Morning, beautiful."

I pulled away instantly. "This was a mistake."

"Mary," George started. "I know you tend to question things. I know you like to go over it and over it in your head, but just don't this time, okay?" His eyes cased down my body, to my breasts, limp from where nursing Alex had stretched them. "The moment is too lovely."

Instinctively, I pulled the sheets up around me, tucking my nipples away. "This doesn't change anything. I'm still—" I said. "We're still—"

"We're still *us*, Mary. A family. You can't just abandon that."

"Like I said, it was a mistake." I pushed the sheets back and fished through my bag for new clothes, haphazardly pulling on a T-shirt and shorts.

I headed to the kitchen, setting the champagne flutes into the sink, pouring the remains of the ridiculously overpriced bottle down the drain, a vision of shoving cash into a blender, watching it pulverize into confetti, running through my mind. I poured myself some water, gulped it down.

I returned to the bed, where George still lay, as if he owned the place. As if what I'd said didn't even matter. Because what Mary says never matters, does it?

"You can't stay," I said. "You need to go."

George raised an eyebrow. "What are you going to do, throw me out?"

"Don't make this harder than it needs to be. I have things to do. I have to get myself established up here. I don't need this . . . this *distraction*."

George's eyes scrunched up. "Up *here*?"

"Yes," I said. "Like we agreed."

His head cocked to the side for a moment, a confused puppy. "You don't mean they didn't tell you?"

"Tell me what?"

George began to laugh. A hateful, bitter laugh. Then he stepped out of bed, pulled on his pants. "Cut-rate lawyers," he said. "I mean, I knew yours was bad, but I didn't think he was *that* bad."

My heart hammered in my chest. "What are you talking about?"

"The divorce," he said. "The one *you* want so badly. You should have received papers from the lawyer. On Friday."

My heart was racing so fast now that I half-wondered if George could hear it. "My attorney was out on Friday. The paralegal—she emailed me yesterday. I tried to check the portal, but—" I said, feeling suddenly stupid. Foolish. Naïve. "But I couldn't remember my password. I got locked out, so no, I couldn't see anything—but you *said*."

George pulled on his shirt, grabbed his wallet from the nightstand, and tucked it into his front pocket. Then he turned to me, looking at me almost with disdain. "You didn't *seriously* think I was going to go for that, did you?"

"You agreed," I said.

"I said that *might* work. Nothing was ever in writing, Mary. And my lawyers wanted me to keep my cards close anyway."

"So what did—what *do*—the papers say?" I asked, my fingers quivering with anger, with fear.

George laughed again, that awful laugh. Then he walked

out of the bedroom and to the front, where he slipped his shoes on, sneakers that cost a month's rent. Finally, he turned back to me. "What do you think they say, Mary? The prenup is airtight. And there's really no need for child support if I have Alex full time."

I walked forward, fuming, as George opened the front door.

"You wouldn't," I said.

"I always made it clear that I would."

"No," I said, wringing my hands together desperately. "Only in the beginning, when you were angry, when things were so new. These last couple of months, you started to be more flexible. You agreed to . . . to everything I was asking for."

"I told you, Mary, my lawyers told me not to reveal all. Did you really think I wouldn't fight you on this? I don't want to lose you. Haven't I made that clear?"

"The courts will never take a kid away from his mother," I said. "Never."

"Maybe not normally, but there are extenuating circumstances, aren't there? You had a hard time of it in the beginning. That's all documented, you know."

My heart cinched up. "You can't be serious." I'd had an awful bout with postpartum depression, right after Alex was born. At George's urging, I'd spoken with the Haywoods' family doctor, a psychiatrist, and later, a therapist. But surely they couldn't use that against me. It was so common—it was *nothing*.

"Mothers have PPD, George. Lots of them do. They don't lose their kids."

"Yes, but leaving Alex alone so you could go out drinking till all hours."

"That was one night," I said, knowing instantly what he was talking about. Cassandra had taken me for drinks when Alex was six weeks old, and it had been so long since I'd been out that the alcohol had hit me horribly. She'd practically had to carry me home. I felt terrible about it, of course. "It was a fluke. A freak thing."

"What about when you ran off to the Hamptons that weekend, leaving your son who needed you on his own?"

I blinked back tears. "*You* told me to take that weekend." It had been a couple of months later, when the pressures of constant nursing and caretaking were getting the best of me. "You set it up and everything. You told me between you and the nanny, Alex would be fine. And he *was*."

"You want to take a risk, really go to court? Fine. We'll see how things shake out. But given how on it your lawyer's been so far, personally, I wouldn't take the chance." George took one step out onto the porch. "But if you come back to me, all of this goes away."

"You're horrible," I said, my voice raised now, my pitch high-strung, what some might call hysterical, tears blooming in my eyes. "You're a horrible, horrible man."

"And yet I'm yours," George said, his smirk returning.

"Get the fuck away from me," I said, and I couldn't help it. I reached both hands up and shoved, sending him back so he tripped over the porch steps, fell, and caught himself with two hands, his body crashing onto the walkway—splat.

I'd never touched George. I'd never touched anyone in anger.

"Oh my god," I heard from a middle-aged woman, power walking by. "God, are you okay?"

Before I could take in her horror, before I could see her rush up to help him, as if he were the victim here, and I the aggressor, I slammed the door.

12

THEN
SUNDAY, JUNE 13
BROOKLYN, NEW YORK

Punishments? Christ. I think we're going to need another round for this," Willa said, signaling to the waiter, who nodded and returned in a few minutes, a pair of sweating glasses in her hands.

"All right," Willa said, lifting the drink to her lips. "Now, give it to me straight. Did he *actually* fuck with you? I mean, physically? Because I'll kill the man, I swear, and no one would suspect little old me." She beamed. "I'm the sort of person who would do *anything* for my friends."

In spite of it all, I laughed, because she was right. No one would suspect her of anything of the sort. It would be the perfect murder, wouldn't it? Willa didn't even know George.

I shook my head, realizing she was still waiting for an answer. "He never touched me," I said. "Not like that."

"Then what was it?" Willa urged me on. "I mean, I *know* it had to be bad."

Suddenly, I was thankful for the new drink. "The first thing was Alex's baby blanket. It was this old one of mine that my mom had restored. A few nights after I approached George about Cassandra's jewelry, I couldn't find it. I asked George if he'd seen it, and he did this whole song and dance helping me look for it. Alex was crying, and I was super upset because my mom had put so much love into it."

"Oh god," Willa said. "I've watched enough bad TV to see where this is going."

"A couple days later, our housekeeper was over, and I saw the blanket, cut up into rags, being used to dust the picture frames. I tried to ask her, but she clammed up, saying it was in the bin where her other dust rags were and she was sorry if she made a mistake." I took a deep breath. "I didn't want to press her further, because I knew it wasn't her fault. We *did* have this bin, which we put some of our clothing scraps into . . . George abhorred paper towels, insisted we not use them. Easy for him when he was never the one cleaning up the messes. Anyway, when I asked him about it, he said he had no idea how it got in there. He even held me when I cried. But after a few minutes, he goes, 'You know, I'm not surprised something like this happened. After all the arguing between us these last few days. You've been so stressed about this mess with Cassandra. You must have tossed it in the wrong bin.'"

"So he *wanted* you to know," Willa said. "Controlling prick."

I laughed, bitterly. "He did, and yet I was so accustomed to doubting myself that I *still* didn't fully blame him. I told myself I'd been sleep-deprived, I *had* been stressed. Cassandra called a few days later, asking me if I'd found the jewelry, and

I told her I'd looked but there was nothing, just to buy some more time."

Willa nodded me on.

"I felt torn up with guilt about lying to her, so I tried to broach the subject again with George. It led to another fight." I looked down at my drink, back up at her. "That night, my journal was gone. I'd started one as soon as I found out I was pregnant. I wrote a little something every few days, kept it up through Alex's first year. I planned to give it to him when he turned eighteen or twenty-one or something. I'm not sure Alex would have even cared about it, but still—it meant something to me."

"George took it?" Willa asked.

"He said he didn't, but I didn't believe him. That was when it really started to sink in. My fears had been right. I couldn't stand up to him. What George says goes, and there's hell to pay if you try and rebel. I started to question everything. I mean, how could I live with someone who would do something like that?" I looked down, then back up at Willa. "Even so, if he'd stopped there, I might have been able to move past it. We could have tried couples therapy, I don't know, but then Cassandra called again, and I couldn't take the guilt, the lying. I went back to George, begged him to give the jewelry back to her, to listen to me, to take my side in this one thing. To choose me over Henry. He didn't get mad. He didn't tell me to leave it. I naïvely thought that he might actually consider it . . ."

"Oh boy," Willa said. "The calm before the fucking storm."

"So a couple of days later, I'm supposed to visit this college class. One of my old editors had taken an adjunct position at NYU, and she'd asked me to come talk about feature reporting—I think almost out of pity because she knew how far out of the game I was. Anyway, George asks the nanny to stay late, I get dressed up, blow-dry my hair and everything. It's the first thing I've done career-related since Alex was born." I took a sip of the fresh margarita, shame rising within me. "I get to the class. I'm a couple minutes late because of a train delay, and then there's someone else there, already speaking at the lectern. My old editor spots me, she comes out, asks me what I'm doing there after I told her I had a scheduling conflict."

Willa's eyes widened. "Oh my god, he *didn't*."

"Did I find actual proof? No, but it's not hard to delete sent emails. Unless I had a full-on nervous breakdown and started canceling things I had no memory of, the only explanation I could come up with is that George went into my email—he knew all my passwords anyway—and sent her that note."

"He fucked with your career?" Willa asked. "Holy shit. I mean, and canceling that late. It could have burned a bridge."

"Oh, I'm sure that it did. I backed out of the class as quickly as I could, mumbling something about a mix-up. I was so embarrassed."

"Wow," Willa said. "Just . . . wow. I mean, that is some *insidious* shit. Like, borderline evil. Did he admit to it?"

"You know," I said, "I didn't even ask. I went home, went straight to bed, didn't even talk to him, but the next day, I said I wanted to move out. He told me it was temporary, that he knew I would change my mind. He insisted I stay in one of his properties because he knew I'd be back, and I agreed, only because the prospect of finding a place in the Brooklyn rental market was overwhelming. I don't think George thought I'd last more than a week or so, but now, here I am."

Willa took another sip. "The journal, the blanket—okay, I mean it's really shitty, but it's nostalgic stuff. Career moves, that has real-world implications. And for someone like you, who's already going to have trouble getting back into the swing of things, after a baby."

"I know," I said, taking a large gulp myself. "Believe me, I know."

"Did you take her jewelry?" Willa asked. "When you left?"

"I should have," I said. "But I was too scared of how George would escalate things if I did. And then as the weeks went on, George began to threaten to go for full custody of Alex." I hesitated, considering, then decided to be out with it. "I saw it all actually, a few weeks ago."

Willa raised an eyebrow. "The jewelry?"

"Yes," I said. "At the brownstone. Right in the wall safe where George always had it."

"Wow," Willa said. "What a motherfucker."

"Do you blame me?" I asked nervously. "For not taking it?"

"Are you kidding?" Willa reached a hand to mine. "I mean, what a set to be up against. What the hell were you supposed to do? It's criminal what these kinds of people do. Just *criminal*."

We were interrupted by the return of the waiter.

"It's last call out on the patio," she said. "I need to close you out, but I can get you another round first, and if you want more, you can always go inside. The bar is open until midnight."

"Oh," Willa said, letting go of my hand. She glanced between our drinks, which—to my shock—were both nearly empty. "Yes, I think we'll be devilish and do one more."

Soon, fresh drinks were before us, our credit cards handed over. The tequila was making time take creative leaps, and it felt like little more than seconds before the waiter was bringing us back our respective bills, both AmEx Black.

I looked down at my bill. *Eric Walton.*

"Wait a second," I said, trying not to slur as I motioned for the girl to come back. "I . . . I think you gave me someone else's card."

"Really?" she said. "Oh, I'm so sorry for the mix-up."

Willa was already waving her off. "Not a problem at all! See, I've got hers, and she's got mine." She pushed the leather holder forward and snatched back the one in my hands before I could give it another glance.

"Eric?" I asked, the moment the waiter was gone. "But I thought your husband's name was Jack?"

Willa scrawled out her signature on the receipt. "That's his middle name. And I've told him a million times he ought to use it on things like this—or hell, just change his legal name to Jack and be done with the rest. It only leads to confusion, but alas, he's old-school that way. Eric was a family name, you know."

I nodded, then quickly signed my own receipt, staring at the numbers on the check, math already seemingly out of reach. "Sorry," I said. "I didn't mean to pry."

"Not at all," she said, and then Willa lifted her drink, swirling the fresh margarita. The moment I signed, she clinked her glass against mine. "*Anyway*, we should celebrate," she said.

"Celebrate?" I asked. "After everything I just told you?"

"Yes," she said. "Because you're leaving the bastard behind. Getting the hell out of Dodge."

"That's the problem," I said, clutching the glass like it was a life raft. "Sometimes I fear I'll never find a way to get out."

"You will, Mary," Willa said reassuringly, tipping her glass back and drinking. In spite of the fact that the room was already beginning to spin if I stared at one point too much, I followed suit. "I really believe you will. It's you versus a total prick. I mean, at some point, good has to prevail. And if it doesn't, well . . ." Willa raised an eyebrow. "You know who to call."

13

NOW
SUNDAY, AUGUST 15
WOODSTOCK, NEW YORK

I headed into Woodstock that afternoon, desperate for sunshine, for fresh air, for a drink, intent on putting George out of my mind.

In the middle of town, I found a beer garden speckled with picnic tables, right behind the main parking lot, where a long-haired hippie was crooning on a makeshift stage up front. I ordered a double IPA and a large fries, craving numbness.

I'd spent the hours after George left leaving messages for my lawyer, trying to get into the portal, Googling custody battles and reading Reddit threads on divorce, trying to figure out how in trouble I was, the notion always at the forefront of my mind: George was going to win. George *always* won.

I kept my eyes peeled for other Brooklynites, but I didn't see the woman from my baby group—or anyone else—and tried to enjoy my beer.

I was deep into the next round when I spotted Willa on the other side of the field, tanned and relaxed, cheerful and seemingly content, in a polka-dot dress and a wide straw hat. She was dancing, spinning that little girl round and round as the man next to her tipped back a beer, tapping a foot along to the music, like this life of hers up here was the most natural thing in the world.

A flame of rage flickered within me. She was the one who'd pried and prodded, who'd ordered all those margaritas. She was the one who'd wanted the whole miserable story, but when I told her everything, she just . . . left.

Screw her, I thought. Screw her and screw George, and screw all these kinds of people who think they can get away with murder, who think the rules don't apply to them.

I set my beer down, and I stood. This had gone on long enough.

My heart raced as I approached her, one foot in front of the other.

"Willa," I said, her back to me.

I saw it, in the quick jolt of her shoulders. Recognition. A name she'd answered to many, many times before.

She didn't turn. But I didn't move.

It took him a moment, but the man I'd seen last night finally sensed that something was wrong. He scratched at the back of his head, stared at me like I was an intruder, reached instinctively for the little girl.

"Willa," I said again. "Answer me."

"Can we help you?" the man asked.

I ignored him. *"Willa."*

Finally, she stood fully, turned around to face me. "Like I said before, you must have me confused with—"

"You can't pull this with me anymore," I said, my voice desperate, pleading. "Willa, it's *me*. You don't have to pretend."

Her lips parted, as if to speak, but then the man crossed his arms. "Listen, her name's not Willa—it's Annie."

The moment was broken. Willa looked down at the grass.

I glanced around, saw that people were staring. In the periphery of the beer garden, I spotted a dad I might have seen at one of the playgrounds in Brooklyn. I shuddered to think how I must look. "Fine," I said. "Fine. Do whatever you want. *Be* whoever you want."

I turned on my heel, seeking only escape, but as soon as I was out of the place, I heard footsteps behind me, then felt a hand brush against my arm, soft, warm. "Mary, wait."

There she was. Sun on her hat. Chest rising and falling from running to catch me. Sweat beading against her chest. "I told Rich I had to go to the bathroom to compose myself, I just—"

Her presence hit me like a shock. Only moments ago, I'd been begging her to acknowledge me, but now here she was. Doing it.

"I wanted to say I'm sorry," she said finally.

That did it, that sent budding, drunken tears right over the edge, streaming down my cheeks.

"Oh god," Willa said, stepping forward. "God, I'm making it worse."

She wrapped her arms around me, and for a moment, I let her hold me. Smelled her musky Tom Ford perfume, a hint of the Altoids she popped like candy. Then I came to my senses, pulled back almost viciously.

"Who *are* you?" I asked. "What is going on?"

"I can explain, but . . ." Her eyes darted around. "I can't do it here, okay? I'll slip out this evening. Eight o'clock? The place you were last night. Right next door is a proper wine bar. There are seats tucked in the back where we won't be seen."

"You saw me last night?" I asked.

"Of course I saw you," Willa said. "Take it from me, Mary, never try to moonlight as a spy." Then she grinned, and for a moment, it was like I had the old Willa back. "I didn't expect you to follow us all the way home, though." She squeezed my hand. "Listen, I have to go, but tonight, okay? I'm not a total monster, I promise you. I told you I was your friend, and I meant it . . . I still do."

It was overcast as I left the house, just before eight.

I knew that Willa wouldn't be able to help me in the mess I was in with George, but still, I couldn't resist a chance to know who she was, to finally get answers. Closure, even.

I found her at a lone table on the bar's stone patio, seated beneath arced branches, as if she'd carved a little opening out of a copse just for us. She smiled at me, as if nothing in the world was wrong. Anger bubbled up from deep down, rushing up my spine as I took the seat opposite her—how could Willa *still* act so *normal*?—but before I could say a word, a waiter was there: "Can I get anything for you, ma'am?"

"The pinot gris is fantastic," Willa said. She plopped the glass in front of me. "Go ahead, try it."

I pushed the glass back at her, then nodded to the waiter. "Sauvignon blanc, please." I knew that whatever Willa had was probably better, but I didn't want to give her the satisfaction of taking her recommendation.

"And another of these for me," Willa added. "Oh, and two waters." She smiled, nodding to me. "This one is a total mom about it, in the best way, always making sure you alternate booze with true hydration." The waiter smiled politely and dashed off.

"I know you have to hate me right now," Willa said, diving right in. "I mean, *I* would hate me, at least." She laughed, finished off the remaining wine in her glass. "And I *am* going to tell you everything, promise. But I want to know how you are. I've been thinking of you, these last two months."

"How I am?" I asked, dumbfounded by her nerve. "Really? Let's see. I've been living on my own with Alex with basically no friends, no one to talk to. We celebrated his second birthday alone, just him and me—you were going to do that with me, remember? *Paw Patrol* decorations and Doritos?"

"I remember," Willa said gently. "And I'm sorry."

"It doesn't matter," I said. "I'm here now. *You're* here now. What is going on?"

Willa's head tilted to the side. "But *why* are you here, Mary?"

"Because I wanted out of the city," I snapped. "And George agreed to me moving here with Alex. But—"

The waiter returned then with two glasses, cutting me off. The condensation was so thick, I could have reached out a finger and written a message on the side. I grabbed mine quickly, suddenly eager for the drink.

"Ma'am," she said to Willa, delivering the wine to both of us. "The card you gave us to open the tab isn't going through. Do you have another we can try?"

Willa's eyes widened, only for a moment, and she leaned

over, digging in her purse, and quickly came up with another. "I've been having issues with the chip on that one. This should work fine."

"What was that about?" I asked as soon as the waiter was out of earshot.

"I know," Willa said. "Swiping the card at the beginning? What do they think, we're Thelma and Louise or something? Going to get the booze in us and run off?"

"Are you using a stolen card?"

Willa huffed. "No, Mary, I'm not using a stolen card." She laughed and shook her head, like I was a kid employing toddler logic. "The chip is having issues. Like I said. *Anyway*, is George up here with you?"

"What?" I asked, thrown. "How did you know—"

"Oh," Willa said. "I mean, you seem *so* upset, and usually, when you are, it has something to do with him." Her eyebrows narrowed. "Hold up, hold up. Don't tell me you *slept* with him or something."

"No," I said, practically jumping for my wine as heat rose to my face. "No, of course not."

"Oh my god," Willa said. "Oh my god, you little hussy! I was joking, but you did, didn't you! You really did?"

"It's none of your business," I said.

"So did you tell him about me?" Willa asked casually. "About seeing me here in town?"

"No," I said, eyebrows narrowing. "Why would I?"

"I just figured you'd want to tell someone, and I know you don't have many people to confide in. You must have been so shocked. Meeting *Annie*, you know."

"George isn't exactly the type to run to in a crisis," I said bitterly. "But enough about him," I said. "Why are you going by Annie? What happened to Jack Senior? What happened to your *son*?"

Willa's smile faltered at the last word. She almost seemed to wince. And in that moment, it was like I could hear it, while the crickets around us chirped and the glasses of white wine sweated, the sound of Jack Junior's little voice: *Willa! Willa!*

"Oh my god," I said, setting my drink down. "*That's* why he never called you Mama. You told me he liked to say your first name, and I *bought* it. But you were never his mother at all."

"To be fair," Willa said, tossing her hands up like we were arguing about little more than who took the last slice of pizza. "I never *technically* said I was."

My mind flashed through all of the memories she and I had made together—lazy days at the swing set, sticky tequila-soaked nights—and I remembered so much. Her telling me that three was a good age, her calling Jack Junior pet names, divulging the secrets she used to get him to sleep at night. But she hadn't said it outright, had she? And who did that, anyway? All, *Hi, this is Alex, and I am his mother.*

"What are you, then?" I snapped. "Some kind of messed-up nanny?"

Willa half rolled her eyes, but even as I said it, it didn't compute, either. I had met Jack Senior, he'd swooped in and kissed her, almost passionately, right there on the edge of the path in Prospect Park. Willa's silver fox. Impossible to forget.

"A nanny who screws her boss, I guess?"

"Easy there," Willa said. "I get your point. But, no, I am not a nanny. I'm a lot more than that. I was there when Jack needed someone. And I was everything to Jack Junior. I was the one reinforcing his potty training, teaching him his letters, signing him up for summer camp, planning his perfectly portioned lunches—I may have been a salty snack queen, but you should see how many fruits and veggies I chopped up in tiny little pieces for his lunch—getting him the right-sized, right-*looking* clothes for every season, buying bougie toys that would keep him engaged, researching pediatric dentists because Jack Senior's insurance changed. *Me.* Now, does it really matter if we shared blood or not?"

"Where was his mother?"

Willa eyed me, as if making a decision as to how much to divulge, then pressed her lips together, readying herself to swallow a bitter pill. "She died at the end of last year."

"She *what*?"

"Oh my *god*, Mary, get a hold of yourself! I didn't kill the woman, if that's what you're thinking. It was a car accident, apparently. I never met her—*obviously*."

"So what happened then? You were with them, calling yourself Willa. And now you have a new name. And, what? A new family?"

"I know how it looks, trust me," she said. "But things went south with Jack, and way before I expected. He kicked me out, and I had nowhere to go. And like I said, one damn sapphire necklace isn't going to do shit for a security deposit in Brooklyn. So I bailed town, and then I met Rich up here. And—"

"You created a whole new identity?"

"Jack turning on me—it screwed me up, okay? I wanted a fresh start. Anne's my middle name. I didn't buy a fake passport on the dark web, promise. It was a little name change. Happens every day."

"Then why did you pretend not to recognize me? This guy doesn't know your past, does he? He doesn't even know who you really are."

In a flash, I remembered that last time we ever went out together, the way the waiter had given me a credit card that said *Eric* on it. Eric Walton. I cocked my head to the side. "You've done this before, haven't you? This is . . . this is your scam. Shacking up with dudes, getting their money, bouncing? That credit card you used that last night we met up. It's not that Jack is a middle name, as I foolishly believed. It was from some entirely different guy."

"Eric gave that to me," Willa said firmly. "He told me I could use it whenever I needed anything. It's not my fault he was too wrapped up in his world, too flush in money to need to worry about those things, to remember to get it back after we broke up."

"Oh my god, Willa, how many times have you done this? How many . . . men . . . have you *manipulated* like this?"

"I'm good at being who men want me to be, who they need. When women leave, they leave a big gaping hole, and men start to realize just how much these women were doing to keep their world afloat. I mean, mental load—hello? It's not a crime to fill that hole, Mary."

"And that's why you hide your real identity behind nicknames and lies? Because it's all so aboveboard?"

"Listen to me," Willa said, and for once, her voice wasn't

charming, jovial. It was strained, and it was like I was seeing a glimpse into the real her, one tiny layer pulled back. "Things right now . . . they're tenuous, okay? I can't entirely explain it, but I have to lay low, and it certainly wasn't in my grand plan to run into you." She reached out her hand to mine, and for a moment, I let her take it. "And I hope, based on the fact that we really *were* friends, that we really *did* care about each other, I hope, after every walk we took and every joke we made about all the uptight Brooklyn moms around us, you'll let me do that. Because I swear to you, on every damn season of *The Bachelor* and *The Bachelorette*, that your friendship did mean something to me. For a little bit, it meant everything. I didn't want to ghost you, but I didn't have a choice. So in honor of that, I hope you won't go kicking up drama with Rich. With anyone."

I gazed at her a moment, and I wanted to believe it, I really did, but the hurt ran too deep. "You didn't ask me here to connect, not even to explain. You asked me here to secure my silence," I said. "You can say whatever you want, but that's the truth, isn't it?"

"Mary, my dear. *Please*. I care about you. I promise."

I whipped my hand away, disgusted. "You wouldn't have done what you did if that was true."

"Mary," Willa said, frantic now. "Just do me this favor." Her hands swept around, and I'd never seen her so off-kilter. "I have a lot to lose. You don't get it, okay? You can't *possibly* get it."

I stood so fast, my chair almost tipped over. "Maybe your sob story would have more sway with someone who wasn't already losing everything. I'm leaving, Willa. I'm sorry I came."

It was only after I'd backed away that Willa stood, and she said it so firmly it almost felt like a threat.

"Just keep this secret for me, and I'll make everything up to you," she said.

"Help me out, Mary. You won't regret it."

14

The night's tequila still pulsing in my veins, I stumbled out of the cab Willa had put me in and onto 19th Street in Brooklyn, my temporary home. I made my way up to the second floor and into the apartment, crashed into bed. Willa and I had spent our last drink in a mood almost jubilant, clinking our glasses to how much we hated George and men like him, how it was right for me to leave, to get away, even if the road ahead promised to be bumpy.

I was *drunk*. Drunk as that night Cassandra had had to take me home, right after Alex was born.

Yet I felt lighter, somehow. Willa knew my secrets now. All of George's awful punishments. She knew—and understood—why I could never go back.

She knew what I'd done, how I'd failed to help Cassandra. And she forgave me. She understood.

I pulled out my phone, tapped into messages, started a new one to Willa.

Thanks so much for listening tonight. Love ya.

Her reply took only seconds to come back.

Anytime, girlie. I'm sorry he's doing this to you.

I remembered the way Willa had joked.

I'll kill the man, I swear, and no one would suspect little old me.

Not for the first time, the thought shot into my head.

Sometimes I wish . . .

All jokes aside, it was a horrible thought to have. Who in their right mind could think that about the father of their own child, no matter how awful he was?

Only right now, it also felt like a *logical* thought to have.

George had made it so clear he would punish me and punish me until I came back. And if he really made good on his threats to take Alex away, how was I going to stand up to him and the Haywoods? It was David versus Goliath. As Willa would say . . . *yikes.*

The life insurance alone. It would give me freedom from them, all of them.

I could build myself a new life.

It was a horrible, terrible, evil thought.

And yet, hadn't George done terrible, evil things? Destroying beloved items. Messing with my career. Trying to mold my own son into yet another person to walk all over me?

What more would he do, if I gave him the chance?

Who would he turn Alex into if he had him, day in and day out?

Sometimes I wish . . .

Suddenly, it felt like it needed to be out, just as all the rest of it had been, and the tequila lured me, and as the room spun around me, I felt the pull, desperate, to rid myself even of this.

I typed it out to Willa, hit send before I could stop myself.

Sometimes I wish George were dead. It would make all of this easier. I would finally be free.

I saw the dots immediately, Willa typing, and I struggled to stay awake, but the room spun faster, and the phone fell from my hand, my lids suddenly heavy.

Then I was out.

15

The call came the moment I opened the door to the rental, still reeling from my meeting with Willa.

George. I held the phone in my palm, considered ignoring it, but on the off chance there was an issue with Alex, I felt I had to answer.

"Hello," I said.

"Mary." George's voice was warm, open, every hint of anger and antagonism drained from it, like a sponge squeezed out.

"Is Alex okay?"

"He's fine," he said. "That's not why I'm calling."

The line hung blank for a moment, and then: "We need to talk," he said. "I was too rash this morning. I thought when you let me sleep over, that meant . . ." His voice trailed off. "But I've been thinking, maybe you're right, about all of this. This whole last year. I made so many mistakes. I want to fix everything."

"What do you mean? How would you even—"

"Let me come over tomorrow," he said. "I'd ask you over here, but Henry's place is being renovated, and it's a mess. I can fix this, Mary. I can give you what you want."

"What I want?"

"What started all this. Her jewelry. You can give it back to her yourself."

"It's—it's with you? Now?"

"No, but I'll get it. *Fuck Henry*. I'm tired of cleaning up his messes at the expense of my own family. I'm tired of listening to him—to all of them—instead of trusting you. I just have to get some things in order first. I can come around eleven. Noon, latest."

"It's not just the jewelry, George. It's . . . everything. You never let me make a decision. You never even let me have my own voice. You . . . you punish me every time I go against you. You messed with my work. Do you know how scary that is? The thought that you could, would, destroy my career just because you wanted to?"

A pause on the line, and I found tears in my eyes. They were words I'd wanted to say to him for so long, had never found a way to.

George's voice was tender when he finally responded. "I know, Mary. You're right, about everything. I wasn't raised with the best influences. I was raised to get my way . . . always. It's not an excuse, I know, but it's the way it was. And I want to change that. I want to loosen up. I want to listen to you. I want to make all of this right, starting with this. *Please*."

The tears spilled down my cheeks, because they were

words I'd dreamed of, words I'd never, ever expected—not coming from him.

"Okay," I said. "Okay. I have something to do at ten, but by eleven, I should be back to the rental. But this doesn't mean—"

"I know, Mary, I know. It doesn't fix everything, but it's a start, isn't it? I'm going to make this up to you, as best I can," George said, taking a quick sharp breath.

"At least, I'm going to try."

I woke just after eight the next morning, full to the brim with nerves.

George would be here in hours. George would be here with Cassandra's jewelry. We had been fighting about it so long, I could hardly believe that he was actually going to relent, that I was going to have the chance to make things right with Cassandra.

I showered, tidied up the rental, in disarray from the day before, and unpacked my suitcases. Then I drove to the pre-school for the tour, spent an hour listening to a chipper woman who looked like she could front a Grateful Dead cover band show me Montessori-style learning centers, an art room, a toddler meditation space, and acres and acres of property where the kids could run. I tried to focus on the gorgeous all-wood playground, the coop where the kids helped raise chickens, the sheet of numbers she handed me, detailing tuition costs (still steep, but better, by far, than Brooklyn), early-bird registration, and sibling discounts. It was no use, of course. My mind was only on George. On what today would bring.

On whether I could believe my husband when he said he really wanted to change.

It was eleven fifteen by the time I pulled back in front of my rental. George was nowhere to be seen.

For a moment, I wondered whether he'd changed his mind. Was this whole thing another charade, a lie, a game? Was he screwing with me? But he'd said he'd come by noon, at the latest, so I forced myself to take a breath, to wait.

Eleven fifteen turned to eleven thirty, eleven forty-five, noon, and then twelve fifteen.

I called him then, his phone ringing endlessly. And again fifteen minutes later. Fifteen minutes after that. Finally, at one thirty, I'd had enough. He couldn't toy with me like this. Make promises, get my hopes up, and then not show up.

Besides, if he had that jewelry, I wanted it. Before he changed his mind, decided to align himself with Henry again.

Quickly, I googled Henry's address here in Woodstock again, found it in my maps.

I walked up to Tinker Street, then up a block until I hit Waterfall Way, taking a left. I wandered past a creek and waterfall, until I found a little blue house, tucked among the trees. Not very large or anything, but big enough that with modern amenities and a little bit of a revamp, Henry would make another killing when he sold it.

Once I was at the door, I spotted the swath of paint—Farrow & Ball Lake Red—and knew, without a doubt, I was at the right place. I knocked, but heard nothing. Knocked again. Tried the bell. Then I called George again. It rang and rang. No answer.

There was a small window at the top of the door, and I stood on my tiptoes, peered through.

Red. All I could see was red.

On instinct, I tried the door, found it unlocked. I threw it open, stepped across the threshold.

Red was everywhere. Raked across the off-white walls. Caking onto all that original wood—an elaborate chair rail, an exposed beam ceiling. Dripping, even, onto a tufted otto- man, a sheepskin throw. Droplets on an antique mirror. Splashed across all the décor added to make this place look cozy. A mounted Gibson guitar. Antique snowshoes. A topo- graphical map of Esopus Creek. Red, destroying what would have been a picture-perfect image, something you could pin up in the windows of the real estate office in town. I stepped forward, pulse pounding in my ears.

What the hell is going on? What happened here?

My eyes focused, and I spotted the open paint can in the corner, the brush dipped inside.

It wasn't blood; it was paint.

And before me, scrawled in huge letters across the wall:

DIE RICH PIG

A break-in, of course. Another break-in. But what happened?

Was . . . was he here when it happened?

Oh god, oh god, oh god.

I turned to my right, but as I did, my toe caught on some- thing soft and heavy, weighty and, and . . .

I fell forward, reaching out and scrambling to catch my- self, my knees smashing against the hardwood floor, my hands barely breaking my fall. I struggled to push myself up, but once I did, I screamed.

Because there it was, red again.

But not paint this time. Blood. Spatters and splatters and splotches and pools.

And in the midst of the blood, a body.

Splayed out and large, frozen in horror.

My husband. The one I'd loved, the one I'd hated, the one who had seemed, for once, like he actually wanted to change.

The one I would never, ever get to talk to again.

George.

PART TWO

PART TWO

16

WILLA

Sometimes I wish George were dead. It would make all of this easier. I would finally be free.

It was nearly eleven, dark apart from the streetlamps that lined the edge of Prospect Park, and I was situated on a bench, paralyzed with indecision. Nothing but huge oak trees behind me; electric bikes, scooters and cars, zipping across the avenue in front.

I'd poured Mary into a cab fifteen minutes ago, then stopped when I'd gotten her last text.

The words were a shock, coming from her. From sweet, play-by-the-rules Mary. Course, it was still Mary through and through. So cautious. So careful.

I could kill the bastard, that's what I would say if someone was fucking with my things, my work, trying to take my kid from me. None of this conditional wishing shit.

I sized up the brownstone. How absurdly large, how incredibly unfair. That one family should have so much when so many others were barely getting by. When the taxes on this place alone could cover all my parents' yearly mortgage. When I was growing up, even into my twenties, I thought rich people were smart or special, clever or at least very business-savvy. Then I met them. Then I lived with them, slept with them, cared for their children. And what I learned was that most of them were just lucky. Lucky and aware enough to know that they *had* gotten the biggest slice of the pie, ready to cling to it with clumsy, greasy hands.

Looking at the brownstone now, it wasn't that I didn't feel bad, course I did. I liked Mary, truly. Liked the way she seemed to genuinely care for me, to insist I drink water, to grab me before I stepped into a pile of shit. I liked the way she trusted me, even though she barely knew me. I liked the way she looked at Alex with nothing but earnest love in her eyes, like all she wanted was to not fuck him up, but she worried that she—or her situation—might do it in the end. I even liked what she'd told me tonight—here she was, mothering a kid who could have it all, have anything, and what she was worried about was not how she'd get him into Harvard, but whether he'd grow up to be kind, kinder than his dad.

Mary hadn't asked for this, and she certainly didn't deserve it. It was unfair, obviously.

But life isn't fair, is it?

It's a transaction. One person wants one thing, and another gives it, getting something in return. Some transactions, we're okay with. Some we even celebrate, no matter if they're good for us or not. Marriage, packing a venue full of best friends in ill-fitting chiffon dresses, propping tables with chalkboard signs and ranunculus blooms so everyone can cheer on a piece of paper filed with the local government. A hoped-for new job, a contract signed that promises you'll answer to them, day in and day out, fifty-two weeks a year minus two for vacations and a few personal days (if you're lucky!), a vow to spend more time with your coworkers, kissing your boss's ass, working the career ladder like a woodworker with a chisel, than you'll ever devote to your family, your friends, or even yourself. The purchase of a new home, a thirty-year promise crafted of equity and escrow and flood insurance and a now-empty savings account, the ubiquitous house-keys-and-champagne-flute photo inevitably to follow on social media. *We did it! We looked the man straight in the face, and we said, yes sir, we will play your game, and we'll smile while we're doing it.*

Other transactions, we look down on. Bankruptcy filings. Sex work and separations. Foreclosures and any number of nonviolent felonies that leave a bad taste in society's mouth.

We don't like the things that show us that it's all a trade-off. That people want sex and are willing to pay for it. That substances are addictive. That the so-called American dream is stacked against you from the start. That breaking the rules is the only way to even the score.

But at the end of the day, we're all just humans. Humans with wants, with needs. Ones who never evolve past trading homemade peanut-butter-and-jelly for another kid's Cool Ranch Doritos.

Maybe a better me, a more naïve me, would give it all up—abandon this particular transaction—so I didn't have to toss a grenade into what had become a real friendship with Mary. And maybe there was some part of me, however small, that still was good. Maybe that was why I was sitting here on a hard bench on the edge of the park, running my nails over a bit of peeling paint and staring at my damn phone. Deciding.

I flicked through Mary's texts—her drunken confessions— and there was that stupid feeling in my stomach again. Guilt. God damn it.

I tapped out of her texts and back to his. Ones that had come in just as I was loading her drunk ass into a cab.

Dying to see you, come over?

And the address beneath, the address of the brownstone across the street.

Behold it now, in all its glory. The red door. The perfectly manicured plants. A light on up in the second story, a bedroom waiting for me.

A bedroom that Mary, herself, had slept in for so many years.

I took a deep breath, then thought, fuck it. Shot off the text.

Rounding the corner, be there in 2.

I stood, straightened my silk dress, reapplied my lipstick.

Maybe a better woman would have walked away, left it all behind.

But I wasn't a better woman. I was me.

Besides, I thought as I crossed the street against the light, daring one of the bikers to try to hit me, George can't get away with *everything*, can he?

17

MARY

Mrs. Haywood. Are you Mrs. Haywood?"

I jolted at the sight of the woman in front of me, standing out amid the chaos, the flash of the crime-scene photographer's camera, the blood still on the ground, remnants clinging to my own hands, to my pants, the paint that looked like blood on the walls around me. And people, so many people. Paramedics, police, and photographers.

Chaos, all around me. Chaos, and carnage.

I blinked twice, trying to pull myself back to the present. It had all happened so fast. Finding George. Scrambling to get my hands on my phone. Dialing 911 with bloody fingers. Telling the dispatcher everything I knew. Waiting by his body, feeling for his pulse, for breath coming from his mouth. Knowing my husband, Alex's father, was dead. Knowing nothing would ever, ever be the same again. Then the sound of the siren and all the people invading this place.

People who asked me questions and took evidence off my body. People who looked at me like this was all my fault.

"Mrs. Haywood?" the woman said again.

"Yes," I said finally. "Mary."

"Detective Morales," she said.

My eyes widened, taking in her glossy dark-brown hair and Elizabeth Taylor eyes. The sort of posture that made her medium height seem taller. I hadn't taken her for a detective, and yet, of course she was. Because here *I* was, my dead husband's blood on my hands. Of course there would be a detective. And of course she'd want to talk to me.

"Perhaps we can go somewhere a bit quieter?" she prompted.

I nodded, then followed her, the click of her heels leading us into a kitchen, cabinet faces off, glossy tiles half-applied on one wall, and to a small table surrounded by four chairs.

"We'll need your shirt and pants to go in here." She opened a large zip-top plastic bag with *EVIDENCE* printed across it and set it on the table, gesturing to my blood-spattered jeans.

"What do I—"

"There are some sweats in here," she said, placing a shopping bag on the table as well. "Should tide you over for now."

"Okay," I said cautiously. I scanned the kitchen, looking for a door to a bathroom, but the detective only turned around, clearly waiting for me to undress right then and there.

Cooperate, I thought. Just cooperate. Don't make this look worse than it is.

Carefully, I slipped off my sandals, then slithered out of my jeans and tank, tucked them into the evidence bag, and grabbed a pair of oversized sweats and a large T-shirt that read *Woodstock Police Annual 5K*.

When I was done, I cleared my throat, and Morales turned around. She grabbed the evidence bag, pressed the top shut, and pulled out a notebook instead. "Tell me everything that happened, then."

"I already talked to one of the officers."

"I know," she said, all business. "But I want to hear it myself."

I nodded, my heart thumping loud in my chest, the cacophony of sound still banging on in the front room. "Can I sit?"

Morales didn't say no, and I sank into the chair, spent. She didn't take a seat herself, making the power dynamic even more off, but there was nothing to do about it now.

"Start from the beginning," she said. "What was the plan this morning?"

"George was going to come over to my place. He was supposed to get there around eleven or noon."

"And what about the hours leading up to that? What did you do?"

I bristled, knowing the implication. She wanted an alibi. My god. "I had a meeting, at a preschool on the edge of town. Woodstock Kids Academy. The woman there, the director—Janice, I think—she showed me around. We met at ten. I left a little before eleven."

"Yes," Morales said. "I know Janice well. We'll speak to her. And before that?"

"I was at my rental," I said. "Tidying up. Unpacking. Making coffee, you know."

"So no one else saw you then?"

A chill ran down my arms. "No."

"Right," she went on. "Back to the meeting. Why were you and your husband staying in separate places? Neither of you live here, correct?"

"Oh," I said. "Sorry. I figured someone would have said. We're separated. I was planning on moving up here, and I came to look at possible rentals, daycares. That's why I was at the preschool."

"So why was Mr. Haywood here, then?"

"He wanted to reconcile. He . . ." My voice trailed off, briefly. "He wanted us to give the marriage another chance."

"And you didn't?" Morales raised an eyebrow.

"We've been apart since February. I guess I thought it was time to move on."

The detective didn't ask why, only made a note. "But you agreed for him to come over. Why?"

My heart thumped heavily as I thought of my conversation with George last night. The way he'd insisted he'd actually wanted to change. Was it real, or was it another game of his? I would never know, and I ached with the grief of it. Tears filled my eyes, and I felt, almost, like I would never know who my husband really was.

"He was going to bring over some jewelry," I managed, swiping away the tears. Morales tossed a pack of travel tissues on the table between us, and I took one.

Then she took a seat herself, on my level now. "What jewelry?" she asked gently.

"George was holding on to jewelry that belonged to his brother's wife. Henry and Cassandra. They're caught up in a messy divorce," I said, blotting beneath my eyes. "George and I had been arguing about it. I thought he should give it back to her, but he kept taking Henry's side. Until last night. He called me, said that he wanted to give it back, that he"— more tears, more blotting—"that he wanted to change a lot of things, start actually listening to me."

"Was it valuable jewelry?" Morales asked.

"Yes," I said, nodding. "Yes, very valuable. And then George didn't show up, and I tried calling a bunch of times, and at one thirty, I decided to come over here instead, and I got here, and I knocked a bunch of times, and I looked through the window in the front door, and I saw—it looked like blood—I guess it was paint, but I didn't know." I gasped to catch my breath. "I saw the graffiti first when I opened the door, and I thought it was another break-in, but then I turned—" I paused, the tears gushing forth now. "I turned and I tripped," I blubbered. "And I fell, and—it was him."

Morales nodded gently, then glanced at my hands, red still caked into the creases of my skin.

"It was from the fall," I said. "I called 911 right away, I promise you. Then everyone got here. And now here I am." I sniffled, grabbed a new tissue, crumpled the other one in my palm.

"Yes," Morales said. "Here you are." She paused, then flipped a page in her book. "Did you find the jewelry, when you arrived?"

I shook my head almost viciously. "No," I said. "No, of course not. I saw him, and I completely forgot all about it."

She cleared her throat, obviously changing tack. "Okay, then. Did your husband have any enemies?"

"No," I said quickly. "But Henry did. He was always arguing with people online. And then all his properties were getting broken into, and there was graffiti at all of them. And this is *his* place. Someone could have mistaken George for Henry. They look a lot alike." My voice cracked. "But I don't know why someone would kill him. It's only ever been break-ins before. Nothing——" George's dead eyes flashed again to my mind, and I felt like I might throw up. "Nothing like this."

Morales raised an eyebrow. "Things do escalate. We will look into the break-ins. Speak to the rest of the Haywoods."

"Henry was here Saturday. I don't know if he's still in town or back in Brooklyn. George's parents are in Montauk. My son is there, staying with them. They don't even know—should I call them? I didn't even think to . . ."

"We'll send an officer to inform them today. Make sure they know before the news gets hold of it."

News, I thought. I imagined vultures pouncing. Descending on the most obvious of obvious suspects—me. The estranged wife, tied up in a bitter custody battle. This was bad. Very bad.

"I didn't kill him," I said, my voice earnest, desperate, tears streaming down my cheeks. "No matter what was going on with our separation, I couldn't—I wouldn't—kill him. He's the—he was the—the father of my child. He said he wanted to change—actually work things out between us."

Morales's eyes caught mine, and I couldn't tell if she believed me. I knew, deep down, that there were so many reasons not to.

"What about anyone close to him?" she asked. "Was there another girlfriend, an affair partner?"

"No," I said, rearing back. "God, no. Our separation had

nothing to do with that. George wasn't a cheater. I'm not, either."

"What about since the separation?" she pressed. "If that was in February, then it's been six months already. Was Mr. Haywood dating? Seeing anyone? Anyone at all, even if it was only casual?"

My shoulders seized up, and I crumpled the tissues even tighter in my hand, like if I could turn them into the smallest ball possible, somehow, this would all go away.

The thought of George with someone else had never seriously occurred to me, he'd always been so desperate to win me back. After all, who threatens to go for full custody solely to force someone to return if they're distracted and newly in love, if they're living up a single, bachelor life?

But now, the idea was like a flashing neon sign, one that couldn't be turned off. I inhaled, feeling foolish, because suddenly it seemed clear. George and all his efforts to get me back had cooled off a bit, hadn't they? Right around the middle of June. He'd seemed less desperate, more . . . distracted. Then in early July, he'd become so much more reasonable. He'd agreed to joint custody. Agreed for me to come up here. Encouraged me to book the place in Woodstock to get it all sorted. He and I had spoken less from that point on, knowing things were on the way to finally resolving.

But then, this. Something had changed between then and now. Something that had caused him to go back on everything we'd agreed to. To want me back more than ever, to go to any lengths to stop me from leaving.

Had he met someone this summer? Had things gone wrong between them, somehow?

Was there a woman, out there, who hurt my husband?

"Did you think of something, Mrs. Haywood?" Morales prompted.

"No," I said automatically. "I mean, I guess I don't know." I swallowed back a rising feeling of dread in my chest. "If George was seeing someone, I never met her."

I took a deep breath, then used the crumpled ball of tissues to pat my eyes one more time.

"I never knew anything about her at all."

18

WILLA

Y ou're gorgeous, you know that." George kissed me
one more time on the mouth, biting the edge of my
bottom lip as he pulled away. "I have to hop in the
shower. Don't rush out."

He crossed the wildly spacious bedroom in three strides,
his body, right down to his bare ass, lithe and strong. People
with money always hired the best personal trainers. Even
Jack's ass was more toned than mine, despite his age. Then
George slipped into an en suite bathroom that was bigger
than my entire bedroom growing up. Closed the door behind him.

A distinct turn of the lock. Presumptuous much? Did he
think I was going to follow him in there and beg for another
go? Still, I decided it was a good thing. The lock itself was
super loud. A little warning for me before he opened the
door again.

My phone buzzed with a text from Jack—**Hope you had fun and aren't feeling it too hard this morning! Jack is asking for you ❤**—but I ignored it, hopping out of bed to the sound of water running. I stuffed my dirty underwear in the bottom of my purse and pulled my silk dress over my head.

I scanned the room, looking. Classic Brooklyn. Crown molding. White walls. Black chandelier. Framed modern art. Fiddle-leaf fig. Rich-people décor. Mary had said the safe was in the bedroom, but where? A few quick steps and I was in front of the big art piece. Carefully, I lifted the corner an inch off the wall—nothing but drywall and dust. Then I turned, looking at the bed. *Bingo.* Flanked by nightstands, each beneath a small framed print. With this much space, you'd think they'd get another big painting or even some huge mirror so they could watch themselves fuck.

No, these prints seemed purposely put there to cover something.

Listening to the pulse of the shower, I beelined to George's side of the bed and slid the frame one inch, two inches, and then . . .

Jackpot. The wealthy truly were such clichés. Hiding valuables in a wall safe like this was a goddamn Agatha Christie novel.

The thing was black steel, simple. Didn't even look biometric. Basic, like the ones they give you in hotel rooms. Mary had once called George a Luddite. Apparently, that was going to work in my favor.

The shower was still running, and my fingers pulsed at the thought of what must lie mere inches away. I glanced at the safe's ten-digit keypad, a keyhole beneath. Two nightstands. George wouldn't write the code down, would he?

Leave the key? Not likely, but I had to check. I tugged on the handle of the nightstand, found a mess. Loads of cash, for one thing, wads of it, crumpled and tossed in. No way he even knew how much was in there. To guys like George, cash came out of wallets and went into drawers. Privileged fuck. I took two twenties and slipped them into my bra, then tried to sort through the rest: Business cards. Cuff links. Nothing unexpected.

Another squeak of pipes. My shoulders jolted. Was George one of those speed-showerers? If so, it would totally throw me off. A moment, and then the sound of water continued. He must have been adjusting the temperature. I popped the frame back into place, went around to Mary's side. This one was neat and tidy, full-on Marie Kondo–ized. Not one but two vibrators (good for you, Mary!), plus some serious-looking book that proudly proclaimed its National Book Award Finalist status with a gaudy gold label. *Huh*. I'd always pictured her as a mystery kind of girl like me, all Gillian Flynn and Patricia Highsmith, but maybe she was an intellectual at heart. Underneath the book: a receipt from Blue Bottle Coffee and a tag for bougie lingerie. And at the very bottom, black velvet, a *Made in Italy* sticker on the back. Clear, crystal edges. A picture frame, the kind a Great-Aunt Lydia would insist on giving for a wedding. I flipped it over, saw Alex first. His soft brown curls, his overeager kid smile. The laughter in his eyes. Behind Alex, George. Next to him, Mary. There it was again, that slick and oily feeling from last night. Guilt.

I'd never duped a woman before. Never pretended to be someone's friend.

Never actually made a friend entirely by accident.

She doesn't deserve this.

The thought was strong, cutting, as I looked at the photo, Mary's hair tousled by the wind, flipping out slightly at the bottom. But what was I supposed to do now? Leave? Never see George again? Stay with Jack, love on Jack Junior? Go to the park with Mary and Alex? Actually *be* the person I'd done such a good job pretending to be?

It wouldn't last, anyway. Jack would get tired of me, or I would get tired of him. Then I'd be on to the next one, yet again.

I wasn't getting any younger. I couldn't keep this up forever . . .

My phone buzzed, and I jumped, dropping the frame back into the drawer.

It was so good to hang last night, feeling it this morning though! Love ya, and sorry about my drunken ramblings. Obviously I was just joking. Tequila, you know!

Mary. God. Mary, whose husband I'd just fucked. Whose things I was picking through right now.

Why did she have to be so nice? So lovely?

My stomach roiled, the guilt sloshing around like a poison.

It still wasn't too late to stop. George would never tell her he was sleeping with other people. But my eyes locked back on the print, on the safe waiting behind it. On the trove of jewelry within.

How could I walk away now?

The Haywoods had to pay for what they'd done.

And I was happy to cash in on that payment.

19

MARY

NOW
MONDAY, AUGUST 16
WOODSTOCK, NEW YORK

I stared down at my now-clean hands, no hint of George's blood left. I was sitting in a hard plastic chair that was half-cracked and clicked anytime I so much as breathed, in an empty room in the Woodstock police station—an interview room.

Once Morales was done with her questions, a baby-faced officer who'd never even told me his name had driven me off the scene, not back to my rental, as I'd hoped, but instead to the police station several miles outside town. He'd asked me to put my phone and purse in a clear plastic bin up front and then deposited me in this room, swiped the inside of my cheek for DNA, insisting that since I'd been at the scene, the only way to rule me out was to have access to that information, and I'd been too afraid of looking even more guilty to object. Then he'd carefully cleaned my hands with alcohol wipes before taking my prints on a digital reader. When he was done, he'd asked me to go over everything again, for a statement, and I'd told him what I'd told Morales, and what I'd told the officers who'd first arrived to the scene before that, careful to say it all in the same order, to not mess up any details, already scared I was somehow flubbing it up, knowing how it would look if I made even one mistake. The officer had typed everything up on a dinosaur of a laptop, then left me alone in the interview room.

Now I looked up at the ticking clock, askew on its hook on the wall. It was four thirty. I'd been sitting here, alone, for a half hour now, nothing to do but return, in my mind, over and over again to George's dead body. To realize that nothing on earth would ever bring him back, would ever let me know if he really was sorry, if he really had wanted to change. And wondering, too, just how much trouble I was in. If I was truly a suspect, or if this was all a formality? My sweet little boy had lost his father. He was going to grow up now on a completely different trajectory, to live with the knowledge his whole entire life: *My dad was murdered. My dad is gone.* Was there a chance, even small, that Alex would lose not only his dad, but his mom, too?

Should I be calling a lawyer already? And who would I call anyway? Ron Davis and his associates couldn't even manage to pass on the initial divorce offer before George told me himself. I had no money for someone else. I barely even had the money for him. There was George's life insurance, but that would probably take forever to pay out and would only serve to count as another mark against me. Real motive. I could call Rachel or my mom, but they hardly had a few dimes between them, Rachel content to work in retail, my mom saddled with a slew of medical bills from her recent fall. No, the only ones in my life who had money—and quick access to it—were the Haywoods. And what would they think? Had an officer already informed them that their one-time daughter-in-law had called the police with their son dead in the room and blood literally on her hands?

God, had they already told Alex?

He needed me now, more than ever.

I needed him, too.

The door clicked, then burst open. The baby-faced guy was back. He eyed me, then crossed his arms, a power stance. Oh god, I thought. They're going to do it now. They're going to charge me with my husband's murder.

I could only think of Alex. How badly I wanted to see him, to squeeze him, to kiss his chubby cheeks and smell the distinct powdery scent of his Buzz Lightyear Pull-Ups. To brush Cheerio crumbs off the bottom of his lip and feel the quick pulse of his heartbeat on mine, delight in the way he said, "Mama, don't go." Would the next time I see him be in some jail cell? God, would Ruth and Frank even bring him to visit if they thought I'd killed their son?

The officer's arms uncrossed. "You're free to go now. But you need to stay in the area. Detective Morales will want to talk to you again."

Relief flooded through me. They weren't arresting me. They weren't going to keep me from Alex.

The officer leaned against the doorjamb. "Do you have someone you can call to come get you? We were going to have an officer drive you back, but he just went out on a call. I can take you at the end of my shift, but it's not for a couple of hours still. Unless you want to wait."

"No," I said, shaking my head almost viciously. "I don't want to wait. But I don't even have my phone."

"It's up at the front with your other things. I'll leave you to it, then. Got work to do. And like I said, stay close."

I wandered into an empty hallway, retraced my steps until I was back at the front, the beeping of walkies, the shuffling of papers, the symphony of sound an eerie mundanity when everything in my world was falling apart.

"Excuse me," I said to the woman up front. "I think my things are up here."

"Mary Haywood?" she asked.

I nodded, and she pushed the bin toward me. I grabbed my purse, my keys, my phone, tapping the last to life. The battery was nearly dead, but I opened a car service app. I set my location, tried to call a ride, but the closest car was forty-five minutes away. I checked another app. No cars on there at all.

I looked up at the woman. "Is there a taxi service in Woodstock?"

"Not really," she said matter-of-factly. "There are some by the train station, but that's across the river in Rhinebeck, they won't come get you out here. You can try the apps, but it can take a while for a car to show up."

"I tried them. There's nothing."

She shrugged, as if this wasn't remotely her problem, and I suppose it wasn't. "One of the officers can drive you, but not until the shift change at seven. There's no one you can call?"

No, I thought. I didn't know anyone in town. Henry was probably gone by now, and he wouldn't help me anyway.

Only I *did* know someone. Someone who'd asked me to help her only last night.

A shiver ran up my spine. I wanted nothing to do with her, her and her lies. But I wasn't about to sit here for two hours, either.

So with shaking fingers, I tapped into my contacts, found her name. A name that wasn't really her name at all.

It rang only twice and then there she was. "Hello," she said, her voice warm, yet surprised. "I didn't think I'd hear from you, not after last night."

I struggled to find the right words.

"Mary," Willa said. "Is everything okay?"

"No," I said. "No, it isn't. Listen. I'm at the Woodstock police station. I need you to pick me up."

"What . . . what happened?"

"It's George," I said, my voice choking with emotion. "It's George. He's dead."

A pause, a distinct one—or was I imagining it?—and then Willa gasped. Immediately, I heard a shuffling in the background. "Oh my god," she said. "Oh my god."

More tears came down then, and I found myself struggling to catch my breath.

"It's okay, Mary," Willa said. "I'm only ten minutes away. Just hang tight. I'll be right there."

20

WILLA

Headed out to the playground, maybe I'll see you there?

I flipped my phone over, balancing it on one thigh. Little Jack zoomed around the living room like a plane on steroids.

It had been four days since I'd seen Mary. She'd texted me once each day. All of the mesages earnest. Unreciprocated. Half of me wanted to grab Jack, get him onto his scooter, text her that I'd be right there, put her out of her misery.

I couldn't. Not until I fully made a decision. Because despite everything I'd felt when I found George's wall safe, now I found myself waffling. Unsure.

I tapped my nails against the back of my phone and adjusted myself on the Italian leather sofa.

My cold heart, apparently, wasn't totally made of stone,

because I'd missed her this week. And I swear it wasn't guilt or my barely functioning moral compass. I actually missed *her*. No one knew, not one of the men I'd been with, how much I missed having a real friend. A woman. For moral support and margaritas. Gossip and girl talk.

"Willa! Willa!" Jack Junior yelled, flailing his arms about wildly.

"What is it, buddy?"

"You weren't *looking*."

I put my phone in my pocket—out of sight, out of mind. "I am now."

Jack was cute, he really was—Jack Senior, too. I'd only slept with George once. It wasn't too late to give it all up. Pass on the big payday. Stay friends with Mary. Get Jack to buy me some jewelry instead. Why was it my job to punish the Haywoods? I didn't owe anyone anything. The world was unfair. Period.

Yes, I wasn't getting any younger. Yes, I needed some security—eventually—but I wasn't exactly decrepit yet. I didn't have to blow it all up now. I could wait . . .

Jack Junior came in for a crash landing. Overhead, the sound of Jack Senior's footsteps. After his *very important call*, we were off to Red Hook for the day with Jack's work buddy, Brad.

Jack and Brad would spend the afternoon pounding buckets of beers and sucking meat from crab legs. I'd be stuck taking care of both Jack Junior and Brad's kid, but I didn't really mind. This was the business I'd chosen, right?

The stairs creaked, and then there was Jack, his silver hair glistening, his face barely flushed. "Shall we, then?"

A lesser woman—or perhaps a more self-respecting woman—would have needed time to check she had everything. Touch up makeup. Pack a bag with snacks and waters, extra tissues and baby wipes, a visor and sunscreen. A different woman might have asked what the rush was. Not me. I made it easy for them—always.

"Let's." I stood, opened my arms so Jack Junior could rush into them. I pulled him to my body and in the living room's gilded mirror, I looked at myself, at my designer black jumpsuit, at my perfectly applied lip stain, at the espadrilles Jack had gotten me last week. Jack Junior's blond curls tumbled onto my shoulder. We were a picture of familial bliss, one that looked easy but required so much to maintain.

But when Jack walked up behind us, completing our family with his massive frame, he frowned. "You look tired," he said.

I blinked. He'd never said something so clipped. So *resentful.*

"You must have really gone hard with your friend the other night."

The sun was shining, and the place was packed.

The crab shack was painfully hip. It had all kinds of Nantucket vibes, even though we were still very much in Brooklyn, overlooking IKEA, not the Atlantic Ocean. Everything was bright. Bright-colored umbrellas. Bright crab shells. Bright faces, flush with sunshine and alcohol. Families out with their kids, tossing beanbags into cornhole boards. Twentysomethings clinking Coronas, lipstick already smudging. OGs who missed the old Brooklyn, when Nathan's hot dogs were ten cents and there were *real* freaks at Coney Island.

We were packed around a picnic table, and Jack Senior and Brad were making a dent in the second bucket of beers on the table while I de-shelled crabs and cut corn off the cob so the two little princes could eat without choking. Wiped butter off their faces and pulled packs of apple juice from my purse just for them.

"Now, this is a woman," Brad said, the alcohol quite obviously going to his head. "Gorgeous. Sexy."

"Hey now," Jack said.

"Sorry," Brad said to Jack, wiping a bit of sweat off his brow. "I just mean she's got it all," he said as if I weren't sitting right there. "Like Mary Poppins but hotter."

I looked to Jack, waiting for him to tell Brad to shut up. But Jack only leaned in, grabbed my chin with a cold finger, and turned my face to his. He kissed me, then didn't pull away, darted his tongue into my mouth and circled within, biting my tongue hard enough that I wanted almost to cry out, right there in front of the kids. Brad. Everyone.

When he pulled away, he was grinning, like a boy who'd made his mark, shot through the heart of a doe. "She sure is," Jack said. He stood, grabbed my hand in his. "Show me where the bathroom is, will you?"

Brad raised an eyebrow.

"Watch the kids a minute," Jack said before turning, tugging me along.

We made our way through the crowds, Jack never letting go. Then, suddenly, we were in the back, and there was an all-gender restroom without a line. Jack whipped open the door with gusto and practically pushed me inside.

"What are you doing?" I asked.

"You look so fucking hot right now," he said. "I can't help myself."

"You're drunk," I said. It was bold. I didn't usually question him outright. But he was being especially dickish.

He cocked his head, looked like he was going to tell me never to talk like that again, but then shrugged, leaned in, pressed me against the driftwood-and-shiplap walls of the bathroom.

I could have told him no, could have pushed him away. Jack was a lot of things but he wasn't a rapist. Still, I didn't. I liked this part. The excitement. The thrill. Jack pulled my skirt up and his own zipper down, pressed inside me, hard as a rock.

When it was over, he pulled away, zipped up, stared at me.

"I want you out of my house by the morning."

My eyes narrowed, and for a moment I couldn't even believe I'd heard him right. "What?"

"I know about your little sleepover," he said. "I know you weren't with a friend."

"I wasn't—"

"Spare me the lies. I *know*."

"But how—"

"It doesn't matter," he snapped. "I'm not going to be a fool."

"What about Jack Junior?" I asked.

He shrugged. "It sucks, but he'll get over it."

I opened my mouth, my jaw agape. This was not supposed to happen. Not until I'd made more progress with George. Not until I'd decided what exactly I was going to do with Mary.

"Jack," I said, my voice pleading. "Jack Junior will be heartbroken."

"Should have thought of that before you fucked another guy." He took a breath, and for a moment, all of the anger was gone, and there was only sadness and pain. "I thought I loved you," he said. "Now, stay the fuck away from us."

He turned then, leaving me there, standing in that dingy bathroom, trying to figure out what the hell to do next.

My phone buzzed, and I took it out, thinking it might be Mary again, asking me what had happened.

It wasn't Mary, though. It was George.

When can I see you again?

I stared at the text, my face burning with shame. I thought I'd have more time.

Reality hit me like a slap across the face. I had no place to live as of tomorrow. A hotel in Brooklyn would eat through my savings fast. I needed someone to rely on. I had no choice.

The bridge I'd thought I could walk right back over only an hour ago had, in an instant, been burned.

George was the only one I had now.

I couldn't ever talk to Mary again.

21

MARY

Willa insisted on coming in with me once we got back to my rental in Woodstock, and I let her, too exhausted and spent to protest—and also more than a little bit afraid to be alone. She was wearing jeans and a black tee and a boho scarf around her neck, and once she got inside, I locked the door behind me, checking the deadbolt twice.

It had hit me fully on the ride back: the police might not realize it, but *I* knew I didn't kill George. That meant someone was out there, someone who'd wanted to hurt him, hurt the Haywoods, maybe. How did I know they weren't going to come after me, too? To the outside world, to anyone who didn't know me personally, George and I were still very much together. The Haywoods had gone to great lengths to keep the whole thing quiet.

Willa disappeared into the kitchen to get us waters, and

I plugged my phone into the charger on one wall, dialed Ruth, eager to talk to Alex. It rang and rang, but she didn't answer. I tried Frank, too. Genevieve, the nanny, who was twenty-six and absolutely glued to her phone. Still nothing. My heart ached again with longing. I wanted to hear every garbled word, every baby pitch, of Alex's voice, wanted to look into his eyes—George's eyes—and know that some-how the two of us would be okay. That there would be hurt, there would be loss, but I would protect him as best as I could.

I wanted to talk to Ruth and Frank, explain that this had nothing to do with me. Make a plan. The cops had insisted I stay close, but there was no reason my in-laws couldn't come up here, bring Alex to me, where he belonged.

Willa emerged from the kitchen with two glasses of water held easily in one hand, a pair of wineglasses in the other, and a bottle of wine tucked beneath her arm. She set it all down on the coffee table with the ease of someone who'd waited on many a customer at many a restaurant.

"I figured you'd want something a little stronger, too."

I guzzled the glass of water, and she retrieved a cork-screw from her pocket and removed the cork in three satis-fying twists. She filled the wineglass halfway and held it out to me.

After a moment, I set the water down and took it, quickly gulping some back. It did help, after all. I followed up with a quick sip.

Willa poured herself a glass and sat opposite me in the small living room.

"What happened?" she asked. "Did you—I mean—were you the one to find him?"

I nodded.

"You went over there?" Willa prompted.

"He was supposed to come to me—I'd agreed to talk with him, one more time—but he didn't show."

Willa took a long, slow sip of wine. "I know it's awful, everything that happened, but part of it at least must feel like a relief." She leaned back into the sofa and stretched out her arms, like a woman in a Matisse painting. Like she belonged here, somehow. Here, with me.

"What must feel like a relief?" I asked.

"Well, it's what you wanted, isn't it?" Willa went on, so matter-of-fact. "It's what you *said* you wanted."

My stomach twisted. "I wanted to be free of him," I said. "Not like this."

Willa's eyes lasered in on mine, and a million words seemed to pass between us without so much as one being exchanged. She probably still had that drunken text, right there on her phone. Was that why she'd agreed so easily to come get me? Why she was inside my living room now?

She wanted my silence about her past. And now she had it, didn't she? Because if I crossed her, she could go straight to the cops, show them those words.

Lord, they could do me in.

Sometimes I wish George were dead. It would make all of this easier. I would finally be free.

"You don't actually think I had anything to *do* with this, do you?"

Willa hesitated, and then her eyebrows scrunched up. "No, Mary. No, of course not."

"Because what I said, that last night we hung out. I was drunk. I didn't mean it."

"Course you didn't," Willa said, but there was a hint, right there in her voice. A hint of *something*.

"Do you still have it?" I asked.

"Have what?"

"The text."

Willa took another sip of wine, her eyes leaving mine briefly. Then she set her glass down, making it clatter on the table. "I don't keep old texts," she said. "Takes too much space on my phone. They automatically delete after thirty days, so you don't have to worry, okay?"

"Okay," I said hesitantly. I cleared my throat. "Do you need to get back to your . . . *family* here? After you already snuck off last night?"

"I don't, actually," Willa said. "Rich—that's the guy— his mom, she had a fall this morning, and she's in the hospital. She's down in New Paltz, and he went there to see her, make sure she's okay. He took Poppy with him." Willa took another sip of wine. "Don't forget your water, Mary. And we should get some food, too. I'm guessing you haven't eaten. That's what grief does, you know. Time for me to take care of you, for once."

I knew I could stop her, tell her to go. I should, shouldn't I? She was a liar, a con artist. Couldn't trust her as far as I could throw her.

But, much as I hated the truth of it, she was also the *only* person in town who might have my back. And already, she was heading to the kitchen, returning with takeout menus presumably grabbed from a drawer. "Pizza?"

I could only nod, watch as she pulled out her phone, got ready to order.

"I won't say anything to the guy, you know, about your past."

"Thank you, Mary, my dear," Willa said, looking up from her phone. "And I won't say anything about that text, either." Her mouth spread into a casual grin. "After all, that's what friends are for, right? Keeping each other's secrets."

22

WILLA

I t was weird as hell.

Sitting at Mary's kitchen island in her massive brownstone, surrounded by her family. Scratching a nail over her bougie soapstone counters. Propping my ass on one of her barstools. Drinking from one of her coffee mugs.

And the worst ones, of course.

Sleeping with her husband.

Pouring Cheerios into a bowl for her son.

"Mo! Mo!" Alex yelled with abandon.

The kid loved abundance, wouldn't touch his Tupperware if it was anything less than halfway full. I guessed it would work out for him, in the end. He was all set to live an abundant life.

You shouldn't know this. You shouldn't know the eating preferences of her son.

This was why I didn't con women. This was why I didn't make friends.

Mary's most recent text had come only last night, when I was in her bed with her husband, enjoying the feel of her thousand-thread-count sheets.

Willa, have I upset you in some way?

It was the most direct she'd been since I stopped talking to her weeks ago.

It had touched me, it really had, how she kept on trying. It was almost like she really cared about me. Not for my looks, for the sex, for the status of having a skinny platinum blonde draped on your arm. Not for the way I shouldered the mental load, took care of the kids. She cared about me for *me*. She laughed at all my dumb jokes. She wanted to know my history. And I knew she felt, as I did, too, that when we were together, there was no need to play a role. Ironic, of course, because I was playacting in so many ways, but in the ones that mattered, I was true true true.

I wanted to respond to her text, but I'd promised myself I wouldn't. Didn't want to give her any hope, much as I missed her. Ghosting seemed the kindest option, all things considered.

"You really are good with kids," George said, breaking my thoughts as he broke eggs into a pan. He wore a crisp white button-down and deep-indigo jeans.

"I used to babysit a lot," I said. "Growing up." George didn't ask where I was from, and I knew he didn't care, so long as I was an easy fuck. Mary had asked.

Alex shoved a handful of Os into his mouth and began to

chomp. It was way too many, and instinctively, I reached my hand out, let him spit out the ones that he didn't want. Tossed them onto my napkin to throw out later like I'd seen Mary do so many times.

"And you won't say anything, right? I mean, should you ever . . . I wouldn't have even had you and Alex meet—I know it's so early—but the nanny had a family emergency." George raised an eyebrow, and I knew that at least part of him questioned the nanny's story, as he would question any working-class person who inconvenienced him in any way. He was bred well enough not to say it out loud—"you just can't get good help these days" was too on-the-nose for his generation—but he was thinking it. They were *always* thinking it.

"Our little secret," I said with a smile, glancing to Alex. "Right?"

Alex nodded and popped more Os into his mouth.

Meeting Alex had been unplanned. Accidental. Most of the time, George came to my place anyway—or his place, rather. A few days after Jack Senior fucked me in a bathroom and hung me out to dry, I told George they were doing renovations in my building, that it was miserable to stay there and that's why I couldn't have him over. That night, he'd offered me the keys to a studio apartment his family owned that was off the market temporarily, told me I could stay until the end of July. Something to do with locking in a higher rental price if you waited until August to let it. Oh, the ways the rich find to screw us.

I'd said yes, obviously. Moved my meager possessions from a hotel in Sunset Park up to the place in Brooklyn Heights. Found myself looking out over the cobblestone streets and wondering how it was so easy for some. Apartments waiting at the ready for the mistress of the moment.

Alex had never been part of the equation. George had texted me at ten last night, just back from a holiday weekend in the Hamptons—because, of *course*—begging me to come over. We'd fucked in George and Mary's bed while the occasional sounds—and lights—of exploding fireworks, left over from the Fourth, went off around us. The only reason I'd agreed to stay the night was because he'd promised that the nanny would be picking Alex up to take him to soccer in the park by eight a.m.

Then this morning, I'd woken at eight fifteen to see George gone from the bed. I'd headed downstairs, frozen at the sound of Alex's voice the second my feet hit the hardwoods, stiffened as Alex came running to me, wrapping me in a hug.

"Wow," George had said. "He's not usually that friendly with strangers."

"I'm Willa," I'd said quickly, before the little guy could give me away. "Nice to meet you."

So now I was sitting here, counting on Alex's very limited vocabulary to not entirely blow up my spot. He wasn't yet at the age where he'd run back to Mary and tell her everything. The most she'd pry out of him were one-word answers, yeses and nos. Or, for Alex, *yeh* and *nuh*.

Did you have a nice time in the Hamptons with Dada? Yeh.
Did you see any fireworks? Yeh.

Did you later run into the woman who I thought was my friend but was actually a con artist intent on scamming your father?

Luckily, Mary didn't know to ask that one.

The front door burst open. A young girl, likely no more than twenty-five, with red hair, vintage overalls, and tattoos circling her arms, rushed in. "I'm so sorry I'm late, Mr. Haywood," she said earnestly, scratching at her elbow. "It won't happen again, I promise."

Alex kicked his feet excitedly and stretched to get out of his high chair. I unclipped him and set him down and he ran to the girl, yelling, "Gigi! Gigi!"

George didn't introduce us, but the girl couldn't help looking my way, her eyes, lined in bright purple, widening just slightly. I could have been you, I thought. I could have nannied, could have earned my paycheck the proper way, and yet I hadn't wanted to cart the kids around and go home to a crap apartment. I wanted to sleep in the proverbial brownstone myself. I wanted the spoils of a lifestyle I never would have had otherwise. I wanted the key to the golden fucking city, and with each new man I got it.

The girl kept on staring, and I shot her a look, daring her to judge me, and she quickly averted her eyes, getting Alex's backpack, a water bottle, and a spare change of clothes together as fast as she could. Alex kissed George, waved to me. Then they were gone.

"Don't worry," George said. "We pay Genevieve loads, and we're connecting her with a Columbia professor so she can get a good reference letter for a master's program. She'll be discreet."

I nodded.

"But with Alex gone," he said, raising an eyebrow, "I don't have to rush anywhere."

So there we were, kissing again. Making our way up the staircase. Pawing at each other.

There we were, lying on his bed after. And then there it was again, the sound of shuffling downstairs.

George leapt out of bed, as if caught. My own body tensed up, too, fearing it was Mary.

He peered out the window, then turned back to me. "The stroller's on the sidewalk," he said. "Genevieve must be back." He sighed. "Let me go down and see what she wants."

"Should I—" I started to get up.

"No," he said. "I'll be right back."

He was downstairs for at least a couple of minutes. I wanted to get up, examine the safe a little more, but it was too risky.

Then the door burst open, and George walked in. "Fucking private soccer instructor has to be paid in cash," he said. "And fucking Gen Z nanny thought she could Venmo him. That's Park Slope for you. Sorry. Mare—I mean, Alex's mom—she usually takes care of it. Give me a second."

Of course Mary does. All the help in the world, but you couldn't pay someone to take on the mental load. It was the one thing you couldn't hire out.

George opened the nightstand drawer first, the one I'd stolen forty bucks from, but evidently whatever was in there was not enough for a private soccer coach for a two-year-old.

My heart beat fast, excited at this gift, this incredible blessing. One I hadn't even had to orchestrate myself.

Without a word, George slid the painting above his nightstand over a touch, my pulse rushing now, my eyes following his.

This was what I'd been waiting for, all this time.

George was making it so goddamn easy.

I needed a reason to stare, a reason that didn't make it seem like I was after the goods locked inside.

"A safe behind a painting," I offered. "How very old-fashioned."

George laughed. "It does the job."

He went at the code quickly. I caught a one to start, then another number I couldn't quite see, but was down—possibly to the right? Then George's finger went back up top, a two. Then a three, another one. The last digit, I couldn't catch, but with all the important dates I'd collected from Mary, I figured I could fill in the blanks.

The safe beeped. The door opened.

I looked at my phone, acted like I couldn't care less about his stupid safe.

But my fingers were tingling. My hackles were up.

I was getting closer now.

It was almost time.

23

MARY

I woke to the sight of Willa, lying in the bed beside me, the sheets pulled up high around her.

It was a surprise to see her there, but only for a moment, like when you wake on the first morning of vacation, in unfamiliar surroundings, light peering through a strange window.

But then your mind catches up to the visuals in front of you. Remembers.

Between sips of wine, bites of pizza, I'd called Frank and Ruth countless times, desperate to see Alex, but had never gotten an answer. Eventually, it was late enough that I knew Alex would be in bed. And so I'd stopped dialing, let Willa reassure me that George's parents were probably in shock, had likely spent the whole evening talking to the police, that it would all be clearer in the morning.

So, reluctantly, I'd let Willa pour me another glass of

wine, let our old, familiar pattern resume. We'd finished the bottle, left our dishes on the counter and headed out to the back patio, wineglasses refilled, conversation strangely flowing, even if there was an undercurrent of tension, the knowledge that she could destroy me if she showed the police that text, that this scheming woman held my freedom in her hands.

There was a moment, in the drunken haze, that wasn't real at all, now that I peered back at it in the harsh light of day, but had felt real all the same. A moment when tears came to Willa's eyes, and she said how much she missed me, when tears sprang in my own as well, and in spite of my better judgment, we held each other, hand in hand. Willa said she was glad fate had thrown us together again, that she hadn't had a friend like me in so, so long, and I said the same. And when the second bottle of wine was empty, when she said she should walk back to her empty house, since she'd had too much to drive, I'd said that was silly, she should just stay, and when she made her way to the couch instead, I said that was silly, too.

I was drunk, of course. I wasn't thinking straight.

Now, daylight beaming, head aching a little but clear, at least, I was.

I stared at Willa, tucked under the blanket, hands beneath one cheek, sleeping like a cherub, like a child. Mascara smeared, but otherwise beautiful.

Was she really here as a friend, or was she planning something now? Getting ready to send that text straight to Detective Morales? But *why*? What could possibly be in it for her?

I pushed back the covers, thoughts swirling. There were only a few real possibilities as to who had killed George.

First, one of Henry's many enemies had actually gotten mad. *Really* mad. Maybe it wasn't even some random person from the internet. Maybe it was someone Henry had screwed over. I had no doubt that Henry screwed over a lot of people. They could have gone to that house yesterday morning, expecting to find Henry, seen his brother, and assumed it was him. They either were responsible for the break-ins, and *DIE RICH PIG* was the whole point, or they knew enough about the break-ins to write that on the wall as a decoy.

The next option was clichéd but obvious. If George had been seeing someone, and maybe he really had, then there could have been some argument between him and the woman, whoever she was. Maybe she wanted to get back together and found him up here, trying to reconcile with me? It was far-fetched, but the possibility couldn't be entirely written off.

And the last one—the truly terrifying one—one that had only even occurred to me in the depths of my drunkenness last night, was that it *was* Henry. Maybe George had told him he was going to give Cassandra's jewelry back. Maybe they'd argued about it, and Henry had killed George in the struggle to get the stash. Could Henry, for all his faults, really murder his own brother over some jewelry? Sure, he wanted to keep Cassandra away from anything that could be liquefied into cash, but he and the Haywoods didn't actually need it. Did Henry's desire to punish Cassandra go above everything else? Or was it so spur-of-the-moment, so casually violent, that Henry had been acting on anger above all? The thought gave me chills.

God, George, I thought. What did you get caught up in?

Carefully, I climbed out of bed and grabbed my phone. I

pushed myself out of bed, dialed both Ruth and Frank—
again, nothing. What game were they playing?

The ache in my head came on stronger, pulsing, as I
stared at the phone in my hands, unsure what to do next. I
found my bag on the floor, dug around for my toiletry bag,
thankfully located a pair of Advil. In the bathroom down
the hall, I scooped water from the tap, swallowed the pills in
one gulp, my mouth sticky from the wine, then used the
bathroom and made my way back to the living room.

I paused, frozen to the spot. There, in the corner, was
Willa's purse.

I thought of her phone. She'd promised the text was gone,
but for all I knew, that was a lie.

I knew my first priority was Alex, but Ruth and Frank
weren't answering—and this was a priority, too, wasn't it? I
peered into the bedroom to check that Willa was still asleep,
and then without hesitating, without even stopping to put
pants on, I set my phone on the hall table and bolted for the
bag. It was a basic leather tote, not at all the sort she would
have carried when I knew her back in Brooklyn. Nary a designer label in sight.

I dug in, looking for an iPhone. The bag was deep, dark,
and cavernous, way too big for anyone, really, and knowing
I had very little time, I tipped it all over onto the rug so it
wouldn't make too much noise.

Coins spilled out, rolling over the rug and across the floor.
There was a receipt, a cheap wine opener, a pill box, and a
book of matches. Hand sanitizer and bug spray, sunscreen
and travel tissues, baby wipes and training diapers. A paperback novel—Patricia Highsmith—and an Amtrak ticket from
the city to Montreal, dated in July, just over a month ago.

No phone.

"Should I put a pot of coffee on?"

I turned to see Willa, out of bed now, fully dressed in what she'd worn yesterday, right down to the scarf. When had she gotten up and slipped on her jeans? How had I not heard it? How was I the one kneeling here, egg on my face, wearing nothing more than a tank and underwear?

"I needed Advil," I said, spitting out the first excuse I could think of. "My head is pounding."

It was only once the words were out that it hit me properly, the strangeness of it. Willa hadn't even asked what I was doing. She'd only asked if I wanted coffee.

Calmly, coolly, Willa strode around the mess I'd created and plucked up her pill box with two fingers. She twisted it open, held it out to me. A mess of pills, different numbers and colors, but besides the three blue-green Advil Liqui-Gels, the same ones I'd swallowed myself only minutes ago, there was nothing I recognized. They could be roofies or Ritalin, antipsychotics or antacids, and I wouldn't know the difference—I'd never been into pills. Reluctantly, I grabbed two Advil.

"Do you want water?" Willa asked.

I bit my lip, and Willa tilted her head to the side.

"Or did you not really want the Advil at all?"

I hesitated, unable to answer, and she only smiled, twisted the pill box open again, cupped the palm of her hand. I dropped the pills in and she put them away, then reached into her pocket.

"You want to know who I really am, I'm guessing." She pressed a cheap wallet into my palm. "Go ahead," she said. "Look through it."

It wasn't what I was after, and yet, with the chance for answers right here in front of me, how could I *not* look?

I opened it to find an ID from New York State. The name: *Charlotte Anne Williams*.

"My mom called me Charlotte Anne. I hated it, obviously, sounded like something straight out of an *American Girl* book. On the volleyball team, which I was really good at, by the way, we all called each other by our last names. Williams. And then, when I left home, it made sense to go by Willa. Yes, sometimes I go by Annie, or sometimes even Charlie, and when I have legal stuff, yes, Charlotte, but the truth is, I think of myself as Willa. That's who I am."

I opened my mouth to speak, but Willa continued.

"There are three credit cards in there. All mine. I have a bad habit of maxing out balances, which you caught me in the other night."

I pushed the wallet back at her. "It's not this," I said. "I wanted to check your phone, to make sure that text wasn't on there."

"I told you it wasn't," Willa said. "And even if it was, I wouldn't do anything. Don't you believe that?"

I stepped back, slowly. "How can I know what you'd do, when you've lied to me so much?"

"Listen, Mary," Willa said, voice calm now, smooth. "I know the prick deserved to die. After everything he did to you. Everything he did to your sister-in-law. And even if you *did* kill him—"

"I *didn't* kill him," I said. "Jesus Christ."

"Okay, okay," Willa said. She stared at me a moment, then nodded. "But even if you did—"

"I *didn't*. He was finally talking about changing, he was

admitting he was wrong. Why would I kill him when he had actually started listening to me for once?"

"Okay, okay," Willa said. "All I'm saying is, never in a million kajillion years would I want *you* to go down for it. This isn't a fucking Highsmith novel." She raised an eyebrow, then kicked the paperback on the floor. "And believe me, I've read enough of them. I don't want to pin anything on you, or god, *frame* you. I just want to know you're okay."

I stared at her, trying to understand. There was something missing there, something I wasn't seeing. Something that should be so very clear. Maybe Willa didn't want to pin anything on me. But she did want something, I could see it there in her eyes.

"Willa—" I started.

My words were swallowed by a loud knock on the door.

I rushed to the front. Was it the police? Officer Morales? Lord, I was hungover. Half-naked. Were they really here—already—to arrest me, take me away? I hadn't even talked to Alex yet.

I peered through the peephole to see a smooth black dress, elegant pearls, silver hair cut into a clean, perfect bob. At first, relief. It was my mother-in-law, Ruth. I would finally get to talk to her. To demand to see Alex.

But to the left of her, Henry.

The hairs on my neck stood up as the knock sounded again, loud, persistent. Desperate and grief-stricken.

"Open up, Mary," Henry said caustically, as if I were a criminal, hiding out. "We know you're in there."

24

WILLA

It was hot as all get-out in Brooklyn, but today was the day. Only forty-eight hours since I'd seen George open the safe, but no time like the present, right?

My heart drummed. My fingers tingled. I stood on the brownstone steps, sweat beading on the back of my neck. I'd chosen my accoutrements carefully:

Small tote, slung across my shoulder. Brown paper bag, smelling strongly of garlic, sesame, and yeast. An act, but a good one. George had a meeting in the city, and I'd waited around the corner to make sure the town car came and got him, but if someone should come by for whatever reason, I'd say I wanted to surprise George with breakfast.

I scaled the steps with purpose, like I belonged. It was amazing what you could get away with when everyone saw you a certain way. Chloe flats. Tailored black romper. God damn if I didn't look the part. Here I was, a well-to-do trustworthy woman. The kind you could hand the keys to an unoccupied apartment. Who you didn't even ask to leave the room when you popped open your safe. Who you laughed with about the absurdity of a private soccer tutor. Oh, New York City, never stop being you. This world was wild. No matter how long I'd played inside it, I'd never quite get used to it.

I set the bagels down and knelt to the Master Lock. Pulled out my phone, like I was checking the code for an Airbnb or rental.

Like I said, when you look the part, no one questions a thing.

I was moving fast, but also taking a well-timed opportunity. See, I *had* to do it on a Wednesday. Between George and Mary, I'd put together most of the schedule. The cleaning service, the name of which Mary had given me over a month ago, came on Tuesdays and Fridays, something I'd confirmed over the phone. It wasn't hard to call them up, say I was George's new assistant, that I was merging his home and work calendars and wanted to get everything in one place. Tell the girl on the other end of the line that he actually *had* mentioned the schedule to me, but I'd forgotten to write it down and didn't want to ask him again. I could practically hear the smile in her voice, the recognition. "Oh, I'm sure you don't," she said with a laugh. "No problem. I've got it right here."

Working-class solidarity. Another tool in my toolbox.

And then Thursday, the landscapers came. Why they needed landscaping for a few hedges and a rosebush was beyond me, but hey, it wasn't on me to question the schedule.

No, Wednesday was the day. The nanny, Genevieve,

wouldn't be a problem, since Mary had Alex during the week, picked him up from the soccer teacher on Monday and kept him until Friday.

Fingers shaking slightly, Master Lock secure in my hand, I tried George's birthday first, narcissist I knew him to be.

One. Zero. Two. Three.

It took me a moment to get the silver numbers just right. Then I pulled at the black tab, the one that would open if I had it right.

Nothing.

A deep breath. Another try. Mary's birthday next.

Click. Zero. *Click, click.* Two. *Click.* One. *Click, click, click, click, click.* Eight.

A shuffling behind me. I turned, but it was only a mother, pushing a stroller, completely wrapped up in her baby's needs. I pivoted back to the Master Lock, pulled the tab. Nothing.

Please, I thought. Please let the next one work.

Alex's birthday.

George didn't really care about his son, at least according to Mary. Still, the date was logical, right? For all I knew, Mary had set the combo to this lock. She was the one who'd interfaced with the nannies in the past—George's frantic unprepared search for cash to pay the soccer teacher made that clear. Besides, it was the sort of unpaid labor that always fell to a woman. The kind of thing I specialized in.

I stared at the lock again. Stand here much longer, and I might look suspicious to a neighbor. I had to be right. Mary probably set this up herself, and Alex's birthday would be an easy one for the nanny to remember. It's the kind of thing *I* would have chosen if I were taking charge of things.

I said a quick little prayer and got to it.

Zero stayed. *Click, click, click, click, click* to the seven. One stayed, too. *Click, click, click* to the five.

I pulled.

Relief swam through me. The box came open.

Two keys, one gold, one silver, on a ring, there for the taking.

I snatched them quickly, stood, and slipped the gold into the lock. It stuck a minute, and I switched to the silver. It stuck, too.

I felt the sun on my back. Sweat migrating to the pits of my arms now. Smelled the yeast of the bagels.

Focus, I thought. Just focus.

I returned to the gold key, then pulled the handle forward, just slightly, as I'd once seen George do.

Just like that, the door opened.

God damn, I was in.

25

MARY

The door quaked beneath Henry's knocks.

"One second," I said. I rushed to the bedroom, pulled on pants and a bra, then returned to the door. I turned the handle, let the two of them in.

"Where's Alex?" I asked immediately, turning to Ruth. "I've been calling you and calling you. Is he okay?"

Ruth ignored my questions, and the two of them pushed past me and into the living room. Henry's eyes widened at the sight of Willa. Ruth's did, too. "Who are you?" she asked.

"She's a friend in town who came over last night," I said quickly. "Now, where is Alex?"

Willa quickly shuffled off into the kitchen, giving us our space.

"I'm serious," I said. "Where is my son?"

"He's fine," Ruth said. "He's with Frank. He's *safe*." Ruth's eyes were sunken, bloodshot, makeup caked into the fine lines of her face, her black dress askew on her shoulders. The implication in her words was clear. My son was okay, when hers was not.

"Then why weren't you answering me?" I asked.

"You think you get to interrogate *us*?" Henry roared. "What the fuck happened, Mary?" His eyes were vicious, his face reddened with anger. And it was like I could see it then, his towering over George, lifting something over his head, bringing it down. *Smash*.

Two pairs of eyes were trained on me, waiting for an answer.

"I don't know," I said desperately. "I don't know."

"The cops said *you* found him," Henry said, his words full of ire. "Care to explain that?"

"I did," I said, looking at Ruth, not Henry, willing her to understand. "George was supposed to come over here yesterday morning, but he didn't. So when enough time had passed, I went over. And I called the police the moment I found him, Ruth. I didn't hurt him. I *wouldn't* hurt him. Whatever was going on between us, I never wanted anything—anything like this—I *swear* to you."

Henry scoffed, but Ruth's eyes locked on mine, and even if part of her wanted to blame me for everything, there was a hesitation there, too. "I know about the custody offer he sent you," she pressed. "Our lawyers drew it up. You must have been furious."

I looked down, then back up at her. The woman who'd had far too much champagne at my wedding, who was a wonderful grandmother to Alex, in spite of everything. "I didn't even know about it until George showed up. We—George spent the night on Saturday," I said, knowing I shouldn't keep anything from her that would eventually come out, not if I wanted her on my side. "When I woke up Sunday morning, that's when he told me. He thought I knew. Of course I was angry. But not enough to—god."

"A mother will do a lot to keep her kid."

I stared at her, caught her cool blue eyes. "How could you, Ruth? How could you let your lawyers do it?"

"You think you get to question my mother?" Henry snapped.

I pressed on, looking only at Ruth. "You *know* how much I adore Alex, how much he adores me. Why didn't you tell George to stop? To agree to joint custody? You know I belong in my son's life."

"I did," she said, her voice raised now. "I'm a *mother*, okay? No matter what you might think of me. I might have had all the help in the world to raise my boys, but I'm still their mother. George assured me that it was a negotiation tactic, that you would eventually come back."

I shook my head, moisture springing to my eyes. It was all such a waste. So much arguing, negotiating. So many harsh words, bitter threats.

It felt like, if George had only let me go, none of this would have happened. George would never have come up here. He never would have been killed.

"Why were you two meeting yesterday morning, if you *weren't* reconciling?" Ruth asked.

I looked at Ruth, then at Henry, who was standing beside her, eyes sharp. Finally, I turned back to my mother-in-law. "Can we speak privately?"

"Whatever you have to say to her you can say to *me*," Henry practically spat.

"Mother to mother," I said. *"Please."*

To my surprise, Ruth's face softened. She turned to Henry.

"You *can't* be serious," he said.

"I want to hear what she has to say."

"Fine," Henry said, tossing his hands into the air. "I'll be out front." He stalked out quickly, slamming the door behind him.

I peered through the peephole, waited until I saw him walk all the way to the street, and then I turned back to Ruth.

"Look," I said, my voice soft. "I know you don't want to hear anything bad about your son, but Henry and Cassandra—"

"Cassandra?" Ruth said, rearing back. "What does that vile woman have to do with any of this?"

"She's not vile," I said. "She was my friend, you know."

"Everything that went wrong with this family started with her. She's cruel, you know. Violent."

"Violent?"

"You don't know the half of what she did to Henry. She never tells you that part. Screaming at him, pushing him around. I saw her actually hit him once, you know. Smack him straight across the face like it was *nothing*. Left a mark and everything. Just because *she* didn't think he should have another cocktail. As if she didn't go quite hard on the sauce herself."

My eyebrows narrowed. "When was this?"

"Oh, years ago," Ruth said. "Before you met George. Henry said it wasn't an isolated incident, either. Not in the

slightest. Little different than the perfect picture she pre-
sented to you, isn't it?"

I couldn't imagine Cassandra actually *hitting* someone,
could I? She was hot-tempered, sure, I knew that well, but
that didn't mean . . .

"What does Cassandra have to do with this?" Ruth asked
again.

"It was her jewelry," I managed. "George was going to
give it back to me, so I could return it to her."

"The jewelry she *lost* and tried to blame on Henry, tried
to use as a pawn to hold up the divorce?"

"No," I said, voice earnest now. "Henry took it. He gave
it to George to hide for him so she couldn't get it back. He
knew she was going to sell it so she would have money for a
fresh start. He didn't want her to have a dime."

"No," Ruth said, voice firm. "My boys wouldn't do that.
Maybe . . . maybe Henry . . . but never George."

"They did," I said. "And *he* did. I saw the pieces myself,
locked in our safe in the brownstone."

Ruth's eyes widened, but then she pulled herself together.
"You must have misunderstood."

"If it's any consolation, George was finally going to give
it back."

I hesitated, replaying the thoughts, the suspicions, that
had been trotting through my head this morning, decided I
had to ask, since she was here. "Ruth, is there a chance
that—that Henry found out George was going to give the
jewelry back to me—that they argued, that Henry took it,
that George tried to stop him, and—and—"

"And what?" she snapped.

"And Henry got angry and—"

"My *god*," Ruth said, backing away from me, as if I were poison, as if she could catch something vile if she stood too close. "He's my only living son. How *dare* you?"

"I'm sorry," I said. "I didn't mean to—"

"Oh, I know exactly what you meant to do. You've made yourself quite clear. Henry told me you weren't on our side, you know? And I didn't want to believe him, but now—I can see he was right."

Ruth turned for the door.

"Wait," I said. "What about Alex? Where is he? I need to see him."

"He's with Frank and the nanny in Brooklyn," she practically spat.

"But—"

"This is no place for him, Mary. And right now, you're not even thinking straight. Saying these things about Henry." She crossed her arms. "Alex will stay with us for the week, just like we planned."

"No," I said. "No. I need to see him. Now."

"Really? Because the police have told us that they've strictly forbidden you from leaving town."

"So bring him to me," I said.

"You think *this* is a place for him right now? Any mother could surely see that with a murderer on the loose, with random women we've never even met crashing with you, this is no place for him. You smell like booze, Mary. Take a few days and pull yourself together. We're not keeping him from you. We're just protecting him from all this." She eyed me then, dead serious. "Besides, it will give you time to rack your brain, think of anything, anything, that you can share with the police to help the investigation. To figure out who did this to my son."

"Ruth, I—"

"I'll have Frank call you this afternoon. You can see Alex on FaceTime. That has to be enough for now."

"Ruth, please—"

Already, she was walking out the door, pulling it shut tight behind her.

Her words rang in my head as I peered through the peephole again, watching her go.

Any mother could surely see.

Rack your brain. Think of anything.

Already judging me, sizing up my reactions, building her case as to why I wasn't fit to care for her grandchild. Figuring out ways to punish me. For finding George. For accusing Henry. For daring to go against the family.

"That sounded awful."

My shoulders jolted, and I turned to see Willa, eyes wide, kind.

"Are you okay?" she asked.

I turned away from her, back to the door. Of course I wasn't okay. My son was hours away, and I was stuck here, practically waiting for the cops to pin everything on me. And even if Ruth did believe me for now, I had a feeling she wouldn't for long, especially with Henry whispering in her ear, maybe even trying to cover his own tracks. What if whoever had seen me push George on Sunday morning came forward? What if the police somehow got their hands on the history of my texts? And if Henry really had done it, what would that mean, anyway? The Haywoods would throw me under the bus before they ever let one of their own go down for anything.

There was something else, too. Something in front of me, something that very much didn't fit. Something that was bothering me, something off, like a misplaced sock.

Finally, it hit me.

The door, the one Ruth had just swept out of.

When I'd let the two of them in, I'd only had to turn the doorknob, and then there they were.

The deadbolt, the one I'd checked multiple times when Willa and I had come in last night, had been unlocked.

I turned back to Willa, my heart racing. "Did you go out the front door last night?"

"No," Willa said. "Just the patio off the kitchen, with you. Why?"

"The deadbolt," I said, a sick feeling in the pit of my stomach. "It was unlocked."

I struggled to catch my breath as fear sliced within me.

"Someone came in here last night."

26

WILLA

I closed the brownstone's front door. Engaged the deadbolt and the chain.

Through the foyer. Into the living room. Alone in here, the place felt even larger, even richer. High ceilings. Ornate medallions around modern lights. Velvet and leather sofas. Windows that curved out, like beer guts spilling over tightened belts.

A smell of orange oil and lemongrass. Glossy parquet floors. The cleaners had come yesterday, no mix-up there. Good.

I went straight up the stairs, then stopped two from the top, jumping at a noise. My phone.

A text from Mary.

Give me a call, ok? We can work it out.

Christ, it was like the girl had radar trained to notice any-time I was in her house.

I took another two steps, leaving the first floor behind me.

Forget Mary. Forget guilt. This was big-time, the kind of score I'd never even *thought* to hope for. This wasn't a Moncler coat, a pair of designer shoes. This was life-changing money.

I beelined down the hallway. Past George's office. Past Alex's room. Hugging the left side of the wall so a nanny cam, if there was one, couldn't catch my movements.

And then, at last, the bedroom—*her* bedroom.

No one here. No chance. Still, I gave a cursory glance to the bathroom and walk-in closet.

No one hiding, no one watching. Just me here. *Go time.*

I surveyed the print—George had slid it aside when he'd opened the safe in front of me that morning, but this could take some time. A hand on each side, careful not to mess it up, I took it off the wall, popped it onto the neatly made bed.

I'd done a little research. Most wall safes gave you five attempts before locking you out completely. Some more, some fewer. Either way, I figured I had three solid guesses at the code before I was cut off. If I used all three and it *still* didn't open, I wasn't sure what to do. I was the new person in George's life. If he came home to a locked-out safe, I'd definitely be a suspect. If I didn't crack it this morning, there was no reason I couldn't simply slip the print back onto the wall, steal away, and continue to work on George.

I knew enough to narrow the combination down. The first digit was a one, the second, unknown but lower on the keypad, followed by two-three-one and a final unknown digit.

I pulled out the slip of paper I'd jotted it all out on last night.

1_ 2 3 1 _

George's birthday was 10-23-83. I'd gleaned that from Mary, and the 1-0-2-3 could align with what I'd seen, even though the last two didn't. It's possible he used his own birthday and added another number of some importance, but I had a feeling he was too smart to put the month and date of his birth in the combination.

I also knew from Mary that they'd moved into the brownstone right before they were married, which made me reason that little Alex's birthday wouldn't factor in.

Besides, this was George's domain, *his* side of the bed. He was narcissistic, for sure, but he coveted Mary. She was his prize.

I looked down at my first guess, jotted down on the paper.

1-0-2-3-1-8

A 10 to nod to their wedding anniversary, September 10, something I'd learned on my own, sifting through the *New York Times*. Followed by the day of George's birthday. Mary's at the end.

I took a deep breath, then punched it in.

The beep was instant and all wrong. Low when it should have been high. Two dashes appeared on the digital pad, and even though I grabbed the handle, it was clear that the thing was still locked.

My next guess was in the same vein, just Mary's birthday and the wedding date transposed.

1-8-2-3-1-0

I hit each number carefully but quickly.

Another low-toned beep. Another two dashes.

Fuck.

I looked at the next number I'd written down.

1-7-2-3-1-8

A shoutout to their *dating* anniversary, June 17, which I'd been lucky enough to get off Mary and had the benefit of not being public, if something like that mattered to George. Not to mention if they'd gotten the safe before the wedding, that date would maybe be fresher in the mind.

One more quick sharp breath. Then I keyed it in.

It didn't work. Shit.

My heart raced. Should I turn back? Cut my losses? Try to get more information from George before all of this blew up in my face?

No, I thought. I was so close, and if I couldn't crack it now, after two months of friendship with Mary, after seeing George open it in front of me, I probably never would.

I looked at my next guess written down.

1-8-2-3-1-7

Mary's birthday. George's birthday. Dating anniversary.

Carefully, I punched each digit in.

I didn't think it would come, I didn't think it *could* come, but then there it was, that high-pitched beep.

Fingers itching with anticipation, I pulled it open to see stacks of cash on one side, a passport and papers on the other.

Carefully, I grabbed the passport, moved it over, reached my hand even farther back.

There was a chance nothing was in here. No bracelets. No diamonds. Not a single jewel. That it had all been moved since Mary last saw it.

My fingers brushed something soft. Velvet.

I pulled out a black drawstring bag—large, too, maybe eight inches square—something you might imagine sitting at the end of a rainbow, filled with gold.

Fingers quivering, I pulled it open, suddenly desperate.

There it was, right on top.

The bold and mischievous emerald eyes. An onyx nose. A chiseled jaw and pinned-back ears, coated with diamonds.

Panthère de Cartier. Gleaming white gold, verdant emeralds, ink-black onyx, and diamonds clear as anything. The crème de la crème. Rich, even for rich people. Wikipedia had told me it was a design first created for the Duchess of Windsor—and of course it was. Modern-day imperialism and capitalism went hand in fucking hand. An icon. One that had stood the test of time.

I lifted it, heavy in my hands. This wasn't the original, of course. *That* was worth millions, tucked in a museum somewhere. Still, it was Cartier, no less. The real deal. The shine and shimmer confirmed as much. The sheer clarity of every stone. God, to be so rich. A bracelet, something you took out into the world with you, worth half the cost of a small house. A little over a hundred grand. One Mrs. Cassandra Haywood had popped casually across her wrist when she'd been with Henry. I'd seen it in photos online, after all.

The riches, the sheer insanity of it, didn't end there. It went on, like stepping into a cave of gems. A simple Cartier Love bracelet in rose gold, one that cost a cool ten thousand.

A Tiffany & Co. tennis bracelet—diamonds like a river—that had to be worth at least fifty thousand.

And even more beneath. Colors and gems and *wealth wealth wealth*.

Emerald drop earrings. A sapphire pendant, one that dwarfed the one I had around my neck. A viper-shaped Bulgari ring, littered with diamonds. Earrings from Harry Winston.

So much sparkle. So much flash. So many different high-end labels. It was no wonder Mary thought her sister-in-law was flashy—there was nothing even remotely modest about a single one of these pieces.

They all existed to say *Look at this money. Look at all I have.*

More than half a million in jewelry, tucked in the back of a wall safe.

Looked like I would get my fresh start after all.

27

MARY

I stared at the door's lock. My little Woodstock hideaway, which should have been so safe. My face felt hot, as if I were an old thermometer, temperature rising, the glass about to explode, mercury spill out.

I turned back to Willa. "You promise you didn't go out there?"

Willa shook her head solemnly. "I promise."

She could be lying—she lied about *everything*—but this was seemingly such a small detail, such a random thing to lie about. She might not be telling the truth, but if she was?

"Then I can't be here," I said. "We have to go."

"Okay," Willa said, obviously trying to instill some calm into a situation that was very quickly spiraling out of control.

"Can we go to your place?" I asked.

A moment of hesitation, impossible to ignore.

"I mean, you said that no one's even there, right?"

I had to be out of here, but I also didn't want Willa out of my sight, not so long as she still potentially had that text.

"Yeah," Willa said. "It's just, it's a bit of a mess. Maybe I should walk over first? Just give me an hour to clean things up?"

"No," I said, quickly. Firmly. "I don't care about the mess. I don't want to be alone right now. Not with a killer out there. Not when someone has come into this place."

Willa blinked, one time, then two.

"Is that a *problem*?" I asked, a slight edge in my voice now.

"No," Willa said, plastering on a smile. "No. It's not a problem at all."

Following Willa's car, I backed out onto the street and toward the main road. I found myself clenching the wheel at the perfect ten and two, checking and rechecking for oncoming cars and pedestrians, teeming in the streets this time of year.

I missed Alex—desperately—wanted to squeeze his thick toddler thighs, feel his weight in my arms, see his smile. As soon as I was at Willa's, I would call Frank. And if he didn't answer, then Genevieve. I had to talk to my son.

I followed her onto the main road, left toward her house.

My heart sank. There, right on the corner, next to the turnoff to Henry's place, to George's murder scene, was a news van, unmistakable, with a satellite dish on top, logos plastered on all sides.

This is it, I thought. They're descending.

Another minute, and we were in front of the deep-blue farmhouse, as proud and stately as the mountains behind it.

Willa got out of her car, then came back to help me grab my bags, and led the way up the porch steps. She fished in her purse for her keys and slipped one into the lock, turned, and opened the door. The light was the first thing I noticed. Bright, warm sunshine, pouring through the front windows, illuminating wide floorboards, pockmarked with age, with life, casting hard shadows where the windowpanes were.

I saw the mess next. Children's books tossed onto the bottom steps of the staircase, Legos littered across the rug in the living room to the right, dishes and cups still stacked on a large table in the dining room to the left.

"I told you it was a wreck in here," Willa laughed. "Poppy and Rich cleared out pretty quickly when they got the call about his mom."

It was all so normal, so familial, so pedestrian, almost. The couches were deep teal and looked cozy, lived-in. The dining table's fancier modern chairs were set apart with a plastic high chair. The only thing I wasn't fully expecting was a set of books on the coffee table—a biography of Karl Marx, the *Comprehensive Guide to Workers' Rights*, *The History of the Modern Labor Movement*.

"Make yourself at home," Willa said. "The guest room— just about the only thing that's clean—is the first door up the stairs on the right. I'm going to run a load of dishes and vacuum up Poppy's Cheerios before they fully meld into the rug."

"Thanks," I said, and I grabbed my bag from Willa and headed toward the stairs, then turned back.

"I'm sorry," I said. "But I can't relax until I see that that text is gone from your phone."

"Of course," Willa said. She dug in her pocket, then pulled out her phone. "Shit," she said. "It's dead. See?"

She turned it to me, and I saw nothing but black.

"I didn't charge it last night. Let me just pop it on the charger, okay? Then I can show you."

She turned and walked to the kitchen, not looking back.

A slight chill crawled up my spine, but what was I supposed to do? Follow her in there, rip the phone from her hands? No, I had to play nice with her. Had to keep Willa on my side so long as there was a chance she still had that text. Because if she did have it, if she showed it to *anyone*, Ruth and Henry would find a way to destroy me. Make it so I'd never see Alex again.

I headed up the stairs, finding the room at the top. It was simply outfitted, with a double bed and a small nightstand, and painted a pleasant shade of gray. I tossed my bags on the bed and pulled out my phone, trying Frank first, calling and FaceTiming, but got nothing. I sent a quick text:

I saw Ruth and Henry, she told me Alex is with you and Genevieve. Just want to say hi to him. Please call me back. And please don't tell him about his dad until I can do it myself.

I waited a couple of minutes and then texted Genevieve, as well.

Mary here. Just want to see Alex for a minute. FaceTime me when you can, please.

Please god, let them do the right thing. Please just let them call me, let me see Alex.

I stared at the phone, willing it to ring, but when it didn't, I tapped back into my contacts.

Thinking of the news van, I made the other call I knew I needed to make.

Rachel answered on the second ring. "Mary! I was just thinking about you. How's my little boo-boo?"

My voice caught in my throat at the sound of my sister. My sweet dear sister who had no idea of the mess I was in. "He's with—" I hesitated. "With his grandparents this week."

"Oh, he's not with you? I'm sure you mentioned that. Sorry, I've been so busy with Mom . . ."

"No, it's okay," I said. "I just, I called because—" There was no easy way to say it. "It's George."

"Lord," Rachel said. "What did he do now? He's not fighting you on custody again, is he?"

I would have laughed if I hadn't been so close to panicked tears. "He's dead, Rachel. He's been murdered. It happened yesterday."

A pause, brief. And then "Oh my god. Mary, you can't be serious, he can't be—"

"He is," I said. "I found him."

"Jesus Christ," Rachel said. A patter of her feet, shuffling to a different room, protecting my mom from this until Rachel could explain it calmly. "What happened?"

I told her the story, the one I'd trotted out to the police multiple times now.

"Oh god," Rachel said. "What should we do? And is Alex okay?"

"Yes, he's with Frank and his nanny in Brooklyn." Saying it like it was my own plan, not Ruth's, made me feel the tiniest bit better.

"But why don't you go get him?" Rachel asked.

My chest tightened. "Because I still need to sort all this out with the police. They said I shouldn't leave town yet."

Another pause, and I could practically hear Rachel's wheels turning. "You're not—you're not a *suspect*, are you?"

"I don't know," I said. "I hope not, but—"

"Do you have a lawyer?"

Then I really did laugh. "I have no money for a lawyer. Everything is tied up with the Haywoods."

"We can get a second mortgage on Mom's house," Rachel said. "I have a little bit saved. We can—"

"Stop, Rachel. It's too early for all that."

"Should I come down? I mean, Mom isn't supposed to travel, but—"

"No," I said. "Stay there. Hopefully they'll catch whoever did this, and it will all blow over soon."

"You really think so?" Rachel said.

I could hear it, the fear in my little sister's voice. A sister I'd always done my best to protect.

So I lied. "I do, Rachel. I really do."

I spent the afternoon watching bad TV with Willa and dialing Frank and Genevieve, waiting for them to call me back.

Willa had shown me her newly charged phone as soon as I'd come downstairs, and like she'd said, there were no texts older than a month, yet it still didn't put me totally at ease. I knew she could have saved them, plenty of places. But there was nothing else to do. So we'd changed into loungewear, and I'd done my best to distract myself while I clutched my phone, waiting for a call. From Frank or Genevieve, letting me speak to Alex; from Detective Morales, asking me to come down to the station again.

Two calls did come. One from the CEO I was supposed to interview for *Forbes*, which I'd completely forgotten about in the chaos; another from the real estate agent I'd been set to meet. I'd mumbled "family emergency" to both, had gotten off the phone as quickly as I could.

Eventually I went back upstairs, dialing Frank and Genevieve yet again, then falling asleep at some point, the weight of everything practically melding me into the covers. When I woke, it was well after seven.

I checked my phone immediately, my heart leaping at a text from Frank.

Sorry to miss you before. Been busy here. Thinking of hiring our own investigators. Alex is doing just fine, fell asleep early. Will call you tomorrow. And don't worry, we haven't told him anything yet.

Beneath the text was a photo of Alex smiling, unaware that his father was dead, that his world would never again be the same.

I sighed with relief and let myself relax. Alex was fine, Frank and Ruth weren't keeping him from me, they were just grieving. Processing what had happened to their own son, deciding how best to throw their masses of money at the problem. I wiped the sleep from my eyes and stole down the stairs to find a smell, rich and earthy, and tinged with meat.

"I made Bolognese," Willa said, turning from the gas stove, where a red sauce bubbled in an oversized skillet.

"Wow," I said. "Smells amazing." I looked around. Everything in the kitchen was gorgeous, right down to a stainless steel fridge, littered with pictures of the girl I'd seen, plus an *Occupy Wall Street* magnet that fit in with the books on the coffee table. "I have to say, I never saw you dating a socialist."

Willa laughed. "I know, right? And Rich is really, *really* serious about it. He somehow found a way to make his contractor business co-op and everything, so the guys he works with get a share of the profits. Besides Poppy, it's what he cares about more than anything. Anyway, this is just about ready. You hungry?"

I nodded.

"Grab a seat at the table. I'll take care of the rest."

Within minutes, a steaming plate of pasta was before me, sprinkled with cheese, blood-red wine sitting in a glass next to it. We dug into the pasta, barely talking, both of us having two servings—I don't think either of us had had anything all day. When we couldn't eat anymore, we pushed our plates to the side, and Willa topped off my wine without asking, then took a gulp—and a deep breath. "What I said last night," Willa started, taking another sip. "About you being relieved, it was callous, I realize that now. I'm sorry."

"Thank you," I said. "And it's okay. George really did sound different the last time I spoke to him, like maybe he was going to change. And now I'll never know."

Willa hesitated, and then her face softened. "Maybe he was. That must be so hard, Mary, I'm so, so sorry." She paused a moment, then took a sip of wine. "Do you really think someone came into the house last night?"

"I know I locked the deadbolt, I know I did."

"Christ," Willa said. "That's terrifying. Who do you think it was?"

"I don't know," I said. Because it didn't make sense. If some angry vandal had killed George, mistaking him for Henry, why would they come to my place? Perhaps an ex-girlfriend had some reason to be angry at me—and I suppose she could have gotten the info for my rental off George's phone, but I had the only key. How would someone even get in?

Then something struck me. I thought of Henry, walking down my street that first day, the way George had told me he'd slipped in the back. I'd assumed that Henry had used the key and put it back into the lockbox, that the key I had with me now was the one he'd used, but what if there had originally been two? What if Henry had taken one, never put it back? I thought of him, just this morning, the rage in his eyes, as if he were out to get justice for his brother. What if it was all an act to point me in the wrong direction?

"You okay?" Willa asked.

"Yes," I said. "I mean, no." I took my phone from my pocket, searched for the instructions to the rental. I opened the email, suddenly desperate to see, scrolled down to the check-in instructions. There was the code to the lockbox, a note about always locking the doors behind you, and then, the last line of the paragraph: *There are two keys in the lockbox. They both go to the front door.*

"Oh my god," I said. How had I missed this? How had I not put it together?

"What is it?" Willa asked.

It was so clear, suddenly, so *beyond* clear, that I felt foolish for not seeing it before.

"Henry," I said. "It had to be Henry."

"George's brother?"

I brought her up to speed on my run-in with Henry on Saturday. "What if the jewelry wasn't there? What if George hadn't even gotten it yet? Or what if Henry thought George had given the stash to me already, and he came in to my rental to look for it? And then he comes back with his mom in the morning, playing the grief-stricken brother."

Willa's eyes widened. "You really think he would?"

"Henry came into the rental on Saturday to set up the flowers. He must have taken a key and kept it. I just checked the rental instructions. There were two keys in the lockbox, but I only ever saw the one. There's simply no one else who even would have been able to come in."

"Wow," Willa said. She looked genuinely shocked. Could I trust her? I didn't know. Could I trust anyone? Not really.

That didn't matter. Not compared to this.

I grabbed my phone, googled the number, got an answer after a few rings.

"I need to speak with Detective Morales," I said. "I've got new information. Something she absolutely needs to hear."

28

WILLA

It was gorgeous out here. Just gorgeous.

I loved trains, had ever since my first ride to the city.

Romantic. Old-fashioned. No stress. No driving.

We chugged along at a steady clip. Hudson River on my left. Trees and brush and *land, land, land.*

No more city. No more sensory overload. Bye bye, Brooklyn. It's been real.

Problem was, despite all the peace, all the beauty, I couldn't find a way to relax.

I couldn't stop scratching. Might have been the Amtrak's textured seats. Or the pulsing early-July heat. Still, it was relentless. My arms. The backs of my knees. The place on my neck where the baby hairs grew.

Hell, maybe I was just nervous.

The last few hours had been a whirlwind.

Stuffing the jewelry into my bag. Cabbing it back to the apartment in Brooklyn Heights. Packing up my passport, my ID, my credit cards and computer—all the things worth taking. Tossing my life into a pair of duffel bags.

I'd coated my hair in mouse-brown L'Oréal. Waited forty-five minutes for it to process. Clipped a few inches off the ends. Put on my cheapest Target clothes and a pair of over-sized sunglasses.

I'd locked the door behind me, leaving the bed unmade, some things behind. The place would look lived in if George came by. Prevent him from drawing the wrong conclusions just yet. And even when he *did* figure out I wasn't coming back, he wasn't going to go and report me—his *mistress*— missing. He was still trying to get Mary back.

Afterward, I'd grabbed a cab to Penn Station. Bought a ticket on the Adirondack Amtrak line, headed north, with cash. Final destination: Montreal. I wasn't sure if I'd go that far, but I wanted to keep the option open.

Now I looked around.

The train was full. Had been since leaving the city. The borough-dwellers were getting the hell out. Setting off on a romantic ride up the river. Escaping the hustle and bustle of the city in the summer. Commuting up to Poughkeepsie. Or trying to see a bit of creek and forest and mountains, if only for a day.

Opposite me, a young couple, heavily tattooed and laden with Apple products, worked in tandem without looking at each other.

Meanwhile, I was the asshole who was taking up two seats, but I didn't dare put my bags up top. The cargo was too precious.

The train slowed, approaching our next stop: Beacon. The hip couple began to pack their devices.

I unzipped my own bag, reached beneath underwear and T-shirts, jeans and socks. Felt a touch of velvet.

My fingers worked at the drawstring, tugging it open. I reached inside, relief flooding me—a catch of breath—as I touched the jewelry. Facets and prongs. Smooth and sharp. The emerald eyes of a panther. Vicious, vindictive. Money money money.

My shiny new life.

No more running. No more bouncing from place to place. Man to man. Child to child. No more worrying about how many years I had left in me for this kind of life. Mary thought I was late twenties, and I'd never disabused her of the assumption. I was actually thirty-five, only a few years younger than her. But I'd always looked on the younger side, and the men I'd been with had been happy to hand over their credit cards so I could get a facial. I never told them that those facials came with Juvéderm and Botox, as well.

Getting out of this game was absolutely what I needed, but it was scary, too. I'd been pretending so damn long. Contorting myself into boxes men created for me. Working myself into corners. Expanding to fill the spaces.

Who was I without all that?

My phone buzzed, and I jumped.

Quickly, I closed the bag, zipped it all tight.

The train slowed.

What if it's George?

What if he's already been home, seen what's missing?

What if I've already fucked it all up?

I took the phone out of my purse, fingers shaking.

The train stopped. The couple stood up, bodies moving in tandem.

Relief. It wasn't George, but Mary.

Hi again, it's me. Just give me a call, ok. I'm worried about you.

My fingers hovered over my phone's keyboard. God, I wanted to text her back. Tell her everything.

Hey, Mary, I've got half a million bucks worth of your sister-in-law's jewelry. Grab Alex, come with me, take a cut, and we'll build our own life up north.

Laughter bubbled within me. How silly and absurd. How fun. Drinking wine. Cuddling Alex. Spending money. Just Mary and me, two strangers who'd met on a playground—no men to want or possess us.

No expectations, just us.

The train doors opened. The cool couple got out. Movement and shuffling. New people getting on board.

I trained my eyes on my book. Another old detective novel. My favorite.

"These seats taken?"

I looked up to see a man and a little girl. Matching grins on their faces. Bags and ephemera in the guy's arms. He gestured to the seats opposite mine.

"No," I said. "Please. Go ahead."

I stole glances their way as they shuffled in—couldn't help it.

He was tall and lanky, due for a shave but in a way that sparked curiosity. One that almost made him more handsome. He wore a *Medicare for All* T-shirt, but that didn't

mean anything, did it? Plenty of people with money considered themselves progressive.

The girl—probably about three?—had a mess of Shirley
Temple curls and a look of absolute amazement in her eyes.

He went to work folding up his stroller, wedging it above.

Meanwhile, the girl stared, slack-jawed, as if she'd never
seen a human before. As if I were the face of god.

I never got tired of that, no matter how many men, how
many children. The way they could look at you with such
love, such awe, such guileless care in their eyes. As if they'd
known you forever and at the same time had never seen anyone like you before.

Kids were amazing. *Truly*.

I let my book fall to my lap, waved at the little girl, unable to help myself.

"Hi," she said proudly.

"Hi there. What's your name?"

"Paw-pee."

The man tossed a bag reading *DiaBeacon*, the museum
up here that all the Manhattanites just *loved*, above, then
put a backpack with loads of pockets, clips, and straps
onto the floor. He pulled the little girl into his lap and
went to work sifting through the bag for what I'd guess was
a snack.

I could see the girl's patience began to falter as the prospect of food made her hungrier. Finally, the man reached
down far enough and found a package of half-broken crack-
ers, which the girl took with a wilted smile.

I could organize the hell out of that backpack, I thought.
Make it so much easier to find what you were looking for. I
was so good with kids. A gift, really.

He opened the Ziploc for her, and she began to munch. I was about to turn back to my book, but the man smiled my way again—a kind smile, really. "She loves the train. It's got to be her favorite thing in the world."

"Who wouldn't?" I said, smiling back.

He's probably married, I thought. Probably on a Daddy-daughter outing, nothing more.

Besides, I was past all that. I was moving on. Away from all this.

The man looked at me a moment, and then I saw it—I did—as I had learned to pick up on, the drift of his eyes down to my hands, bare—not a ring in sight. "Her mom's out in Ohio. Not many trains there, so it's a treat when she's with me, during the summers. We pick a destination and do a day trip. I've offered to drive her to amusement parks, out to Legoland. She only wants to go if it's by train." He laughed. "Kids, you know."

I let myself chuckle, feeling the prick of recognition, my hackles rising. Knowing what this could be . . . if I wanted.

"What am I saying?" he went on. "You're far too young to have kids."

There he goes, I thought. Just like Mary. Making assumptions about my age. I let myself laugh again, louder this time. An encouraging laugh. "Flattering," I said. "But not the least bit true. I don't have any, though, much as I love them."

The man smiled, and Poppy did, too.

"I like her," the girl said. That was the other thing about kids. They wore every emotion right there on their sleeves.

The man and I both laughed then. "I'm Rich," he said.

I hesitated only a moment, decided it was best to cover my ass—we were still close to the city, close to George and

Mary's world. "Annie. Nice to meet you," I said. "And you, too, Poppy."

The girl grinned.

Don't go any further, I told myself. *You're done with this life. Getting off this hamster wheel.*

I looked at the girl, at her clothes, clean and bright and nicer than something you'd find at Target or Carter's. At the stroller up top, one of those Instagram brands that was too expensive for its own good. At the man, a little unkempt, but in a way that was almost affected. His jeans looked nice—*expensive.*

There was money there, plain to see.

It would be nice, wouldn't it? To have a little companionship while I got everything together? The buyer for the jewelry wasn't yet lined up. I needed to wait, lay low for a bit.

"Where are you headed?" I let myself ask.

"Woodstock." The man grinned. "Well, the Rhinecliff stop, but that's where we live. Old farmhouse right in town."

That did it, if the rest hadn't. Woodstock wasn't cheap. Especially not in the middle of town.

I stepped into the box, into the role, as I had so many times before.

"That's funny," I said casually. "I'm headed there, too."

29

MARY

Not leaving town, are you?"

I turned to see a police officer in uniform at the end of Willa's driveway. The morning light was bright—it was just after ten a.m.—and the man squinted into the sun, eyes on me. Where had he even come from? Were they following me? The thought and its implications were terrifying. If their eyes were only on me, what else were they missing? How could this possibly be resolved if they weren't looking for the real killer at all?

"We're going to the police station, actually," I said, nodding to Willa, who, when I'd told her that I was tired of waiting for Morales to call me back and was going to just drive down there myself, had insisted on coming, for moral support. I still didn't think I could trust her, but I didn't mind having her close, keeping an eye on her if nothing else. "I tried calling Detective Morales, but I haven't heard back."

"Oh," the officer said, shuffling back and forth on his feet. "Well, she'll want to be speaking with you anyway. She sent me to fetch you."

"Can we drive ourselves?" Willa asked, a hand on her hip. "Last time, Mary got stuck there. There was no one to drive her back."

The cop's gaze ping-ponged between us, but then finally he shrugged. "Sure," he said. "You can follow me there."

Inside, the officer led me past the front desk and down a long hallway. Willa had promised to get us iced coffees and meet me back in the parking lot when I was done. Part of me admired her optimism, her certainty that I would be coming back out before the coffees melted.

Or was even that some sort of a game to her? A reminder that she could ensure I never came out of the station if she only walked in and showed them that text.

I followed the man to an empty room with a sad table in the middle and chairs on each side. The placard on the door read *Interview Room 2*. I felt a nervousness in my gut, a prickling of anxiety, but I stepped in quickly, took a seat like I had absolutely nothing to hide.

"Coffee?" he asked.

"No," I said, thinking of the cold brew waiting for me when I got out. Telling myself it would be, that this was all just routine, that once they knew about Henry breaking in, they would be pointed in the right direction.

It was fifteen minutes before Morales came in, hair pulled back, a folder in her hand. "Mary," she said. "I got your message. And like my colleague said, I was hoping to speak to you today, anyway. Glad he caught you."

My spine went rigid at the word *caught*, but Morales pressed on. "This is being recorded, so you're aware." She gestured up to a camera in the corner, as if it were nothing.

Was I supposed to object? Ask for a lawyer?

"That's fine," I said finally. "I want to help however I can."

"Good," Morales said, folding her hands together. "So first off, what is it that you wanted to share?"

"It's about Henry, George's brother. You didn't find the jewelry at the crime scene, right?"

Morales didn't answer my question, but from the look in her eyes I would guess the answer was no.

"Yesterday morning, when I woke up, the deadbolt was unlocked. And I'm sure I locked it the night before. One hundred percent positive. Someone came in."

"Okay," Morales said. "And what does that have to do with Henry Haywood?"

"If George told his brother he was going to give it to me, then maybe Henry came looking for it, assuming I had it. Plus, he had a key to the place."

Morales's eyebrows shot up.

"Henry came into my rental on Saturday afternoon. I saw him as I was arriving. He set up a vase of my favorite flowers and left the back door unlocked. Then when George got to town that night, he went in himself, was waiting for me, to surprise me, with champagne and all that."

Morales shook her head. "I'm sorry. You are telling me

that Mr. Haywood and his brother both broke into your rental on Saturday?"

"Well—" I started. "I mean, I guess technically it was a break-in, but I'd sent George the info about the rental, which had the lockbox key code in it. When I arrived on Saturday, there was only one key in that box, but last night, I read through all the instructions, and I learned that there should have been two. That means that Henry must have taken it before I arrived."

Morales sighed. "And why are you are only just telling us this now?"

"It was all one of George's ridiculous grand gestures, that's all. Yes, it freaked me out a bit, but I let him sleep over that night. I didn't think it would count as a break-in if I let him stay."

Morales narrowed her eyes at me.

"Mrs. Haywood, what do you think these allegations actually prove?"

"That Henry wanted that jewelry. Maybe he got angry when he found out George was going to give it back. Maybe there was some sort of . . . incident, I don't know. But then the jewelry wasn't there. So he came to my place to look for it."

"That's quite a story, Mrs. Haywood, one with absolutely no evidence to back it up."

"I bet Henry still has the key on him," I said. "You could search him, search his things—"

"And what about your sister-in-law, Cassandra?" Morales asked, cutting me off. "It was *her* jewelry, after all. Yes?"

"Cassandra?" I asked, rearing back. "But she's in Pennsylvania."

"Supposedly," Morales said. "But we are unable to find a valid address for her. In fact, we're unable to locate her at all. And Ruth Haywood says she and Henry had a *tumultuous* relationship."

Ruth's words rang in my head.

She's cruel, you know. Violent.

"How would Cassandra have gotten a key to my place, even if she *was* up here?"

"People have ways of getting in, Mrs. Haywood," Morales said. "Especially people who have broken into places before."

"Broken in? But you don't think that Cassandra was responsible for all those other break-ins, do you? I mean, the graffiti. She would never write anything like that."

Morales scratched at her temple. "Could be a diversion. Cassandra Haywood was at odds with the family. Of *course* we're looking at her. At anyone who had a beef with them." Her eyes locked on mine. It took a moment for it to hit me properly, but then it did.

"I didn't do all that vandalism, if that's what you're implying. I don't care at all about Henry. And I don't even know where half the properties are. The only reason I brought it up is because of the graffiti that was there when I found George."

"Ruth Haywood claims there are cameras at every property, and yet those crimes have never been solved. Perhaps someone knew about the cameras, knew where they were, worked around them."

"What does it even matter?" I asked. "If you think it's all a diversion anyway?"

Morales folded her hands, then unfolded them just as quickly. She tapped her nails against the cheap tabletop. "It

speaks to a pattern of anger, of violence. A vendetta against
the Haywood family is certainly worth noting."

"No," I said. "There was no *vendetta*, god. Cassandra was
rightfully angry at how they treated her. And she wouldn't
go and break in to some random place. That's not who she
was, who she is. She's kind. She's caring. What would you do
if you'd quit your job for a man, if you had relied entirely on
him and all his wealth, and then you left him, and he was
working to make sure you wouldn't have a penny to your
name? She wanted the jewelry, which was rightfully hers, so
she could sell it, get back on her feet." My eyes glistened
with moisture, and suddenly, a new idea occurred to me. It
hadn't quite made sense that Henry would kill George just
to get his hands on some jewelry, especially when he and his
family had so much. But what if that wasn't even the plan?
What if killing George was the ultimate way to punish Cassandra? Because if he could somehow pin the crime on her,
that could be worth more even than his relationship with his
own brother. Henry was vindictive, above all. He wanted to
make Cassandra pay. Desperately.

Morales cleared her throat, interrupting my thoughts.
"That's why I asked my colleague to come get you today,
Mrs. Haywood. Certainly *you* must have been *rightfully angry*
as well?"

My head shot up, and fear prickled the nerves of my skin.
Suddenly, it felt like the whole of our conversation was nothing more than a way to put me off-kilter. Morales didn't care
about Cassandra, about vandalism at Henry's properties. She
cared about me.

"Ruth Haywood shared the details of the divorce and custody offer with us. It was enough to make anyone furious.

Especially a mother with a young son. Having your husband out of the way would certainly make that easier, wouldn't it? Custody automatically goes to you. And then there's a hefty life insurance policy, you being the primary beneficiary. Ruth Haywood shared those details with us as well. She also explained that you didn't even want to come up to live in Woodstock, that that, in and of itself, was a compromise. That you would have preferred to be up with your own family in Old Forge. All of that becomes feasible with Mr. Haywood dead."

I shook my head, my pulse pounding violently. It was eerie, horrifying, just how much Morales's words mirrored the text I'd sent to Willa that awful, drunken night. If she got hold of it . . .

"Is there something you want to share, Mrs. Haywood?"

My face went hot. "No," I managed.

"Because any relevant information would really sound best coming from you right now."

"There's nothing," I said emphatically. "I've told you everything I know."

Morales sighed, as if she were an elementary school teacher and I was a wayward student. "Have you ever been violent with your husband?"

"No," I said. "God, no."

Then it hit me, like a ton of bricks. Sunday morning. George leaving. The way I'd pushed him. The way that woman, that power-walker, had seen.

"Think of anything?"

Tears were spilling from my eyes now. "You don't understand. George had just told me about the custody situation. I was angry. It was just a little push, is all. I've never done anything like that before. And I wouldn't kill him. I *didn't* kill him. I—" I clamped my mouth shut, realizing I wasn't helping myself now. "Do I need a lawyer? Are you going to arrest me?"

Morales set a folder on the table in lieu of answering my question. "There's a couple of other things I'd like to address. Couple of items that have turned up in evidence."

She pulled out a glossy photo. It was incredibly close-up, taken with a zoom lens. Cotton-like strands, tinged with red. "Any idea what that is?" Morales asked.

"Some kind of fabric?" I asked. "Maybe a piece of George's clothing? There was blood everywhere."

"Not a terrible guess. But it's actually remnants of a tissue-like product. Highly absorbable. Most likely used to clean up some of the blood at the scene. Forensics' best guess is—surprisingly—" Morales eyed me. "Your run-of-the-mill diaper."

My body jolted, and my heart began to race.

"Your son still in diapers, Mrs. Haywood?"

"Yes, but—"

"And you mind telling me what brand he uses? The lab we've sent it off to for processing assures us they can do an analysis that is quite specific."

"Pampers," I said. "But you can't be serious. Half the parents on earth use Pampers. It doesn't mean—I didn't even have Alex with me up here."

"You keep an extra in your purse? When my kids were younger, I always did, just in case I forgot the diaper bag."

I swallowed, my skin practically on fire.

"This is absurd," I said. "I'm a mother. You can't pin a murder on me because I keep diapers in my purse."

Morales simply shrugged. "We'll see what the lab says. Should have results in forty-eight hours, hopefully sooner." She pulled two sheets of paper from the folder, but held them in front of her, so I couldn't see. "There's something else I'd like to talk about, something I would like you to help us with. Mr. Haywood's phone calls and text messages."

"I thought his phone wasn't found at the scene," I said.

"That's right," she said. "And we are still searching, hoping it, along with a solid murder weapon, will turn up. But in the absence of those things, we're working with what we've got."

"Doesn't it take time to subpoena phone records?" I asked.

"It does. And as to the actual content of texts, it takes several weeks. But the owners have access to the bills, with call logs and records of who has sent and received messages. And they are of course within their rights to release them to us."

"But George handled the cell phones, not me. I didn't even have access to that. How could he release them to you? He's dead."

Morales sized me up, as if seeing how much I knew. "The phone was registered to the Haywoods. His parents."

"Oh," I said. How had I never known that? And I still was on their plan. Christ. That meant Ruth and Frank had access to whoever I was calling.

I replayed what Morales had just said. The actual content of each text doesn't show up on the phone bill. That takes several weeks to get hold of. Morales was obviously going to subpoena George's messages, but what about mine?

Even if Willa had deleted the text, all she had to do was go and tell the police about it, and they'd subpoena my phone for those exact dates. I'd trusted my biggest secret to an actual con artist.

Christ. I'd screwed up. I'd screwed up bad.

"This is a record of George's texts and calls in the days leading up to his death."

I stared at the pages, one listing all the numbers the messages went to, the other with all the outgoing and incoming phone calls. Next to the numbers, Morales had added names.

"As you can see, some of the numbers we've been able to identify. The Haywoods have provided as many details as they can, but there are some we're still working on. Do any of these names look familiar to you?"

I scanned the list. My name was on there. And Henry's. And Ruth's and Frank's. Business associates George or his parents had told me about. At the bottom of the call page, I saw a name I didn't recognize, next to two incoming phone calls Sunday night: *Wright Holdings LLC*.

"I don't know what this company is," I said.

"A lot of people register even personal cell phones to their companies these days," Morales said. "We're looking into it."

"Okay," I said, my eyes moving to the page of text messages next. "There's nothing really out of the ordinary."

I stopped myself, pulled the paper closer with a shaking hand. Every muscle in my body tensed, and all my thoughts, all my suspicions, how sure I'd been about Henry a moment ago, suddenly shot from my mind, a bird taking flight.

What if it wasn't Henry? What if it wasn't some angry vandal?

Oh god, what if it was *her* all along?

There, at the bottom, were five outgoing text messages, from George to a number with a name right beside it. And two incoming, from that same number to George.

Heat rose to my face. I held back a retch.

She had stayed with me Monday night. I had stayed with her last night.

She had poured me wine and fed me Bolognese and pretended to be there for me.

And for months this past spring, she had been around Alex.

All the while, there was this.

I stared at the name, written out in Detective Morales's handwriting, complete with a question mark beside it, a person who had yet to be identified.

Charlotte Williams.

Willa's real name.

30

WILLA

want ice cream," Poppy cried. "You promised ice cream!"

I held Poppy close to me as I booked it away from the Woodstock flea market, where Mary had just confronted me. Didn't stop walking until we were back on the main drag. The sun was bright. Poppy was shielding her eyes with her hands. My heart was racing. Brutally.

It had been just over a month since I'd met Rich and Poppy on that train headed north. Since I'd made the split-second decision to become a part of their lives. And it had been a good month. Rich was kind. Poppy was adorable. The buyer for the jewelry was still being lined up, and their home was a safe place to crash until everything was a go.

George had texted and called shortly after I left Brooklyn but must have tired of the effort. I never responded once. The only reason I didn't block him was because I wanted to get a window into his thoughts, if he *did* decide to take action. So far, he hadn't. There was no real chance of him coming here, either. He preferred Montauk, the Hamptons—classic old money. Yes, I knew there were lots of people from the city up here. That hiding in plain sight *was* a risk. But my dalliance with George had been secret; I doubted anyone besides Henry and Alex's nanny even knew.

Not to mention, I made a point of not making real friends in the city.

Mary had been my one exception.

I made my way down Tinker Street, Poppy heavy on my hip. Should have brought the damn stroller.

Mary had said she didn't even *like* this part of upstate. Thought it was a bougie extension of the city. She missed Old Forge. Her family. So why was she here now?

The streets were teeming with people as I carried Poppy past the bakery. Past the hippie bookstore. I felt suddenly exposed. Wished I had those ridiculous sunglasses I'd been wearing when I'd met Rich. Even with dark hair and different clothes, Mary had picked me out easily. Was there a chance she'd bought my lie? Doubtful.

What if, against all odds, she'd gone back to George? What if he'd told her all about me, what I'd done? What if he somehow found me, got the jewelry back? I still had the whole trove in Rich's house. *Fuck*.

"You okay, Annie?" Poppy asked.

I couldn't help it—I smiled. Poppy was the most empathetic little girl. I cared for her truly. She could always sense when something wasn't right.

"I'm all right," I said, forcing some cheer into my voice. "A little worried, that's all."

"About what?" she asked plainly.

"Nothing you need to concern yourself about, sweetheart," I said, squeezing her chubby thigh.

She squirmed in my arms. "I want to walk."

"Okay," I said, setting her down.

She took my hand, hers giving mine warmth. I tried to focus on the sun, the feeling of her little fingers in mine. Tried to calm myself down.

All this was a wake-up call. I couldn't get too comfortable here. Had to get things moving. Had to put the pressure on.

This is fine.

Poppy walked slowly, but we made our way up the block. Past the town parking lot. Toward the pub on the corner, inhabitants loud and vivacious, spilling out onto the summer streets. Taking advantage of this lovely August weather. Drinking craft beers made in towns ten or twenty miles away.

I'd avoid Mary for as long as she was up here. Soon, it would all be behind me. I'd be nothing more than a memory to this sweet little girl.

Sad, I knew, but she was going back to her mother at the end of the summer. It wasn't my fault that Rich had invited me into his life so quickly. I doubted his ex even *knew* the extent of our arrangement. That I was actually living with the two of them.

This is fine, I told myself again. Meanwhile, Poppy hopped over a crack in the sidewalk.

In front of the pub, Poppy stopped. "There's a rock in my shoe," she said, her voice already turning to a whine.

"Okay," I said, kneeling down. She balanced on my shoulder, and together we took care of the rock.

When I stood up, there was George.

I did a double take, making sure. It was him, all right.

Sitting in the corner, facing us. A beer in front of him. Flicking through his phone.

He looked up as I grabbed Poppy's hand. I pulled her forward, frantic, and she protested loudly—"Wait, wait, I wanna walk, I don't wanna hold your hand!"

I scooped her up, and she writhed in my arms. Let out a screeching wail, announcing her discomfort to every resident within a mile radius.

I kept walking, never turning back, knowing that already I'd played it wrong. Her tantrum would draw more attention, not less.

I didn't turn back until I was at the crosswalk. Until I was making a right onto the street that would take us home.

"No," Poppy cried. "You said I could have ice cream. You *promised*."

"We have to find your daddy first," I said.

I set her down, and her wails ceased the instant her little feet hit the sidewalk.

Tucked behind the oversized hibiscus plant in front of the noodle shop, I let myself look for any sign of George. As far as I could see, he wasn't there. He hadn't followed.

I didn't know if he'd recognized me or not.

But I knew one thing without a doubt: if he had, it could change everything.

I pulled out my phone, shot off a quick text.

I fucked up.

31

MARY

Charlotte Williams.

The name I'd seen only yesterday on her driver's license.

My mom called me Charlotte Anne. I hated it, obviously. When I left home, it made sense to go by Willa.

"Are you okay, Mrs. Haywood?"

George knew Willa. Willa knew George. And Willa knew men for one reason and one reason only . . .

When women leave, they leave a big gaping hole.

It's not a crime to fill that hole, Mary.

My heart ached, the betrayal searing, hot and raw. I had left a Mary-shaped hole in George's life, and Willa had crawled right into it, hadn't she?

Then more thoughts came, spinning out, rolling apart, like a ball of yarn unraveling, the web of lies turning to nothing more than string. The way George had backed off, had almost . . . lost interest . . . in me, beginning in mid-June, right around when Willa stopped answering my texts. The way Morales had asked me if there were any women in his life, the way I'd figured maybe there actually *was* someone, someone angry, maybe, or jealous. Someone whose own relationship with George had gone south.

Then I could almost taste the memory, acidic and dry as a chilled glass of white wine. Willa sitting opposite me Sunday night, only a few days before, the Woodstock air August-balmy. She had asked about George, almost immediately, whether he was up here with me, whether I'd slept with him. I'd believed her pathetic excuse—that I seemed upset and she figured it had to have something to do with my ex—but looking back, it was ridiculous, far-fetched. George had been on her radar, top of mind. Had she been jealous? George was a good-looking man. He was smooth and suave, and he had all the money in the world. Could Willa actually have wanted him . . . for herself?

Another thought hit me—the way she'd asked, almost earnestly, whether I'd mentioned to George that I'd seen her. Why?

"Is there something you want to share with me, Mrs. Haywood?" Morales asked, breaking my train of thought.

I looked up, caught the detective's eyes, the beige tones of the interview room, the screech of the chair legs against cheap tile as I adjusted in my seat. It was suddenly like looking at an entirely different world.

Only moments ago, I had been so sure. It had been Henry. A fight over jewelry. About how to treat Cassandra. A turned deadbolt, the thought leading me straight to my brother-in-law.

What if Willa had turned the deadbolt herself, made it out to look like someone had been in the rental when they hadn't? Point me, and all my suspicions, toward someone—anyone—who wasn't her?

"Mrs. Haywood," Morales said again, her voice firm, annoyed. "Whatever is going on, I have to insist that you be more forthcoming."

"I'm sorry," I said, and I felt it then, tears on the edges of my eyes, making my vision swim. I brushed them aside with the back of my hand, finally looked at the detective. "I know her," I said. "Charlotte Williams."

"Okay," Morales said, carefully. "How?"

"We met at a playground in Brooklyn," I said. "Back in—" I racked my brain. "Back in April. We both had—" I cleared my throat. "We were both taking care of kids around the same age, and we became friends—pretty quickly, I guess." I opened my mouth, ready to let the rest of it spill out. *She wouldn't talk to me for months and then I found her up here, using a different name, with a different family, and she's a liar and a con artist and she could have killed George, for all I know.*

I hesitated, my shoulders seizing up, my heart pounding fiercely.

Could she *really* have killed him?

And why would she? For money, for love?

It didn't matter, did it? It was the perfect murder, wasn't it? After all, who's going to suspect you when no one even knows about your relationship?

It flashed at me then, in all its horror, her words when she'd asked if George had ever gotten physical with me.

I'll kill the man, I swear, and no one would suspect little old me.

I'm the sort of person who would do anything *for my friends.*

And her words, too, only a few nights ago, as I'd stormed off from the wine bar.

Help me out, Mary. You won't regret it.

What if this was some sort of perverted way to keep our friendship intact? Maybe some part of her cared about me—even a tiny bit—and she'd thought she was doing me a favor, thought Henry or someone else would go down for it if it came to that. After all, she hadn't shared that text with the police yet. Something had to be holding her back.

Willa hadn't known that George and I had spoken, that he'd been ready to give that jewelry back to me, that he'd promised me he wanted to change . . .

Willa had perhaps taken my drunken words far more seriously than I ever meant them.

"What is it, Mrs. Haywood?" Morales prompted.

I couldn't give up Willa, not until I knew her motivation. Not until I had something. Some sort of proof that she was involved. Because as much as she claimed to be a ride-or-die friend, I knew that she wasn't. She wouldn't have ghosted me if she was. I had no doubt that if suspicion did fall on her, she'd use that text to protect herself. And if she did, the police would stop digging. Their case would be airtight.

I forced out a lie—of omission, if nothing else. "She and I kind of lost touch, but I ran into her up here, and we reconnected. She's the one who picked me up after my interview on Monday, took me home. I'm actually staying with her right now, because I got so freaked out by what happened with the lock on the door."

Morales cocked her head to the side. "So you two are friends? Did she meet Mr. Haywood through you?"

"Possibly," I said. "I don't know."

"Would she have had any reason to contact him, as far as you know?"

"It's hard to say."

"Mrs. Haywood. I'm sorry, but a moment ago you seemed absolutely in shock and now you're acting like this isn't a big deal."

"I am . . . surprised," I said. "But I don't want to jump to conclusions."

Morales stared at me. She knew I was lying, that much was clear. But she didn't know why. And I had to keep it that way. "I suppose I could ask her. Why she called George."

The detective sat up straighter. "I'd rather you didn't."

I straightened, too, feeling, for the first time, like maybe I had *some* sort of leg to stand on. "Why?"

Morales cleared her throat. "We don't know that any of these people are aware that we have the phone records. Giving her, giving *anyone*, a heads-up—it isn't wise. We'll be reaching out to everyone on the call list in the next couple of days. We just have to clear up a few outstanding questions first. It's best that when I speak to her, I can get an answer that hasn't been rehearsed."

"Okay. Can I go, then?" I asked, shifting in my seat, drawing on all the courage I could possibly find. "I don't have anything more for you. And you obviously don't have a case against me right now, as much as you're trying to make me think you do."

Morales eyed me, then nodded.

"This isn't over, Mrs. Haywood. Don't think these stories of yours have put you in the clear."

"I know," I said. I turned on my heel, walked out of the room, my heart beating fiercely the whole time.

This wasn't over. No one knew that more than me.

It wouldn't be over until I got something more out of Willa.

Until I found out exactly what she'd done.

32

WILLA

R ich was downstairs when I got home from the wine bar where Mary had stormed off, flicking through his phone.

"How was the event?" he asked. As a cover for meeting Mary, I'd told him I was going to the local bookstore for a talk, which I'd found in the *Daily Freeman*. If he'd checked, he would have found a perfectly normal event for some up-and-coming fiction author. The lie was necessary, because as far as he knew, I had no friends in Woodstock, and I wasn't about to explain to him that the woman who'd been following us around was actually correct about my identity.

"Great," I said. "Free wine, too."

He stood up, kissed me lightly on the lips, then sank back into the sofa. Obviously exhausted. I'd only been living with Rich a matter of weeks, but already, he'd grown so used to me. The way I could get Poppy to sleep better than he could.

The way I organized our meals and shopping lists. The way I seemed to Rich like I'd always been a part of the family. His words, not mine.

Sometimes I wanted to give it to him straight. This wasn't some great love or cosmic connection. He missed having a wife, a mother, a primary caregiver so he could relax in the evenings without having to worry about the ins and outs of caring for a child. He only even *had* Poppy in the summer, but it was a lot for him.

It was a lot for all of them.

See, what I'd said to Mary over wine hadn't been a lie at all, even if I didn't give her every nitty-gritty detail.

When women leave, they leave a big gaping hole, and men start to realize just how much these women were doing to keep their world afloat.

No guy was cut out for it. Not even Rich, who deeply cared about other humans but still needed hand-holding when it came to the domestic stuff.

And it's true, whether Mary was ready to admit it or not. Women and girls—we're raised to expect the sacrifice, to know that family life will be hard work. Men and boys? They're told to spread their seed and reap the benefits. Bask in the offspring around you while someone else does the li-on's share of the work. Do a little here and there and receive all the praise for being "such a good dad."

"Poppy give you a hard time?" I asked, pulling myself back to the present.

"Wanted Mr. Snuffles, then her little frog, then to switch it back. I must have gone in there six times."

I joined him on the sofa and squeezed his shoulder. "You indulge her too much, you know. That's why she pesters you."

"I know," he said. "But I don't have your magic touch. I've never seen someone so good with kids as you are. Christ, you could probably teach my ex a few things."

"Careful," I said. "If she hears you say that, she'll fly right over and strike me dead."

Rich laughed, and then he shifted his weight on the sofa, and I could see it, in spite of the tiredness, the stress. I could see what was so familiar to me, what I'd built a life—hell, a pseudo-career—on: desire.

It was too much right now. Not after everything with Mary, which had hurt me deeper than I'd expected. It was one thing to have her out of my life, confused and hating me, but hating me from afar. It was another to see her scorn, her judgment face-to-face. I felt awful about what I'd done. Wished there were a way to make it up to her, to restore a friendship I'd truly adored.

I reached my hand to my head, like I was a tired wife in an old sitcom. "I think the book-event chardonnay got to my head a little bit. I was going to go lie down."

"Oh," Rich said, obviously surprised. But then just as quickly he forced a smile. He was the sort who would never pressure a woman for sex. A refreshing change from Jack the Douchebag, whose credit card I'd actually resorted to using tonight, when the first one didn't go through. Take that, Jackie boy. "Of course. Feel better." He leaned forward, gave me another peck.

"Thanks."

Upstairs, I peeked into Poppy's room, saw her holding tight to Mr. Snuffles, then carefully closed the door. In the bedroom, I paused at the closet, opened it, ran my foot along the floorboards. I'd moved all the jewelry there yesterday, taking it out of its drawer in my dresser, tucking it beneath a loose piece of wood I'd wedged back in and covered up with shoe boxes and an enormous diaper box that held Poppy's old clothes. If George had actually seen me, figured out who I was, I could lose everything. I had to make sure he couldn't find the jewelry, if he came after me.

I shut the closet door and opened the window near the bed. Let a bit of the mountain breeze through and sank onto the mattress. I stared at the vaulted ceiling, lined with beautiful cedar planks. Rich had taken such care restoring this place. I loved it, I really did.

I listened to the crickets. Felt the cool mountain air tickling my cheeks. Nestled into the down comforter and smelled the light scent of begonias wafting up from the flower beds down below.

This was a life, wasn't it? One that many a woman would dream of. And there had been moments, in the last week or so, when I'd wondered, as I always did at one point or another: Could I stay? Could I actually make this my home?

But seeing Mary, seeing the pure horror on her face, brought me back to reality. No one really knew me. Not a single one of these men. I had lied to them all. I'd shrunk myself for them, become squishy and malleable. In a strange way, the only person I hadn't done that with was Mary.

No, no matter how nice Rich was, no matter how easy life was here, I couldn't pass up my chance at starting anew. At seeing who I was, without a man to please.

My phone buzzed, shaking me from my reverie.

Maybe it was Mary, telling me she understood. Promising she wouldn't say another word to Rich. I wasn't going to stay with him forever, but blowing it all up before the deal had gone through was beyond risky.

I pulled the phone out eagerly, but in spite of all that had happened in the last twenty-four hours, George's number on the screen still sent a shock wave through my body.

His words did, too.

Nice home you have there

33

MARY

Willa was leaning against the car in the parking lot of the police station when I got outside, practically sitting on the hood, the iced coffee in her hand, oversized sunglasses covering her eyes, staring at the phone in her other hand.

She was so beautiful, dressed in one of those breezy sleeveless turtleneck summer sweaters I could never figure out how to pull off. So fresh and so young, so much newer, so much more interesting, more captivating than me. I imagined George's hands on her body, his mouth on her neck, drinking her in. I imagined her stretching out in the bed I had called my own, her body lithe and tight in the ways mine no longer was, her belly smooth, no C-section scar. Her legs strong as she straddled him. Knowing, learning everything that I did. The feel of his strong hands against my hips. The way his mouth tasted of Altoids and eucalyptus from the ChapStick he always used. The quiet groan when he came. The tiny little intimacies, the way a towel looked wrapped around his waist, the cowlick just above the left side of his forehead he worked to tame every morning.

My heart ached, sharp and hot, daggers in my chest. How could she sleep with my husband?

How could she *kill* him?

Maybe she only did because she knew you wanted it, deep down.

Was I responsible—somehow—for George's death? Because I had welcomed her into our lives, our world?

Willa looked up when I approached. "How was it?" she asked.

I felt moisture in my eyes.

"Are you okay? What happened?"

I wiped the tears away. "Nothing," I lied, needing to think quick on my feet now. "The detective didn't take me seriously. And I want this whole thing over, because if it goes on much longer, I know George's parents are really going to suspect me. And if they try to keep Alex from me . . ."

"Oh, Mary," Willa said, rushing up to me and wrapping me in a hug. She pulled back. "Of course you're worried. But they can't keep a mother from her son. Anyone can see how much you love Alex. How good you are to him."

I pictured something else then, something newly horrifying. Had Willa been around my son, when I wasn't there? Alex's vocabulary wasn't enough—he wouldn't have been able to betray her. More tears blossomed in my eyes. Had she fed him, wiped his mouth, hugged him when he banged his knee? Sung him "Twinkle, Twinkle," not even knowing to substitute the words?

Had she thought about Alex at all when she killed his father?

"Let's get back," I said. "I need to get out of here."

"Of course," Willa said. "Of course you do. Do you want me to drive?"

"No," I said. "No, I'm good."

I was silent as I pulled out of the lot and onto the road that led back toward town. Willa, too. At the turn to her street, I hesitated. Was I really about to go back with her? Straight into the lion's den? I stole a glance her way. It was so hard to imagine. This woman, who'd comforted me so many times, brutally attacking someone, leaving them for dead.

Was I being paranoid? Was I jumping to conclusions?

"Mary," Willa said. I jolted. I was sitting at the stop sign, and behind me, people were starting to honk.

Wordlessly, I turned onto her street, my pulse picking up. I didn't think she would actually hurt me—maybe that was naïve, but I didn't—and if I let her out of my sight, I had no idea *what* she'd do. I had to find out the truth. If she had killed George, I needed evidence, something to take to Morales besides my suspicions. I needed to be able to make my own case against her, and quickly.

At the house, Willa said she was going to tidy up the kitchen, and I claimed to want to try Alex again, but upstairs, as soon as I heard the water running down below, I walked down the hall until I found the main bedroom. I hesitated at the threshold, taking it in. The bed was unmade, the sheets a mess, and his-and-hers nightstands flanked it all, the one on the right holding a pair of silver earrings and hair ties.

I went straight to her nightstand, then pulled open the drawer, but it was empty, apart from a pack of travel tissues and an Agatha Christie novel. I tugged the drawer all the way out, in case anything was tucked behind it, peered into the back of the stand, saw nothing but cobwebs and dust.

I replaced the drawer, then turned to the bed, running my hands between the mattress and the box spring. It was a cliché, sure, but clichés were clichés because they were true. I wasn't even sure what I was looking for. Some proof that she'd been at Henry's place that morning? Tickets to some far-flung island where she couldn't be extradited?

I made my way around the perimeter of the bed, then bumped into a hamper. I dug through it, looking for something covered in blood, knowing, even as I pawed around, that the exercise was futile. Willa wasn't stupid. She wouldn't have gotten this far, with all these men, if she wasn't good at covering her tracks. Murder would be no different, would it? With murder, she'd be even more careful.

I jolted at the sound of a car outside. I ran to the window, peered out to see a shiny black truck pulling into the driveway, right next to mine.

The engine shut off and a man got out. It was the man I'd seen in Woodstock with Willa. Rich.

I didn't have much time.

I rushed to the dresser, rifling through the drawers, looking for something—anything. I found lacy underwear, silky bras, T-shirts and jumpsuits, jeans and yoga pants. Nothing untoward. Nothing secretive at all.

I pushed the last drawer shut and moved to the closet instead.

It had double folding doors, and I opened them slowly,

hoping they wouldn't creak. The right side was full of sun-dresses that must be Willa's, and a stack of shoe and storage boxes sat neatly beneath, one of them an oversized box of Honest Company training diapers, the fancy brand that we'd used until they started to give Alex a rash. *Of course*, I thought. Poppy wasn't too old for training diapers. In fact, I'd seen an errant one when I'd gone through Willa's purse. I pulled out my phone, took a photo of the box—something I could show to Morales.

Was it proof? Not on its own. I needed more.

I opened the top of the box, found stacks of old baby clothes. I dug through to the bottom, in case something was tucked away, but found nothing.

I was lifting the lid of the next box, careful to be quiet, when I heard the approach of footsteps on the stairs—and raised voices, a kid's among them.

I repositioned the boxes, quickly closed the closet, and shot back into the hallway, peered around the corner, just in time to see Rich on the top of the stairs, the little girl in his arms, staring at Willa. "There is no way I'm listening to your stories right now," he said. "I've heard enough. I've seen proof. I don't have time for this, not with my mom in the hospital."

"Daddy, why are you talking to Annie that way?" the little girl begged.

"Wait, Rich," Willa said. "Please just calm down. Please don't be rash."

The little girl squirmed, and he set her down. Then his eyes caught mine, and I expected him to demand answers, ask me to explain what I was doing in his house, but he only turned back to Willa.

"Daddy, Daddy," the girl said, tugging at Rich's pants. "Don't be mean to Annie."

He knelt down to his daughter. "Annie has to go, sweetie. Annie was lying to us, telling us stories. Remember how your teacher told you it wasn't nice to make things up?"

The girl nodded, her chin quivering, then turned to Willa. "It's not nice to make things up!"

Willa's face went beet red. "I'm sorry, sweetie." Then she looked up to Rich. "I'm sorry."

"Please," he said. "Just gather your things and go."

"But I don't want her to go!" the little girl cried. "She said sorry! When we make up stories, we say sorry and then it's okay!"

Willa bit her lip, then knelt down to the girl. "You're right, sweetie. But I have to go, okay? Can you give me a big hug before I go?"

"But I don't *want* you to go."

"I know," Willa said. "But I have to, and it's not because of you or because of your daddy, I just have to go, okay?"

The girl's lip quivered again, but after a moment, she opened her arms wide, circling them around Willa's neck. When Willa pulled away, her eyes were wet, and she turned on her heel, rushing to her room and shutting the door behind her.

This is the cost of your games, I thought. Hurting children. Breaking their hearts.

Rich looked up then, and his eyes caught mine.

"You weren't lying," he said. "You weren't crazy."

"No," I said. "I wasn't."

He knelt down to this daughter. "Go downstairs, sweetie.

I'll come down and put *Sesame Street* on in a minute. And we can have ice cream, okay?"

"Right now?" the girl asked, eyes lighting up. "In the middle of the *day*?"

"Uh-huh," Rich said. "Just be a good girl and go down, wait for me."

"Why are you here with her?" he asked, as soon as Poppy had gone down the stairs. "After the way she lied to you? What made you forgive her?"

I haven't forgiven her. I think that maybe she killed my husband. But she could ruin me, if she wants to, and I need to find out what happened first before she gets a chance.

Willa popped out of the bedroom then. "Just give me a minute, Mary. Then we'll go."

I was rooted, frozen to the spot. I hadn't agreed that she could come with me, but at the same time, I didn't want to let her out of my sight. I had to find a way to fix this.

A way out.

"She's not a good person," Rich said, catching my eyes again. "She fools you. She makes you think she cares about you. But she doesn't in the end. I thought she cared about me. About Poppy." He took a deep breath, and his eyes moistened. "But she only ever cares about herself."

34

WILLA

Nice home you have there

George's text practically burned against my hand.

I thought of Rich downstairs. Of Poppy, fast asleep.

I'd never wanted to bring them into my mess.

I took a quick breath. Forced some stillness into my shaking hands.

Maybe it was just a bluff on George's part. Maybe no one was out there. Maybe he hadn't followed me. Didn't know where I lived. Maybe he was only saying this to freak me out. Sadistic prick.

I flicked off the bedside lamp, feeling exposed. Then I walked toward the open window.

I leaned forward, my eyes struggling to adjust.

Darkness. No streetlamps here, even in town. A little soft

light from the porch, a light Rich would turn off before he came to bed. The glow of the moon, washing it all in a sickly yellow color.

I saw the curves of the mountains. The trees across the street. A neighbor's mailbox.

And then, something else.

A shadow, a silhouette.

Tall enough, shaped just right, so it could be . . .

The silhouette moved forward, farther into the light. I still couldn't make out the face, but I knew it was a man.

George.

My heart cinched up. This was all such a mess. The buyer should have been lined up already. I should never have been in this position. Hell, maybe I should have left town the very moment I saw Mary. Or at least when Poppy and I crossed George's path in town.

I'd gotten comfy here, hadn't I?

Now here I was, a sitting duck.

I stepped back from the window. Pulled the curtain shut so George couldn't see in. Stared down at my phone, my thumbs hovering over the keyboard.

Should I ignore him? But he'd seen me—he knew that I knew—and I was afraid of what he'd do if I didn't respond.

Pound down the door? Wake up Poppy? Tell Rich everything?

I didn't want that to happen. Didn't want any of this to happen.

No, I had to say something.

I settled on simple, direct.

What do you want

George's typing was instant, in the dots on my phone, in the bowed head of the silhouette.

I want what you took

I had to lie, didn't I? What other choice did I have? I had to play dumb.

I don't know what you're talking about. It's over between us.
Please just leave me alone or I'll call the police.

I hit send, waiting for a response. What if Rich got up right now, went out to look at the stars, as he sometimes did? What if he saw George? What would he do? What if George came in, incensed with anger, intent on tearing the place apart until he found what I'd taken?

What if they started to fight? What if Poppy woke up and went downstairs, begging for more water? What if we were all there, bouncing off one another, pawns in a game I'd created but was no longer able to control?

Everything felt precarious. Fragile. Terrifying.

Finally, another text came through.

Don't play stupid. You're smarter than that.

The dots kept going. George had more to say.

Bring it to me, all of it, I'm at 12 Waterfall Way.
You have until the morning.

The dots stopped, and I thought maybe that was it. I

counted to thirty—then sixty—and then I crept up to the window, pulled the curtain back just enough to see. To check.

He was still there. He must have seen me, because he waved, taunting me.

The danger of my life, of what I'd been doing for so long, hit me with full force.

I was playing with fire. I didn't know *what* George would do.

Finally, another text appeared.

Bring it to me, or else I go to the police

My heart raced and I turned to my phone, but I didn't text George this time.

He found me. We're fucked.

35

MARY

I found a spot right in front of the rental and put the car into park. I got out, the midday sun practically blinding me. I looked back up the street. There was a black sedan, on the other side of the road, maybe a hundred yards ahead. Was someone following me?

The police? The Haywoods?

I squinted, trying to see if there was anyone in the car, if it was idling or parked, but I couldn't tell. The sun was too bright.

"Everything okay?" Willa asked, her bags in her hands, her purse tight against her hip.

"Fine," I said, turning back to the rental and heading up the walk.

On the porch, I found a sheet of notepaper, folded in half and wedged in the doorjamb.

Instantly I recognized the pearly finish, the monogrammed *H*, the heavy weight of the Haywood company letterhead.

Stop filling the cops' heads with your wild, paranoid theories. I didn't kill my brother. I'm starting to think maybe you did . . .

It wasn't signed, but it didn't take a genius to figure out it was from Henry. It wasn't like he was trying to hide it either, given that it was on the damn letterhead. But he didn't need to hide it, did he? Morales had been uninterested in him as a suspect, and with the revelation about Willa knowing George, I almost didn't blame her.

"What's that?"

Willa's voice was right in my ear, her breath practically warming my neck. I jumped, taking a step from her. "Nothing," I said. "Just the Haywoods being the Haywoods."

I turned back toward the road, looking once more for the black sedan, but it was gone.

Christ, maybe I was being paranoid.

I opened the door and Willa followed me inside. Shutting it behind us, I twisted the deadbolt, imagining, for a moment, Willa turning it herself.

"Well, *that* was horrible," Willa said, setting her bag in the corner. "I'm sorry about Rich. And that you had to see all that with Poppy. I'm going to try and dig up some tea bags. Rentals like this usually have them."

I took a step forward, not wanting to let her out of my sight for a moment, but then my phone rang, and I practically leapt at the name on my screen.

"Ruth," I said, answering quickly, as Willa disappeared into the kitchen. "Ruth, I'm glad you called."

"Hi, Mary," Ruth said. Her voice was tired and flat. In the background, I heard the faint sound of traffic, a siren.

"Are you back in Brooklyn already?" I asked.

"I am," she said, resigned. "But Henry is staying in Woodstock, keeping an eye on the investigation."

"You mean intimidating me?" I asked, grasping the note in my hand. "Leaving me threatening notes?"

"He's trying to find out who killed his brother, Mary. That's all."

I didn't want to argue about Henry. She'd never go against one of her sons anyway. "Can I please talk to Alex? I just want to see my son. Frank never called me."

"Listen, Mary, I'm not going to beat around the bush here. I'm in close contact with the detective. She tells me you remain a person of interest. With that in mind, I don't think you should be talking to Alex, not until this gets resolved."

"What?" I asked, my stomach suddenly heavy, my biggest fear finally arriving. "You can't do that," I argued. "He's *my* child. Not yours."

"No, he's not. Mine is *dead*," Ruth practically spat. "And we *can* do it, actually. We have written permission from you to keep him this week, for one. And our lawyers say there is precedent for this sort of thing, especially when a parent is under criminal investigation."

"I'm not—"

"You are, Mary. You very much are."

"I didn't kill him," I said, tears filling my eyes, spilling across my cheeks. "I swear to you, I didn't."

"Then you have nothing to worry about, do you?" Ruth said.

"But—"

Silence. Ruth had already hung up.

I tried calling her back, but it only rang and rang. I tried Frank three times, and Genevieve, too, then Ruth again, but it went immediately to voicemail—*Hi, you've reached Ruth Haywood.* She was screening me.

So this was it, then. They were going to try to keep Alex from me. It was already happening.

Willa emerged from the kitchen then, two teacups steaming in her hands.

"Are you okay?" she asked, setting the cups on the coffee table.

I stared at her, coursing with rage.

You're the reason they're doing this. You you you.

"Ruth doesn't want me to see Alex," I said. "Not as long as I'm a 'person of interest.'"

"They can't do that," Willa said.

"They can," I said. "And they will. They have all the money, all the power, in the world. And I have nothing."

"Oh, Mary," Willa said. She spread her arms wide, wrapped them around me.

"No," I said, squirming against her embrace. "No!" I said again, and I pushed her this time, and my movements were so strong, so urgent, that she stumbled back. I watched as her feet scrambled for footing, as she fell, one hand sliding into the steaming cups of tea, knocking them over, the other trying to catch herself on the sofa. Then she was on the ground, pulling her scalded hand to her chest, holding it close, like an injured animal.

"Fuck, Mary," she said. "You hurt me."

I stared at her, on the ground, and in that moment, I imagined George, the hatred he must have felt toward her.

We can't all be like Rich, I thought. Calm and collected. Still treating her with a respect she didn't deserve.

"My hand," she said, holding it up. "You burned my hand."

The scene felt so surreal. In our short-lived friendship, she was the fun one, the tornado of energy and humor and margaritas. I was the nurturer, the one who directed her stroller away from potholes, insisted she balance her drinks with water. But now I wasn't taking care of her, I was hurting her.

She pushed herself up, then rushed into the bathroom, flicking the water on, running her hand beneath it. "The tea was practically boiling. You can't just *push* people."

"Oh yeah?" I said. Suddenly, I didn't care about the singed skin on Willa's hand, didn't care about Morales's warning to let her talk to Willa first. Didn't care about pissing Willa off, even with the dirt she had on me. The worst was already happening. I had already lost. "You can't just kill people, either."

"What are you talking about?" Willa asked, her hand still running beneath the water, her eyes, crystal blue and full of lies, looking right at me.

And my eyes, wide open, maybe for the first time.

"I *know* you texted him," I said.

Willa looked away for a moment so brief, I almost thought I imagined it: "What are you talking about, Mary?"

"George," I said. "My husband. You texted my husband, and the next morning he was dead."

She flicked the water off, grabbed the hand towel, and held it against her burn. "I have to put something on this. I—"

"I don't care about your *hand*," I snapped. "Stop playing games with me. Just tell me, for god's sake. *Tell* me."

"You must be mistaken—"

"The police *showed* me his call logs. Your name is there. I can figure out what happened, I can put it all together. But I want to hear it from you. If you're going to ruin me, to kill my husband, to keep me from my son, at least have the decency to tell me *why*."

Willa's eyes flitted back and forth, from her bags in the corner to the fireplace to the door, as if searching for a story, one to deliver straight to me. Then she walked from the bathroom, still clutching the towel, and sat down on a chair in the corner, took a deep breath. "I didn't kill him, okay? I swear to you. But I did text him. After I saw you that night, after you told me what you did, I told George to stay away from you. I was trying to protect you. You were acting like you were going to take him back, and I knew that wasn't good for you, and I was a little drunk, okay? I was feeling protective."

She pressed her hands to her thighs, shaking her head. "I know I should have told you, right away," Willa went on. "But then, it turns out he's been murdered, and how am I supposed to tell you that, oh wait, I was texting your hubby the night before someone killed him? I'm sorry. I wanted to say something, I just didn't know how."

"You really expect me to believe that?"

"Yes," Willa said. "Because it's the truth."

"How did you even have his number, then?" I asked. "Explain that."

Willa bit her lip, wincing in pain. "I'd met him before,"

she said. "We moved in the same circles, I guess you could say."

"When?" I asked. "*Before* you met me?"

"No. *After*," she said. "I promise. I always try to have . . . how do I say this . . . multiple irons in the fire. I meet people. Out, you know. We exchanged numbers. I didn't re-alize."

"So it was *exactly* what I thought, then. He was another guy to screw, a guy who had a wife-shaped hole in his life, one you could fill . . ."

The thought struck me, right in the gut, twisted the knife, oh so deep. I was losing everything—I was losing Alex—because of *her*. Because of a woman I'd foolishly let into our lives.

Willa stood then, crossing the distance between us, to sit beside me on the sofa. "Listen, Mary. You have to believe me. I met George at the end of May, at a cocktail bar in the neighborhood, more than a month after I already met you. We traded numbers. He never even gave me his last name. I didn't realize it was *your* George, okay? I didn't think that the world was quite that small. But that last night we met up, the one in June where we got all those margaritas, you told me he was a Libra, and I remembered that the George I'd met had said the same. I still didn't think it was the same guy, but after I put you in a cab that night, I googled you—I never had before—and saw your wedding announcement. The thing is, I'd already slept with him. I'm so sorry. That made me realize I couldn't be friends with you anymore, that being in your life, after what I'd done, would hurt you too much. So I ghosted you. I know it was a shit thing to do, but I freaked out."

I stared at her, struggling to process this new information. The moment I'd seen Willa's name on that call log, my mind had run wild. Willa targeting George. A torrid love affair gone wrong. Spending time with Alex. Getting jealous. Getting angry. All leading to murder. All my other theories—Henry, some angry stranger mistaking George for his brother—practically flying from my mind.

Was what she was telling me actually possible? Was it all a coincidence?

"Then why didn't you say something?" I asked hesitantly. "You could have told me, when I showed up in Woodstock. You could have told me everything."

Willa's eyes flicked to her bags, but then turned back, trained on mine, held my hand in hers. "I really wanted to. You have to believe me."

"Wait," I said, pulling my hand away and scooting away from her on the sofa. "Wait. I saw the call logs. George texted you first. That means you were still talking to him. Why? Were you still together?"

"No," Willa said. "No, I promise you we weren't."

"Then why did he text you? Tell me. What did he want from you?"

Willa's eyes dashed to the left, and I followed her gaze to the bags in the corner.

I stood. "And why do you keep looking at your bags?"

"Mary," she said, leaping to her feet, too.

I'd struck a nerve, and now was my chance. I needed answers. I needed the truth.

"Screw your lies," I said, lunging for her canvas weekender—I grabbed the zipper, tugged it hard.

"Mary, don't—please."

I turned it over, shaking it all out. And then, with a thud, it fell against the floor. A black velvet bag, one that looked familiar.

"Mary!" Willa practically yelled, lunging for it.

I side-checked her and got there first.

I snatched it, the bag heavy, the velvet secured by a drawstring at the top.

Willa pushed herself up and lunged again at me, but it was too late.

There would be no secrets between us anymore.

I pried a finger into the opening and pulled.

There it was, before I could see anything else.

Shining in its glory, practically roaring.

The emerald eyes. The onyx spots. The diamonds cascading down its powerful back.

Of course the bag had looked familiar. I'd seen it, after all, in the back of George's safe.

I stared at Cassandra's beloved panther bracelet.

Begging me to finally see the truth.

36

WILLA

Baby. Baby, it's my mother."

My eyes fluttered open, the morning light blinding, and for a horrifying half-asleep moment, I thought it was George hovering over me.

But it wasn't George, just Rich. Sitting on the edge of the bed, looking down at me with worry clouding his eyes.

"What happened?" I asked.

"My mom fell. Her hip. Poppy and I need to go."

"Oh god," I said, sitting up in bed. "Shit. Is she okay?"

"She's stable, but she's in the hospital. We need to go see her. My brothers are already there."

I rubbed the sleep from my eyes. "Okay. Okay. You want me to get Poppy up? Make you breakfast?"

"All taken care of," he said, leaning forward to kiss me. "She's downstairs watching *Sesame Street*."

I narrowed my eyes. "What time is it?"

"Almost nine," he said, smiling and squeezing the side of my thigh. "That bookstore wine must have really done you in."

"Oh," I said. "Yes, I think it did." Truth was, I'd pretended to be asleep when Rich came to bed before midnight, but I'd been wide awake for hours, thinking about George standing outside the window. Mind running through possibilities until I'd glommed on to one that might work . . .

"Come down and see us off, though?" Rich asked.

"Of course," I said. "Be right there."

I grabbed my phone, checked my texts, and there it was, a response to the one I'd sent last night.

Take care of it.

Mondays in Woodstock were dead—I'd learned as much from a month of living here—but this morning was especially so. Maybe it was the time—not even ten o'clock.

The walk was short, only fifteen minutes, but still it felt risky. I was glad Rich and Poppy were already gone. Glad that the streets were empty. That there was no one to see me.

I turned when I got to the hat shop, then jolted across the road, taking a left on the side street, walking purposefully past the waterfall, past a small lookout point that jutted above the creek and bluestone rocks below. Briefly, I imagined texting George, asking him to come meet me here, instead. Waiting for the inevitable conflict to follow and then giving him a little . . . push. How pleasingly simple. There were no cameras here, even just a few steps off the main drag in Woodstock. I could slip back down unobserved, grab a coffee and a croissant on the way home.

I paused, briefly, walked up to the waterfall. It was about fifteen feet down, maybe not enough to kill on impact, but the water was rushing this morning, the August earth moist. Surely one of those rocks would crack his thick, privileged skull.

I thought of all the people the Haywoods had hurt. Mary, and the trap she was in. The second woman who'd tried to leave that family and they absolutely refused to let go.

I thought of the trap I was in, too.

The way they all thought they could fuck with people, with their careers, their financial security, their *children*. That they'd never, ever have to pay.

I looked at the sign, posted loosely with zip ties onto the metal fencing.

DO NOT LEAN ON FENCE

One of the zip ties was already broken, so the sign hung askew. I grabbed the fence, gave it a good shake. A part of it buckled, and on further inspection, I saw that the post was halfway out of the ground.

It would be so easy, I thought. So incredibly easy.

A beautiful, cosmically karmic way to go. One little push and the rocks and the water would get him in the end.

I took two steps back, composing myself, then turned right.

In a few hundred feet I found the address.

A little blue cape. Adorable.

I looked side to side. No one out, no one walking by. No dogs. No squirrels. Not a soul.

Not even a mouse.

What's more, this place was set back from the road, ensconced in the lush, abundant foliage of upstate New York in the depths of summer. A little patch of privacy right in town.

Like something plucked from a storybook, almost. Hansel and Gretel.

And who was the evil witch? Me or George?

Me, of course. Because women always are, aren't they? We can pull your life together, make your home lovely, your children loved. We can book summer camps, clip toenails, wipe noses and asses, arrange every last appointment, but step out of line, even for a second, and we're every name in the book.

Men like George, they didn't love women. They used women.

Might as well be exactly who he already thinks I am.

I took a deep breath. Lifted my hand to my necklace. Remembered how much was on the line.

Here goes nothing.

37

MARY

In shock, I dropped Cassandra's velvet bag, and it landed at my feet with a thud, the panther bracelet spilling out, rolling across the floor, as if emerging from its lair.

Willa scrambled to grab it, stopping it in its tracks and then jumping at the bag, too, clutching it to her chest.

Again, I felt so very, very foolish.

The moment I'd learned Willa had been texting with George, I'd imagined such wild things. Her sleeping with my husband, moving in on my life, something going wrong between them. Anger and jealousy. An argument, a fight. Passion and struggle and murder in the end, George's own ego, his own feeling of being duped, only spurring it all on, bringing the conflict to its mortal conclusion.

Or something even more absurd, that she'd killed him out of some sort of twisted, misplaced loyalty to me.

But that was all fantasy, wasn't it? Yes, she had slept with him, but Willa didn't do things for passion. For love. For revenge, even. And certainly not for friendship. She did them for money.

"You were always after the jewelry, weren't you? A treasure trove, too valuable to pass up. You know, after that night in June, I thought it was *my* fault you stopped responding to me. I thought I'd freaked you out, saying how sometimes I wanted George dead. And you let me think that."

"I didn't mean to—"

"You did, though. You knew I'd beat myself up about it. But it was never about that. It was never about how drunk I got, or what I said. It was never about me at all. Once you knew about the jewelry, you got dollar signs in your eyes. You moved in on George. What better payday? I practically drew you a treasure map."

"Mary," Willa said. "Stop jumping to conclusions. Please just calm down."

"Don't tell me to calm down!" I cried, the other pieces of the puzzle clicking together. The way Willa was always prying for details. Birthdates and anniversaries, the name of the cleaning service. The way she had been so quick to become my friend. How she'd always seemed so incredibly pleased to see me. How she'd invited me, only days after meeting me, just a random stranger from the playground, to the opera, to drinks, how she'd offered me such companionship, such curiosity about the nitty-gritty details of my life, and I'd drunk the attention up like nectar.

"I was so stupid to think you actually wanted to be my friend. You always seemed too young, too cool, to choose little old me, but there was a reason for that, wasn't there? Because it was always a ruse, just a way to get information."

"Mary," Willa said. "I *wanted* to be friends with you, I did—I do—care about you. And I'm practically your age, okay? I'm thirty-five. I just look young is all."

"Jesus Christ, stop making excuses," I said. "Stop playing this game! You knew about it all before, didn't you? You knew there was jewelry. Maybe you even had a hint that George had it. Did you fuck Henry, too?"

"No," Willa said. "Christ, no. I would never sleep with Henry. I *hate* Henry."

I stared at her. Had she known my brother-in-law? How deep did these betrayals go?

"Look," Willa said. "Did I know you were connected to the jewelry? Is that why I initially struck up a conversation with you? Yes, I won't lie. But that night at the opera changed everything. I could tell we could really be friends. And I haven't had a friend in so long. I haven't connected with someone—"

"Stop *lying*," I said. "You do it so easily, I wonder if you even believe it yourself. You didn't stop talking to me because you figured out my George and your George were the same person. You always knew that. You stopped talking to me because you got what you wanted, and I was disposable. Just like all those men. All those *children*. Toss them aside, keep the credit cards in your wallet, use them until they catch on."

"I wanted to call you, I did, but I knew if you found out about George . . ."

I tilted my head to the side. "Were you with George when Alex was there?"

Willa's face reddened, and I saw real, genuine shame.

"Oh my god." I'd imagined it, of course, but this monster

with my baby, without me to protect him; the thought took my breath away.

"I didn't mean for it to happen, I promise you. George didn't, either. But the nanny was late one morning, and Alex recognized me, but he's not so verbal yet, so—

"How convenient," I practically spat.

My heart ached as it became clear to me, finally, and without so much of a shadow of a doubt, who this woman was, how she had conned me from the very beginning. "You're good," I said. "I'll give you that. For so long, I believed you. But I was just another person to use. Like you use everyone."

Willa's face was pale now. "I'm sorry," she said. "I know how it sounds, added up all like this, but I promise you, Mary. I swear. There were other ways I could have gotten what I got. I liked you. I enjoyed your company. I loved the way you were with Alex, the way the boys got along. I considered you a friend. That isn't a lie."

"A friend?" I shouted. "A friend? Friends don't lie. They don't use people to pull off some jewel heist. Friends don't screw each other's husbands, separated or not. You are *not* my friend. You never will be. I doubt you've ever had a real friend in your whole miserable life."

The tears burst forth then, and I gasped for breath. Willa stepped forward, put a hand on my shoulder, but I pushed her off. I wiped at the tears, at snot coming from my nose.

It was pathetic, I knew, how much I grieved her, knowing now exactly who—exactly what—she was. And yet I did. Because I'd needed a friend when I'd met her, so very badly, and that was what she'd been to me, even if it was all a lie.

Willa grabbed a box of tissues, and I took one, then looked at her, my mind still spinning. "Did George follow me up here—or was it really about you? Did he find out where you were? Track you down? He told me on Sunday night, the last night he was *alive*, that he didn't have the jewelry but he was going to get it in the morning. Because it was *you* who had it. And maybe he knew that all along, but he didn't know how to find you. But here you are, and so he texts you, and he threatens to—what?—blow up things with Rich? Go to the police? So you go over, Monday morning, agree to talk to him."

"No," Willa said.

"No, you're right. You went over just to kill him. So he'd be out of your way and you could make off with the jewelry."

"I didn't kill him," Willa said. "I swear I didn't."

I knew I was risking so much, but I didn't care anymore. I had to know the truth. "And now, if the cops ever look at you, ever give you a second glance, you can pin it all on me. You have that text, after all. The nail in my coffin."

"No," she said again. "Mary, I don't want you to go down for anything. And I didn't kill George. I'm guilty of a lot, but not *that*."

Tears coursed down my cheeks. "I'll never see Alex, you know? If the police pin this on me? He won't have anyone. Not his father, not his mother. How can you live with yourself? How can you be so . . . so *evil*?"

"Mary," Willa said again. "Please believe me. It's not going to come to that."

"I don't understand," I said as sobs began to rack my body. "Why *us*? Why *my* family? Other people have jewelry. Other people have money. It's New York City, for Christ sake.

You could have targeted someone else. What did we ever do to you? What are you not telling me? How do you know Henry? How do you know the Haywoods?"

Willa looked down at her feet. When she looked up, her eyes were open, and kind, and tears were swimming within them, too.

"I never did anything like this before," she said. "Never in my life. I never tricked a friend. Never in my wildest imagination did I ever think I'd try and pull off something so big. I promise you that. I dated rich men—a lot of them—I took their gifts, yes, and I used their credit cards, if I could get away with it. I grabbed cash here and there, maybe even something valuable—things they wouldn't miss. But you have to believe me, Mary. None of this is who I am, not deep down. All of this is new to me, too."

"Then why?" I asked, practically begging now. Feeling, somehow, that if I could understand the answer to this, it would soften the pain of everything else. "Why Henry? Why us?"

Willa took a deep breath, then sighed.

"Because she asked me to."

"What?" I reared back, trying to understand. "Who?"

Willa's eyes locked right on mine.

"Cass," she said.

She pressed her lips together.

"Well, I guess she goes by Cassandra now."

38

WILLA

My phone buzzed with a text when I was standing in front of the address George had sent me, building up the nerve to go in.

Did you take care of it?

I slid the phone back into my purse, took a deep breath, and walked up the sidewalk, onto the porch.

I'm about to, Cass, I thought. I promise I'm about to.

I approached the door, a part of it painted in a red that reminded me of the door to Mary's brownstone.

I had to go into this with confidence, I thought. It was like putting a toddler to sleep. If they could smell your fear, it never, ever worked.

I knocked twice, firmly.

Nothing. No movement.

I knocked two more times, and then I heard a shuffle of footsteps.

The door opened, and there he was.

George wore a casual short-sleeve shirt, the top two buttons undone, and designer jeans, his feet bare. He was freshly shaven, freshly showered, his hair combed back in that way that looked messy but I knew took ages.

He smiled at me—smirked, really. "You made the smart choice."

I didn't ask, just pushed my way in, taking in the living room, almost comically hip. Every little detail making this look like a cozy-modern cabin where Brooklyn- and Manhattanites would want to come up and spend loads of money. The only thing that threw off the vibe was a can of paint in the corner.

"So?" he asked. "Where is it?"

I clutched my purse to my side, didn't answer.

"Don't tell me you didn't bring it?"

"There's nothing to bring," I said, forcing calm into my voice. I straightened my spine, made myself taller. "I came to tell you to stop harassing me."

He stepped forward, and instinctively I stepped back, my body closing in on a corner where an antique guitar hung.

"I know you took it," George said. "I know that's why you're here. And you're going to give me what's mine."

"It's not yours," I spat.

George laughed. "So you *do* have it."

I stared at him, gaze sharp. "It doesn't matter if I do," I said. "Because, like I said, it's not yours. It's Cass—Cassandra's. Mary told me herself."

I waited for it to hit him, and it took a couple of beats to do so.

He'd terrified me last night, showing up at Rich's house, threatening me like he had, and at first I'd thought he'd surely seen me with Mary, but it was only late into the night, really turning it over, that it became clear.

He'd seen me on Saturday, sitting outside the pub. He must have followed me that afternoon—it wasn't a long walk to Rich's. But that was as far as his knowledge went. George was up here to get Mary back—to him, I was nothing more than a bit of convenience. Win your ex back and catch the slut who ran off with the contents of your safe.

Two birds, one precious stone.

No, George didn't know I was friends with Mary.

If he did, he wouldn't be acting like this.

Not now, when things were actually progressing with her . . .

After so many months of separation, she'd *finally* given him what he'd always wanted—a chance. She'd slept with him, and a man like George would call that a win. He wanted Mary back. His property. His wife. He didn't want to end up like Henry. Drunk and sad and alone. Sleeping with escorts and fighting with people on Twitter. He was the respectable brother, and he had to keep it that way.

But Mary would *never* take him back if she knew that while he was supposedly begging for her return, he'd been fucking one of her closest friends.

"Didn't know I knew her, did you?"

"She never—"

"Mentioned me? And why would she? She met me at the playground after she walked away from your sorry ass."

George's face reddened, sweat beading on his upper lip. "Alex, you—"

"Knew him? Yeah. Another thing you didn't pick up on. Just thought I was exceedingly good with the kid you've barely paid any attention to. Hell, I've probably had more quality time with him than you have."

"Shut up," George said, stepping closer. "Just shut the fuck up."

"Oh, I will," I said. "I'll be out of your life, you'll never have to see me again. Because you don't want me to tell Mary everything, do you? How we fucked in your marriage bed— was it three times that one night? How you let me spend time with Alex. How while you were professing your love for her, how much you wanted her back, you were putting me up at one of your family properties, texting me all sorts of dirty, dirty things?"

"You would never—"

"No, I wouldn't. Because Mary is *this close* to taking you back. She even told me last night," I said, stretching the truth a good bit. "And my silence is worth more to you than some jewelry that isn't even yours."

He knew I was right, and it had him fuming. "I told Mary I would have it for her," he said. "I told her I'd give it back."

"So?" I asked. "I'm sure you'll be able to come up with a lie about that. And I'm sure you'll find a way to fool her into thinking she's better off with you. You're about to get exactly what you want. You don't want silly little me to mess it up, do you?"

"Get out," he said. "Just get the fuck out."

"With pleasure," I said.

I made for the door, reaching for the handle, knowing I'd

done it, taken care of it, like I'd promised Cass I would. I could leave now, I could go. This was done. Cass had said the buyer was set up for next week. It would finally, finally be over.

But I looked back at George, taking in his miserable, entitled, privileged face.

I remembered all that Mary had told me, the mess she was undeniably still in.

It wasn't fair. That he could do this to people. That he could do this and move on, still get everything in the world he wanted.

He deserved to be hit, punched, worse . . .

He deserved all the rage in the world.

Mary's—mine—Cass's—everyone's.

"Mary may not have talked about me, but she sure as hell talked about you," I said.

George's face got even redder.

"How you destroyed her things, ripped your own son's blanket."

"That was an accident," George said. "You don't know anything about it."

"Real big man you are," I taunted. "Fucking up your wife's career because you got mad. Bet your own son is better behaved than you."

"Stop it," he said. "You don't know anything. About her. About me."

"The only thing you've ever accomplished in your whole miserable life is being born into a rich family. You had every chance in the world and look how you turned out. A useless man. Spending Daddy's money. Throwing tantrums when he doesn't get all the *wittle* things he wants," I said, putting on my best baby voice. "But why am I surprised? All you fucks are the same."

I saw the snap. Saw his eyes light up, the violence—the anger—push through them, and I knew I'd made a mistake. I knew I'd gone too far. I knew I should have kept my mouth shut.

It was too late.

He lunged.

39

MARY

Cassandra?" I asked Willa, dumbfounded.

"Yeah," Willa said. "She was my roommate."

It took me a moment, and then, suddenly, it clicked. "*She* was the one you missed, the one you lost touch with from the past?"

My mind spun, putting it all together. It was hard to believe, but at the same time, it wasn't. "It was the two of you, wasn't it? In that shitty apartment in Queens?"

Willa sat down, exhausted and spent. She was still clutching the bag of jewelry to her chest, but her grip had loosened slightly. She looked like she was about to set down a boulder she'd been carrying for far too long.

"Yeah," she said. "The two of us, plus another guy, but we were the ones who were close. Cass and I grew up together, in Pennsylvania. That's why I never told you where I was from. On the off chance you'd put it together." She sighed. "We were friends since kindergarten. The same graduating class, everything. We always talked about how we wanted to get out. She finally did, after years of community college, which she paid for herself. She got her dream, finally, at twenty-six—a PR gig in New York City. I stayed behind. I hadn't finished college, but I had a few credits under my belt; I was waitressing, shacked up with an asshole who wanted to make sure I never left. I was twenty-eight when she pulled me out of that bumfuck town. She gave me a room, fronted me the money for the first month's rent and deposit. She made it so easy, she saved me."

Had the truth really been there, so close beneath the surface, only a light sheen of water shimmering on top?

"We were really happy, or at least I thought we were," Willa went on. "Yeah, our apartment was shit, but Cass loved it. We painted the living room purple together, used to blast Whitney Houston and Mariah Carey and Adele and have the stupidest dance parties." Willa blinked back new tears. "Those two years living together—they were probably the happiest of my life. My family, my ex, my stupid hometown were behind me, but I didn't owe anything to anyone. I was free to be myself. I had no money, but I had so much fun. Life was chaotic and improvised, but I was content. I thought Cass was, too. No, I *know* she was."

"Then she met Henry," I said.

I hate Henry.

"Yeah," Willa said with a roll of her eyes. "She organized this benefit for his family—which you already know—and he came in super hot. It was like he put a target on her back. Like he decided this is the woman I'd like to buy, and went about doing it. I only ever met him once—he was too fancy to ever come to our apartment—I saw him pick her up in his SUV, but that was it. Still, the things she told me, the relationship had red flags all over it. It was clear, even back then, that the guy had a drinking problem. Even worse, he wanted to control her. First, it was that she needed nicer clothes, and how could anyone argue with a man who wants to buy you Celine and Prada? Then it was trips to the stylist that his family always went to. Some French lady."

"Étoile," I said, a tickle running up my spine. Whatever Willa was saying wasn't completely a lie, at least. Étoile had cut George's hair—and all the Haywoods' hair, mine included—for years now.

"Then it was that she was too good to live in that apartment with us, even though she loved it there. And he basically prevented her from ever seeing us. It was like clockwork. Anytime she had something planned with us—a dance party in Bushwick or a trivia night at our local dive or whatever—Henry would call up fifteen or twenty minutes before with some story. He'd just gotten front-row seats to *Hamilton*. Or his family was off to Montauk, and he wanted her to come along. Or maybe he'd had a stressful day at work, a fight with his mother, and he needed her." Willa shrugged. "Pretty soon, she was spending more nights at his than ours. He was on her to leave her job, saying it was too stressful, too many hours. He had his assistant scheduling laser facials for her. He urged her to stop going by Cass, said her full name was much more beautiful, that people would take her more seriously. I swear to god, he was *crafting* her into what he thought she should be—and Cass, she felt so lucky, she didn't question it."

My stomach twisted. All that she was describing, it was the exactly the way George had treated me. Maybe he was molding me into something different—less flashy, less ostentatious—but still he was molding me, like a piece of clay.

Willa crossed her legs and uncrossed them, then rubbed at the top of her neck, scratching beneath the high collar of her top. "I didn't say anything at first—I didn't know how. But when she told me she was thinking about actually moving in with him, I told her he worried me. That he seemed too much like the guy I'd left behind in Pennsylvania." Willa looked down at her hands, then back up at me. "She didn't take it well. She walked out of my room, slammed the door behind her, didn't talk to me for days. I fucked up, I know. I shouldn't have been so blunt, but I was scared. That conversation, it pushed her right into Henry's arms. She moved out a couple of weeks later. I tried to stay in touch with her, but I only ever got one-word responses, and then, not even that."

I looked at Willa. Was this all a way of luring me in, spinning yet another tale? But it sounded so real. For once, I thought, maybe it was.

"So how did it come to this?" I asked, motioning to the bag in Willa's hands.

"I ran into her," Willa said. "At Brooklyn Bridge Park, right in front of the carousel. I was living with Jack then, but he and Jack Junior were on this father-son glamping trip, and I had a day to myself. I always loved to walk the Promenade, see the couples taking engagement photos, tourists snapping up the city views. Cass was thrown to see me at first, but then she offered to buy me a drink. I'd missed her so much, even though things went down badly between us, so I said yes. She told me how wrong things had gone with Henry, how much she'd also missed me over the years. We agreed to meet up again, and we did."

"Did you tell her about your . . . lifestyle?"

"Not at first, no. But the drinks continued, and eventually it came out. She was surprised, but to her credit, she didn't judge me. And then we were at the Royal Palms one night—do you know that place? In Gowanus? People were drunkenly playing shuffleboard, and we were sitting there and her eyes just light up and she says, 'Wait a second, you're the perfect person to solve my problem.'"

"And you agreed?" I asked.

"No, not at first. But you have to understand, Mary, just how much everything was worth. And it was hers. It wasn't even stealing. We just needed a way in. And once she knew, well, the kind of life I lived, it felt serendipitous, you know? I mean, we're talking more than half a million in jewelry. She didn't want the flash of it, the glamour. She needed the money since the Haywoods were taking everything. And she never could have done it on her own."

"So you just befriended me?" I asked. "And then seduced George? I know Cassandra was mad, but I thought she cared about me."

Willa scratched at the edge of the sofa cushion. "Cass *was* furious that you wouldn't help her get the jewelry back. And maybe, at the beginning, I told myself that that was why it was okay, because you hadn't helped her when you had the chance."

"I didn't know what to do," I said. "She put me in an impossible position."

"I know, Mary," Willa said, voice kind. "I know that now. But I didn't then, okay?"

Tears crawled down my cheeks, but I swiped them away with the back of my hand. "How did you even find me?"

"Cass gave me the address of the brownstone," Willa said. "I figured that you might still go to the playground across the street, so I started taking Jack there regularly. It wasn't long before you showed up."

I thought of Alex and Jack, happily playing together, Willa and I stretching our legs into the sun and trading stories. It cut so deep, even after all the secrets and lies, hurts and betrayals.

"Look, there would have been other ways of getting the information I needed to get. But you were refreshing. You were different than the other moms I met. You were fresh out of this marriage and fighting for your new life, and so raw, so honest. And so caring. No one was ever really like that with me, not since Cass. And with you, I felt like I could be me."

"Except you weren't you," I said. "You were lying the whole time."

"I was myself," Willa said. "I promise you. And it was a nice break after so many years of being who all those men wanted me to be."

"So when did you meet George?" I asked, pressing on. "And how?"

"You'd mentioned some of your favorite bars when we first met, and I went to a few of those, but I never ran into him. I knew I was relying too much on luck. So the last week of May, I started sitting outside the brownstone and waiting to see if he'd go out. He did, eventually, to this cocktail bar down the street, and I went, too." Willa shrugged. "We talked a little, exchanged numbers, but that was all. Nothing happened until early June. And then, I felt so bad, I really did. And I thought maybe I'd give it all up, maybe this was going too far. But then Jack figured out I'd been talking to another guy. I had no real money, no place to stay. George was it. That's when I stopped talking to you. I'm sorry for everything. It was never meant to come to this."

So I had been right, I thought. George had been distracted by someone else this summer. By her. The thought cut deep. And not just that, but the fact that Cassandra had at least partially set this all up. The two friends I'd thought I loved most, working together to use me. Willa was trying to make it sound nuanced, complicated, like she was carefully stepping through a gray area instead of boldly crossing a line. But in the end, it was betrayal, pure and simple. The worst kind.

More tears sprang to my eyes, but I wiped my face again, holding them back. I needed to know more. "So when did it end with George?"

"When I took the jewelry, when I came up here. Mid-July."

I shook my head, trying to make sense of all of it. "So what happened on Sunday night, then? How did it get to this?"

"You were right, to a point," Willa said. "George did find me, but I don't think he came here looking for me—I think he came here for you and just got lucky to see me, too. This town is too goddamn small. When I left the flea market where you saw me on Saturday, when I was walking back to Rich's with Poppy, I saw him in a bar. He must have followed me home. Then on Sunday night, he showed up at Rich's house. It scared me."

"So you—"

"No, Mary," Willa said firmly, as if anticipating what I was going to say. "Yes, I was scared, but I *never* hurt him. I texted him back that I knew you, that if he didn't leave me alone about the jewelry, I would tell you about us, and you'd never take him back. That's it. I *swear.*"

My mind turned in circles as I took all of this in. "But who killed him, then?"

"Honestly? I thought it was you."

I reared back. "Me?"

"You had the most to gain, didn't you? Freedom. Your kid. I'm guessing George had a big life insurance policy. Rich people always do. And he was a prick to you. He was a prick to everyone. When you called me, I knew I had to help you, and I thought maybe . . . you'd actually done it."

"Then why didn't you turn me in?" I asked. "You had that text."

Willa laughed then, breaking the tension. "You think that if you did kill him, I'd be anything but proud of you? Christ, Mary, he put you through hell. Cass, too. He deserved it, whatever he got."

"It wasn't me. I couldn't kill my son's father, and he was talking about changing, for once. He was talking about making things right."

Willa didn't say anything, but I could see it in her eyes. She thought a man like George would never change.

A silence fell across the room, and my brain struggled to catch up. Was I really meant to believe this? That, betrayals aside, there really had been an explanation for everything?

That Willa and Cassandra had teamed up to get what should have been Cassandra's all along? That even if their methods had been cruel, their motives had been understandable?

Fool me once, shame on you. Fool me twice, shame on me.

How many times had Willa fooled me now?

Willa scratched at her neck, obviously nervous for me to believe her, and in the bright daylight, I saw something. A red mark, almost . . . like a handprint.

I struggled to remember if I'd seen the mark yesterday, but couldn't. She'd had that scarf on the whole time, like a teenager trying to cover up a hickey.

"What's that on your neck?" I asked. "Did someone . . . hurt you?"

"Nothing," Willa said, pulling up her collar quickly. "This top is just itchy."

I stood up, walked closer to her, and Willa's shoulders tightened as she grasped the velvet bag tighter.

Something had happened. Something she wasn't telling me.

"Willa," I said. "Did he . . ."

I swallowed, trying to understand.

"Who did that to you?"

40

WILLA

George reached up with both hands, and for a moment, I thought he was going to frame my face, pull me in for a violent, forceful kiss—almost how Jack had done, that day in Red Hook—but his hands landed on my neck instead.

He began to squeeze, and I tried to wriggle away, but his grasp was firm, he was pushing me against the wall, the guitar digging into my back, the sounds of music, of strings being rapped, filling the room.

Still, for a millisecond, I thought I held the power. I'd had hands on my neck before. With my ex in Pennsylvania, that one time after we stumbled home from the bar. The night that changed everything, that had me calling Cass, had her telling me to get the fuck out before he killed me next time.

There'd been other men, too. Men who'd wanted it, who'd wanted me to let them. Safe words and handcuffs and blindfolds and *hands hands hands*.

Only George wasn't stopping.

"I can't breathe," I tried to say, but the words came out as a croak.

The heels of his palms pressed in then, against my trachea, cutting off all air, and around me, the room began to blur and spin. I flailed about, my arms writhing, my legs struggling to kick, but I couldn't. Already, the world was starting to slip, blackening at the edges.

I was losing.

He was going to kill me. He was going to kill me right here and now. Over an insult. A taunt.

His hands pressed harder, and then—

I came to on the floor, gasping for breath, my throat aching, my knees banged from the fall, the guitar half on top of me.

I looked up to George, whose face was white with terror. He pulled the guitar away, hung it gingerly back on the wall like some kind of psychopath, decorating the sides of a diorama.

It took a moment to get air back into my lungs, for the world to stop spinning, and then I felt George's hands on me, lifting.

I looked at him. He knew and I knew. He'd come so close. He'd almost let the beast escape. Almost snuffed me out forever.

We'd both been spared the consequences.

"I—I didn't mean to—" he stammered.

I didn't say a word. Just grabbed my purse, one hand on my throat, to stop the aching, to somehow hold it off.

I caught my reflection in the hall mirror. My hair was a mess, mussed up this way and that. My skin was flushed where the blood had rushed back in. My forehead dewy. My clothes rumpled, my purse askew.

See me now, and you'd almost think I'd emerged from some all-night sex fest, followed by a morning tryst.

I stepped across the threshold without looking back. Wondered how many times I'd seen a girl in this state. Assumed she'd consented to everything. Assumed there'd been no violence, no raw male rage.

I'd thought I had power. I'd thought that I could make the men's knees bend, make them give me what I wanted, because they wanted *me* so badly. I'd thought that guys like my ex in Pennsylvania were the exception, not the rule.

But all this time, their physical power, the vast ocean of their aggression, their anger—it had been there, only just beneath the surface, waiting to stir. In that moment, it felt like any of the men I'd lived with could have done this, if I'd only pushed the right buttons.

It felt like I had been playing an awful, terrible game, one I never wanted to play again.

In the street, a black car idled, and embarrassed, I turned away, walked as quickly as I could, pulling the collar of my T-shirt up higher with my hands. Wondering if George's fingers had already made marks on my skin.

Shame filled me as I realized what had happened. How close to death I'd come. All because I had to have the last word, had to tell George what I thought of him. Had to defend not only Mary but Cass, too, in whatever way I could.

What a stupid, stupid thing. To poke a bear just to see what they'd do.

I passed two teen girls on Tinker Street, arms linked together, laughing in the morning sun.

I pulled my collar up even higher, looked down.

Don't become like me, I wanted to tell them. *Stick together and never lose sight of each other. Don't let the men of the world tear you apart. Press you so hard you can't even breathe.*

I turned onto the street that led to Rich's and I forced myself to move past this. It was awful, it had happened, and yet here I was. George wouldn't follow me.

Cass's buyer was nearly ready. We could sell the jewelry. Split the proceeds. More than two hundred thousand for each of us. We could get fresh starts, both of us. Run away where none of these awful men could find us.

It was almost over. All of it.

In the end, it would be worth it. It *had* to be.

I was almost back to Rich's house when I reached up to touch my necklace, my hands still shaky with adrenaline, my skin still wet with sweat.

My fingers ran the length of my neck—one time, two times, three times—and I tugged at my T-shirt, shaking the collar. I looked in the gap between my stomach and my pants. I shook each leg, waiting for a jangle, for something shiny to fall to the ground.

The sound didn't come. It wasn't there.

My necklace was gone.

41

MARY

I stared at the mark on Willa's neck, red and practically searing.

For a moment, there was compassion. No man had ever touched me like that, and I wondered if she'd been scared, if she'd found it hard to breathe, if all of it had flashed before her . . .

"Who . . . who did that to you?" I asked. "Was it, was it Henry?"

Willa's eyes closed a moment, then opened. She shook her head slowly. "No, Mary. No, it wasn't Henry."

Her eyes locked on mine, and for once, I was sure she wasn't lying.

The thought was gut-wrenching. I'd been telling myself maybe George wanted to change, maybe he wanted to be a better man for me. Meanwhile, he was strangling another woman, leaving marks on her neck.

Then the other thought came, one that was impossible to ignore: That meant Willa had been at George's that morning. She *really* had.

Willa stared at me, her eyes wide, her face pale (with shame? Fear?) and it was only then that I realized the other thing that was off.

Willa wore dainty hoop earrings, a silver bangle, and an oversized ring with a stone in the middle. I'd always loved her jewelry, loved the way she could balance something trendy with something classy, loved how her sapphire necklace tied it all together.

"Where is your necklace?" I asked. "Did you lose it, in the struggle?"

"Mary," she said. "Please just let all this go. It doesn't matter how I got hurt, okay? What matters is—"

"Then show me the necklace," I said. "Prove me wrong."

I stood over her now, domineering. Maybe George had hurt her first, but she'd killed him, hadn't she? She'd killed him, and she wasn't owning up to it, and that meant I might never see Alex again.

And that was something I could never, ever forgive.

"Where is the necklace?" I pressed. "Did he grab it, rip it off your neck? Was it left at the crime scene, tying the whole thing to you? Is that why you cozied up to me, so I wouldn't tell the police it was yours? Just tell me—god, please, just *tell me*!"

"Mary," Willa said, scooting even farther back on the sofa. "You're scaring me. It's in my things, okay?"

"Oh really?" I said. "Is it in there?" I snatched the velvet bag before she could stop me, then flipped it over, watching as all that jewelry—all that *money*—toppled down onto the ground with a thud.

"Damn it, that's *enough*, Mary," Willa cried, jumping up and scrambling to recover all the jewelry. "Just *leave* it."

It was exactly what George said to me, every time he told me to stop asking about Cassandra, like I was a dog he could command. What Alex had even parroted himself.

But I couldn't be controlled. Not anymore.

"I'm the pushover, right? The one that people like George—people like *you*—think you can screw over. Where's the necklace, then?" I practically yelled. "*Show* me."

I turned on my heel, went to her bags, one of them that I'd already gone through. I flipped the other one over, feeling the satisfaction of taking my anger out on something—anything.

Clothes went flying. Lacy things and ribbed tees. Birth control pills and facial serums.

"Mary," Willa said again. "Don't do this."

I kept shaking, getting every last piece of clothing out.

Then I stopped, my eyes catching on something pale and white, tinged with red.

A training diaper, one she must have had on her in case Poppy had an accident.

One that had been used to soak up blood.

I looked up at Willa. For once, she had nothing to say.

"It really *was* you," I said, my voice cracking.

Of course it was. The con artist was the killer.

And I was standing here with her.

My eyes scanned the room frantically, until I spotted my purse and car keys on the hall table.

I snatched up the diaper and then lunged for them, jumping over the pile of jewels, over everything, not stopping until the keys were in my hands, then ran for the door, pulling it and slamming it shut behind me.

Willa on my heels, I rushed to the car, frantically clicked the unlock button, scrambled to get the handle as the door to my rental car opened.

"Mary," she said, but I slammed the door behind me, locked it, turned the car on, watched as she banged on the window, kept on calling my name.

I backed up, running into the car parked behind me as I did, then pulled forward, jerking at the wheel to get out of the spot, Willa moving away only at the very last second.

I turned left, then back, then forward again, righting the car around.

I pulled down the street, glanced in the rearview, saw her standing there.

Not running, not chasing, only staring.

I sped down the road, passing a cop car as I did, a man at the wheel. Should I stop him? No. I'd missed my chance. I had to get to Morales. I finally had the evidence I was looking for. She'd have no choice but to listen now.

I found the main road, turned left, then stepped on the gas, not caring about speed limits. About anything.

This was my only chance to clear my name.

To get my baby back.

42

WILLA

THEN
MONDAY, AUGUST 16
WOODSTOCK, NEW YORK

My necklace, my fucking necklace.

I'd worn it this morning. When George had grabbed me, the clasp must have broken—or even the chain. Who knew what had happened when he squeezed me so hard.

Was I going to leave it? Let him take this one thing from me, the one thing I cared about, the one thing that was mine?

No way. Guys like George only ever took took took. He wasn't going to get my necklace, too.

I turned immediately, retraced my steps, doubling back toward Tinker Street. Holding my head suddenly higher, not caring about what might show on my neck. I wasn't the bad guy here. I had been trying to even the scales. I had been one of the only ones to ever stand up to the Haywoods.

Me. Charlotte Anne Williams.

Call me a con artist. Say I used men. But all I'd ever been

guilty of was trying to get some compensation for all the things I did. How much would my labor have cost all those men if I'd actually charged them? But you couldn't charge for things like that, of course. Women were expected to do it for free.

When I got to the main strip, I paused, fear tingling within me, the feel of George's hands once again on my neck.

I wasn't going to go in unprepared this time. Fuck that.

I walked up the main strip until I found the waterfall again.

I spotted rocks—big ones—large enough to knock some-one out if it came to that.

A gap in the fencing, where I could reach through.

Adrenaline coursed through me as I sank onto my knees, wrestled my arm through the gap, stretching it as far as I could go.

I pushed until my fingers scraped the edge of the rock.

George didn't know who I was.

What I was.

What I *could* become if pushed hard enough.

Fucking prick, I thought again.

I pulled the rock back, shimmying it beneath the fence.

Then I stood up, carefully slipped it into my purse, on top of my wallet and a pair of Poppy's fancy diapers.

Rage flared within me as I pictured George. The spittle flying from his mouth as he grabbed me, squeezed me. Want-ing to squelch the life from within me, just because I'd dared to challenge his ego.

You can't get away with it, Georgie. Not this time.

This time your family isn't here to save your rich ass like they always do. Money can't buy you protection—not now, not from me.

I was always going on about how unbalanced it all was, the deep unfairness of money. Of men. And yet I was never really able to act, was I? Even my crimes were so petty. Forty dollars here, a swiped credit card there, like Holly Golightly asking for cash for the powder room.

Why had I doubted my own power? My own worth?

George and Henry and my ex in Pennsylvania—men like them—they deserved to die, because they hurt us. Responding violence for violence was survival. Insurance against them grinding yet another woman down to nothing.

Protection for the next victim down the line.

After all, who would deserve it more than George?

For what he'd done to Mary, to Alex? For what his family had done to Cass? For the way he had just treated me, tried to kill me, then pretended like he was such a nice guy, like it was all a big mistake? For the marks already rising on my neck?

Fuck him, I thought. Fuck him and every man like him.

Finally, I was back in front of the house. I looked left and right—no one.

The car I'd seen earlier was gone. This was my opportunity, my chance. One I wouldn't get again, maybe not ever.

The chance to do something right by Mary. To even the scales.

I stepped up to the porch, reached into my purse, felt the weight of the rock inside.

George would never fuck with another woman again.

PART THREE

43

MARY

I didn't stop looking in my rearview the entire drive to the station, scared Willa was following me, even though that was impossible. She didn't even have a car with her.

There was no denying it now. Not with the lies. The jewelry. The missing necklace. The damn diaper sitting in the passenger seat by me right now.

The parking lot was near-empty, and I turned haphazardly into a spot near the front and grabbed my purse, stuffing the blood-soaked diaper inside. Then I jerked the car door open, slammed it behind me, and locked it twice.

I looked back, scanned the lot, jolted at a figure in front of me, a shadow, the outline blown out by the midday light.

I lifted a hand to block the sun, and that was when I saw him clearly. The tanned skin, the silver-fox hair, the deep-set, deep-brown eyes.

"Jack?" I asked, stopping short. "What are you doing here?"

His shoulders jolted up, and then his eyes caught mine. Recognition. "Mary?" he asked. "Willa's friend?"

I nodded.

Jack stared at me. He cocked his head to the side, like he was sussing something out. After a beat, he sighed. "Willa's been using my credit card. I've stopped the account, but I want to press charges. The company said I had to speak to the local jurisdiction. I tried calling but didn't get very far. I figured it was worth the drive up. I have to talk to the restaurant where she used it, get them to confirm it was her. But then I can help make sure she doesn't do this to somebody else," he said. "You know she does this to every guy she's with? Pretends to love them. Dotes on their kid. Steals what she can. I heard from someone from her past. He's getting in contact with all of us. Telling us who she really is."

I thought of Rich, on the stairs, just this morning.

She makes you think she cares about you.

But she doesn't in the end.

"I know you're friends," Jack went on. "But she's not a good person. I know she makes up excuses. Tells herself we all deserve it, because we have money that she doesn't. But it's not okay."

"I'm not friends with her anymore," I said. I took a deep breath. "I know who she is, maybe even more than you do."

Jack looked back to the station. "They hardly had time to speak with me anyway. The police said there's a murder investigation, someone up from the city?"

"Yes," I said. "My husband. Well, we were separated."

"My god," Jack said. "I'm so sorry."

"I trusted Willa, too, you know," I said, tears in my eyes now. "It's not only men that she's duped."

Jack reared back. "Wait, you don't think—could Willa have had something to do with it?"

I swallowed. "I don't think she had something to do with it. I *know*."

"Really?" he said. "Willa."

"She hides it well, but like you said, she's not a good person."

"Oh my god," Jack said, shaking his head in disbelief. "She was living with me, you know. She was around my kid. Jack Junior loved her. And I just let her in. I let her come into my home. I left them alone, so many times. Christ."

"I know," I said. "She was around my kid, too. It's horrifying. I have to go now. Just stay away from her, okay?" I said. "Protect yourself."

Jack nodded, and then he stepped forward, pulling me into a hug. "I will, and I'm sorry," he said. "I'm so sorry she hurt you, Mary." He stepped back. "I'm sorry she hurt all of us."

"I am, too."

Inside the station, I pushed past the people at the desk, threw my hands against the counter. "I have to talk to Detective Morales."

"Ma'am," the woman at the desk said.

"It's urgent," I said, my voice raising to a fever pitch. "Please. I need to see her. *Now*. It's about the murder of

George Haywood," I said. "I know who did it. And I know I might have thought that before, but I have proof this time. I need to talk to Detective Morales. Please."

A raised eyebrow. A lifted phone. A mumbled conversation.

Then the click of heels. Detective Morales.

"Mrs. Haywood?" she asked. "How can I help you?"

"It was her," I said frantically. "The woman from the call log. She killed him. She had the jewelry, Cassandra's jewelry. She used George, she used me, so she could get it. His blood, it's on a diaper she had in her purse. I have the evidence," I said, pushing my bag toward her. "Look."

Morales's eyes shot up, and she took the bag from me, stealing a glance inside.

"There's more," I said. "Willa—I mean, Charlotte—she has marks on her neck, like there was a struggle. She wasn't wearing her necklace, the one she always wears. I think it was there, where George was."

Morales stared at me, eyes widening.

"Did you find a necklace?" I asked. "At the crime scene?"

The detective's hand found the edge of a counter, as if steadying herself.

"A sapphire one?"

Morales didn't answer, only turned away from me, rushed down the hall.

"Where's Carson?" she yelled, at anyone who would listen.

"He's gone to interview the woman from the call list," another officer said, popping out to meet her in the hallway.

"Call him," Morales said. "*Now*. Tell him to apprehend the suspect. And someone come process a new piece of evidence," she said, setting my bag on the counter. "It's in Mrs. Haywood's bag."

Then she turned around, ran back out the door without looking back.

Going to get the woman responsible for all of this.

44

MARY

The waiting was agonizing. Wanting to know if the police apprehended Willa. If she would really pay for all she'd done. To me, to George, to all of us.

Once an officer had confiscated my bag, taking it away to process the evidence, I was led back to the station and deposited in an empty room, this one with a beat-up sofa and a Keurig coffee maker in the corner. Asked to give a formal statement from the same baby-faced officer who'd taken my words about discovering George's body.

Then my evidence-free bag was returned to me, and I was left alone, one hour turning to two. I had my phone on me this time, but I almost wished I didn't. The news of George Haywood's death had finally hit the media, and my device was filling up quickly with texts from people I hadn't really talked to in years. Friends I'd grown apart from after meeting George, like Sasha. The editor and NYU professor who I'd bailed on, and the one who'd assigned the *Forbes* piece, too.

Acquaintances I'd never been close to in the first place. Kind words, condolences, from people who wanted to help me but couldn't. Calls from Rachel and my mom. And texts from them, too. Rachel asking how I was holding up and if there were any updates about the investigation. I did write back, letting her know that there was a primary suspect now and I would call to update her later, but beyond that, I ignored every missive. I tapped into Facebook for a brief moment, but the deluge of notifications was so great that I disabled the account immediately—and Instagram, too—then put my phone away and promised myself I wouldn't look at it again.

I had three cups of shitty coffee, each one seeming to make the thoughts spin faster: What if Willa got away, yet again? What if she was still out there, waiting to strike at someone else?

What if all the evidence I'd given them wasn't enough to clear my name, and the Haywoods would still fight to take Alex from me just because they could?

Finally, the door opened. Morales smiled.

"Mrs. Haywood," she said. "Thank you for your patience."

"Did you get her?" I asked. "Did you get Charlotte?"

"We did," she said, turning to the Keurig, making herself a cup, too. "Luckily, Officer Carson was already with her, at the home where you were staying, when we made the call."

I thought of the cop car I'd seen as I'd driven away from Willa, the one I'd almost wanted to stop.

"But how did you know she was with me?" I asked.

Morales cocked her head to the side and took a sip of coffee. The look on her face showed she was in it for the caffeine, not the flavor. "We've had an unmarked car on you."

"Oh," I said. So I hadn't been crazy, after all. The thought was, if anything, a relief.

Morales leaned against the edge of the table. "I'm glad you came to me when you did. If Carson had simply interviewed her and left, who knows what would have happened."

I felt a tiny bit of space open up in my chest. "Did you find the jewelry?" I asked.

"We were not able to locate it at the scene. You're sure you saw it?"

"Absolutely. It was in a black velvet bag. It was Cassandra's jewelry, without a doubt." Then I winced. "Will it be enough, without it? Since you have the bloody diaper?"

"We hope so," Morales said. "The chain of custody of the evidence has been entirely corrupted, of course. But still, it's something. Especially combined with the fibers found at the scene. But there's more, too. I'm sorry to be so blunt, but skin particles were found beneath Mr. Haywood's nails. We believe it will be a match for Ms. Williams's DNA. We're rushing a comparison as we speak."

Morales finished her cup and immediately set the Keurig up with another pod.

"Some other loose ends. We're still working our way through Mr. Haywood's call log. One of the deputies finally got in touch with someone from Wright Holdings—that was the one name you didn't recognize. Guy says he was a friend from Mr. Haywood's climbing gym, calling to plan their next workout. Does that ring any bells?"

"That sounds right. I didn't know anyone he worked out with personally, but he went at least once a week. George loved that gym."

"Great," Morales said. "The more dotted *i*'s and crossed *t*'s, the better."

"And what about the graffiti?" I asked. "Do you think—I mean, is it possible—that Willa broke into the other properties, too?"

"We're in the process of figuring that out, believe me," Morales said. "Ruth Haywood doesn't have access to the security camera footage. They were fairly crude home setups that deleted after twenty-four hours, but it's possible the tech company has more in their database. Of course, anything to do with tech is a process. We're still waiting to hear back from them. It's entirely possible that the crimes are unrelated, and that Ms. Williams did the graffiti that morning simply to point the investigation in another direction."

Morales hesitated, then crossed her arms.

"Can I speak frankly, Mrs. Haywood?"

My heart beat fast again, but I nodded.

"One of the most damning marks against you, when you were our key suspect, was just how much you'd been holding back from us. We didn't know about the bitter custody battle until Ruth Haywood informed us. Same regarding the altercation outside your rental."

I felt myself redden.

"Here's the thing. The evidence is stacking up against Ms. Williams, but it's not going to look good for you—or for the state's investigation, to be honest—if we're hit with surprises we were not aware of, especially if the prosecution does not know about them and it's something the defense uncovers at trial. If we are clued into something, our prosecutors can work to keep it out of public record, but not if it's not in the file we pass to the state. Now, is there anything like that, anything at all, that might be relevant here?"

I bit my lip, trying to stay calm, but I couldn't. It was too much.

"There is, isn't there? Something Ms. Williams has on you, perhaps?"

"How did you know?"

Morales laughed. "I've been in this line of work a long time. And I saw the pure shock on your face when you saw her name on your husband's call log, followed by an absolute refusal to open up. I know there's something, and I would feel much better about wrapping up this investigation if I knew what that something was."

I'd thought I could hold back my secret words, the shameful things I'd said, but of course I couldn't. Of course Willa and her lawyers would trot out that text the second they got the chance.

I had to get ahead of it. Just like Morales said.

"I never meant it," I said. "Not really."

"Meant what?" Morales asked.

"I was drunk," I said. "It was all the way back in June. We had gone out for margaritas. George had been threatening to take Alex away from me completely, hadn't treated me well leading up to the separation, and she started it, really. She made this joke, like if he ever physically hurt me, she'd kill him." I shut my eyes, shaking my head. "Late that night, I texted her. I said that sometimes I wished he were dead. That things would be easier. That I'd be free, that I wouldn't have to worry about losing Alex."

Tears came then, and I lifted my hands to my face, let the sobs shake my body. "But I never would have acted on it. I never would have killed him. It was a stupid, drunken thought. He was my son's father. Nothing changes that. *Nothing.*"

Finally, I let myself steal a glance up.

Morales's expression was kind, and she reached into her pocket, pulled out a travel pack of tissues. Gratefully, I took one.

"I'm sorry," I said, wiping my face down. "I was too afraid to tell you. Too afraid that if I pointed you in her direction without evidence, that she'd tell you about the text, and my fate would be sealed."

"I understand," Morales said. "Thank you for being honest with me."

I finished blotting my eyes, crumpled the tissue in my hand.

"And off the record," Morales said, her lips pressed into a firm, thin line. "If someone had threatened to take one of my kids, I probably would have said the same thing."

45

MARY

The call came just after eight, when I was walking across the station's parking lot, about to finally head home. My fingers shook at the name on my screen, and I answered quickly.

"Ruth," I said, my tone cautious, defensive. "Hi."

"I'm sorry, Mary," she said, her voice cracking slightly. "I'm sorry I ever thought it was you."

Her words were so tender, so honest, they stopped me in my tracks. "It's okay," I said.

"It's *not* okay. You've never given us any reason to think you would do anything like this—you're a good person, Mary. I know you are . . . but when you lose a child, you feel so hopeless, so . . . powerless, you want to do something, anything, because you know you can't fix it, but you want to so badly." She broke into a sob. "I spent so many years worrying about Henry. His drinking and partying. Whether one day he'd make a bad decision, piss off the wrong person, get behind the wheel when he shouldn't—I never thought to worry about George. I never thought that I could actually lose my boy. That some woman, some horrible woman . . ." She gasped for air, sobs racking her again.

I looked at the bleeding sky, the sun disappearing behind the mountains, and my heart swelled for what she'd lost. "I'm so sorry, Ruth. I can't imagine what you're going through," I said, and meant it. No matter what Alex did, who he grew up to be, I couldn't imagine a world where losing him wouldn't absolutely destroy me.

"The detective told me you're cleared to leave," she said. "Come get Alex, tomorrow morning. And whatever you want to do, wherever you want to go, we'll make it easy for you. Alex needs his mother, now more than ever."

Relief flooded through my chest. For the first time in six months, there was nothing—no one—standing between me and my boy. "Thank you," I said. I looked around, at the sun already beginning to set behind the mountains, at the sky, gray and dark, like it was about to rain. "Maybe I should come there now?"

As I said it, there was a clap of thunder. The wind picked up.

"George always said you weren't a good driver in the dark," Ruth said. "And there's a storm coming here tonight. I imagine there, too."

"I'm not," I said, and as I did, I saw lightning in the distance. "My astigmatism makes the headlights look like orbs. But still. Then I'd be out of here. I'd be with him."

"Please, Mary. Don't risk your safety just to get here tonight. Alex is already asleep. He won't know the difference.

And I'm sure you'll have plenty to do tomorrow. Get some rest, then come first thing."

"You're right," I said. "I'd like to get my things from where I was staying in Brooklyn, and then I'd like to go up to my mom's in Old Forge."

"Okay," Ruth said.

"And then I'd like to build a life up there. A quiet life, for Alex and me."

A pause, hanging across the line, but finally: "I know, Mary. George told me as much. But we'd like to be involved with Alex as much as we can. We love him, still. We'll always love him."

Hope blossomed within me. She wasn't going to fight me. This was all finally going the way it was supposed to. George's killer had been caught. No one could hurt me anymore. Not Willa, not anyone.

"And you will," I said. "Alex loves you, too."

It was fully dark by the time I got back to the rental, and the rain that the thunder had promised had begun. I rushed up the walkway, shut the door behind me, twisted the deadbolt, tossed my purse down, and flicked the light on.

The place was a wreck, obviously turned over by the police, looking for the jewelry, for anything to pin this without a doubt on Willa. The empty cups of tea Willa had poured for us were still on the coffee table. Remnants of another life.

I was taking it all in—the sofa cushions askew, the art pulled down from the walls—when I heard something. A squeaky sound, like a drawer being pulled out. Then footsteps.

Was an officer still here, looking? Had I misunderstood Morales when she told me I could go?

Heart racing, I stepped forward. "Hello?" I called out. "What's going on?"

Then there he was, standing in the kitchen doorway, smirking at me like he had every right in the world to be here.

"Henry?" I asked, my heart racing. "What the fuck? You can't just—"

"Where is it?" he snapped.

"What?"

"You know what." He stepped forward, and he was so much taller than me, taller than George. His face was white with anger, his forehead beaded with sweat. He smelled of booze. "The jewelry."

"You *liar*," I said. "It *was* you on Saturday night. You did take my key."

Henry shrugged. "I was going to put it back in the lockbox on Saturday, but I forgot. By the time I remembered, you'd already arrived. So I hung on to it, who cares? And then, on Saturday, I came looking for what's mine. So what? The jewelry has fuck-all to do with you. Now, where is it?"

"Why do you even care?" I spat. "She needs the money. You don't."

Henry's head whipped back, and he let out an awful laugh. Then he stopped, shook his head, looked at me like I was a child who just didn't get it. "Because if I let you people take an inch, you'll go for the whole goddamn mile."

"You *people*?" I asked.

"If I wanted to give her money, I would have put it in a fucking trust. But I *bought* that jewelry. I gave it to my *wife*. She doesn't want the title anymore? Then she doesn't get the rewards. Don't you get it? None of it was ever hers. And none of it was ever *yours*. You can't marry into this. You can't work your way into it, either. And yet you still try, don't you? You and her, you still go after guys like George and me. You pretend not to want the money, but you're desperate for it all the same. Hungry."

"I don't care about the money," I said. "It was never about the money."

Henry let out another horrible cackle. "Keep telling yourself that, Mary."

"Give me that key, and then get out," I said. "Get the hell away from me."

"Gladly," Henry said. He reached into his pocket and deposited the key in my hand. "Shit's not here anyway. I looked everywhere."

He turned away from me, made for the door.

Before he left, he turned back. "Have a nice life, then. Spend the generous life insurance—you know, the money that you care so little about. And if that runs out, don't be surprised if you find yourself begging another man to take you again. Once you've had a taste of this world, you can't let it go."

He smirked. "Just ask Cassandra."

46

MARY

I wanted to go, just leave and go back to Alex, but it was nearly nine o'clock now, and the rain was still coming down. I knew Ruth was right. I was exhausted, emotionally wrecked. It was dark, and stormy, too. It would be dangerous, driving now. And I was Alex's only living parent. I couldn't put my safety at risk.

Still, I couldn't just sit here. I was coming out of my skin.

I texted Rachel that the killer had been caught, that I was going to get Alex in the morning and drive straight to Old Forge, and then used the bathroom, splashed water on my face, put on fresh clothes, grabbed my purse and an umbrella, and headed back to Woodstock's main drag.

Rain coming down around me, I passed the turnoff to Henry's place, imagined him in there right now, drinking himself silly. Festering in anger. The news van was gone, at least, but I doubted for good. They'd probably been tipped off that there'd been an arrest and were down at the police station, hoping to get a bit more of the story. Lucky for me, I would be gone tomorrow. Away from all of this chaos. Old Forge was so removed from the city, the story would have less impact there. I could rest, love on Alex, eat Rachel's raspberry pancakes, and figure out how to move forward from here.

I just had to get through tonight.

The place I'd gone to on Saturday was open, and the same girl was there from before. I stuck my umbrella in the stand by the door, shook off the rain, and found an open seat at the bar.

"The writer, right?" the girl asked as she pushed a paper menu in front of me. "I'm sorry, but I forgot your name."

"Mary," I said, taking the menu, suddenly famished. "And you're . . . Blaire?"

"That's me. How have your first few days in Woodstock been? Did you find a rental? And a daycare spot for your son?"

I glanced at the other patrons, mostly summer visitors—worried about what hike to go on tomorrow, whether six dollars was too much to spend for a local pork taco that had been written up in the *Times*, *not* the details of George and the Haywoods and everything that had happened—then looked back at the girl.

"Actually, I decided it's not really for me. Leaving tomorrow."

"Oh," she said, scratching at her ivy tattoo. "I'm sorry to hear that."

"All good," I said, glancing quickly at the menu. "I'll do the steak and fries. Plus a glass of merlot."

"You got it," she said.

I scarfed down the food as soon as it was before me,

slurped down the first glass of wine and another as well. When my plate was near-clean, my second glass gone, she asked if I wanted anything else.

I looked around briefly. The place was less crowded than before but still going strong. Outside, the rain continued to fall.

I knew I had so much to do tomorrow, but still I didn't want to be alone, didn't want to be back at my rental. So I smiled and ordered a dirty Hendrick's martini—George's favorite.

To George, I thought when the glass arrived, feeling the cool condensation on my fingers, tasting the saltiness of the olive juice, the sweetness of the vermouth, the juniper un-dernotes of the top-shelf gin. To George, who was beyond imperfect, but who I'd loved once and who'd given me the greatest gift of my life—Alex.

I was nearly done with my drink when I heard a voice behind me. "Mary?"

I jolted, and immediately I thought of Henry's massive form, hovering over me, but then realized that the words were not slurred, and the voice was too warm, too kind.

I turned to see Jack. His silver hair took on a bluish cast in the haze of the bar lights, and although he wore a smile on his face, one that crinkled the edges of his mouth, deepened what we called wrinkles on women and "laugh lines" on men, his eyes looked tired. Exhausted, really.

"Jack," I said. "What are you still doing here?"

He stepped closer, then raised his eyebrows. "I went to go talk to the restaurant, and I was about to get out of town when the police called me again. They arrested Willa, but I suppose you know that?"

I nodded. "It was based on . . . well, on evidence I gave them. Right after I saw you."

"I figured as much." Jack pressed his hands against the bar. For the first time, I noticed a pale bit of skin on his ring finger, where he must have worn his wedding band before his wife died. "They wanted me to give more details about my history with Willa. They had lots of questions. Whether I knew about some large set of jewelry?"

"Yes," I said.

"Well, I didn't, but still. The questions went on and on, and I wanted to do anything I could to help. She knows where I live. She knows where Jack Junior goes to play-groups, where I have him starting school in the fall. She has to be convicted for me to feel safe." He sighed. "And to be honest, when you said what you did at the station earlier tonight, it took me by surprise. It was almost hard to believe. But then I started thinking. There were times that she got angry with Jack Junior, times I thought—I don't know—that she needed to get a hold of herself a bit."

"Really?" I asked. "With little Jack? But she doted on him."

"I know, but I think when you live with someone like that, when you invite them into your home, the mask slips sometimes. She never hurt him or anything, not physically, but there were times—only a couple, I promise you, otherwise I never would have let her continue to stay with us—that she seemed almost like she wanted to."

"Did you tell that to the police?"

"Yes," he said. "I told them everything. I don't know what good it will do, since she never actually hurt Jack, but if it helps their case at all, even in the slightest, then I'm glad

I did. And who knows—it sounds like she did this with a lot of men—maybe there are other kids out there that she did hurt. If the police know to look in that direction, then all the better, right?"

"Right," I said. I took a sip of my martini. This, above all else, was perhaps the hardest thing to wrap my head around. I could sooner believe that Willa killed George than that she'd hurt a child, even in the slightest. But I suppose I didn't really know her at all. I suppose every face she showed me was a mask, just like Jack was saying.

"I just left the station," he went on. "But I'm a city boy and also a terrible driver in the dark, much less in the rain *and* the dark."

I laughed. "Same."

"There's nowhere to stay in Woodstock, not at this time of year. I called around from the police station parking lot, finally got a room at a Howard Johnson by the interstate, but the thought of whiling the night away there was too depressing, so I came here."

"I was too depressed to be at my place, too," I said. "Trust me, I get it."

"Anyway, I don't want to bother you. After all you've been through. I'll go grab myself a table."

He gazed at me a moment, waiting for me to say goodbye, but the prospect of company was too big a draw. And not just anyone, someone who'd been duped by Willa maybe even worse than I had. Besides, I wanted another drink, and I'd rather talk to him than stare at my phone, trying to avoid all the people popping into my inboxes to offer their condolences.

"Wait," I said. "You can join me. I mean, if you want."

Jack hesitated, and then he smiled. "I would like to," he said. "I would like to very much."

I felt myself blush and masked it by taking a last sip of my drink. There was something so naturally charming about him, a man the world respects. Well-off, well-to-do, with at least a handful of years on me and a bank account that was likely full of zeros. He wasn't desperate for a friend like me. He was a handsome, rich widower, a loving father; hell, he could have had his choice of women in the city. And yet he'd chosen Willa. There was something so validating in having him here, right now. The sheer presence of him forced me to recognize that this wasn't all my fault. She'd gotten under *his* skin just as she had mine, because that was what she did. And she was very, very good at it.

All I'd ever wanted was a friend. All he'd wanted was a partner, someone who loved his son as much as he did.

We both got lured into Willa's web, but the spider had finally been caught. Had played a game that got too complicated for even someone as cunning and clever as she was to keep under control.

"What are you drinking?" Jack asked.

"Dirty martini. Hendrick's."

"Good choice," he said. "Want another?"

"I do."

Jack signaled to the girl, and soon, a pair of drinks was before us.

I wrapped my hands around the glass, feeling a prickle of hope. I had a long road ahead, I knew that. I had to raise my son without a father, mourn a husband who was beyond imperfect but had been mine.

Still, I was okay, and so was Alex. And Ruth and Frank were going to help me, not fight me, were going to be in their grandson's life as much as I allowed.

Maybe all was not lost. Maybe I could find a way forward. A good one.

I looked to Jack, a smart, successful man, one who might not have even looked my way in any other circumstances, one who gravitated toward the blond and the beautiful, the young and the free, not a mom with strands of gray and a soft belly to prove it.

Yet here he was, happy to share a drink with me.

I felt a spark of something in my gut. Desire. *Longing.*

For a brief moment, Henry's words flashed through my head.

You and her, you still go after guys like George and me. You pretend not to want the money, but you're desperate for it all the same.

No, I thought. This was just a drink shared between two people who had been hurt. Nothing more, nothing less.

"To this nightmare being over," I said, catching Jack's eyes and lifting my glass. "To never seeing that bitch again."

"I'll drink to that," Jack said.

And we did.

47

MARY

We talked about anything and everything, trying our best to avoid mentioning George or Willa.

Our kids, Jack Junior's affinity for mac and cheese and chicken nuggets and Alex's insistence on new words for classic songs. Jack's work, a boutique investment firm and a recent set of fresh-out-of-college grads who demanded more from their bosses—remote work, overtime pay—than the prior generation had. My experiences with journalism, the handful of stories I'd actually truly cared about, ones written years ago, that felt part of a different professional world, one I knew wouldn't be easy to get back to. The *Forbes* piece I was still hoping to write and the CEO I planned on interviewing, when things calmed down. The single life, bingeing TV shows, ordering too much takeout. How Jack had been too nervous to get back into the dating game, how he wanted a woman's presence in Jack Junior's life but knew he had to choose the right woman this time.

Knew he had to be more careful. I laughed, mostly. Jack was funny, his wit dry and almost biting. I laughed and I smiled, and caught in our own world—in the fishbowl of gin and olives and trauma we were doing our best not to discuss—I felt almost absurdly happy, all things considered.

One round turned to two, and soon the place was about to close. Jack insisted on both picking up the bill and walking me home.

I didn't protest, and we made our way down the street, rain still falling, our umbrellas bumping against each other.

"Well, here we are," I said as we approached the rental.

Jack pulled open the gate to the picket fence, ushered me through, and followed behind and up onto the porch and in front of my door.

I turned to him then. It was almost entirely dark, the moon and stars our only light, and a calm breeze whispered through the trees and shrubs, making the foliage dance.

"Thanks for walking me," I said. I tossed my umbrella onto the covered porch and shifted my weight back and forth as I pulled the key from my purse, my head light and bouncy from all the booze. "I would say you didn't have to, but I'm glad you did. I'm still a bit freaked out."

"No way I would have let you out of my sight," Jack said. "Not after everything that's happened."

Jack let his umbrella fall to the ground, his head cocked to the side. His eyes didn't leave mine, and I remembered, suddenly, the first time my college boyfriend and I kissed, standing in front of my dorm on one of those early fall nights that feels like summer. Air warm and balmy, skin sticky.

He was still looking at me. "I had a good time, you know. I'm glad I ran into you."

I tried to still my breaths. "Me, too."

He didn't look away, and I didn't either, and then it was too much, the tension too thick to bear, and I was about to look down when Jack leaned in and kissed me.

At first it was slow, and I felt a hint of stubble on his chin, tasted the salt of the olive juice still on his tongue, but then it was fast, urgent, and I found myself turning, pulling away to fumble drunkenly at the lock of my rental. Wanting to be inside, wanting to be with him. Jack's breath, hot on my neck, sending shivers up my spine, as I scrambled to get the key inserted just right.

Then finally, it was open, and we were in, and I'd barely turned around before his lips were on mine again, hungry, urgent, his hands firm on my back, mine wrapped around his neck.

It felt so good. So incredibly good. Like a drink of water on an unbearably hot day. Like those moments when the kid is in bed and the dishes are done, and you have two full hours to yourself, giddy with overwhelming relief.

I kissed him back, hard, and as his tongue explored my mouth, as his hands tugged at the button of my jeans, I flashed back to that first day I'd seen him, that silver fox on the loop in Prospect Park, a hot dad if I'd ever seen one. The way he'd leaned down and kissed Willa enough seconds to have to count, the way my stomach had lurched with jealousy at their display.

I'd thought Willa had everything, but she had nothing, really. She had built it all on a foundation of sand.

She'd told me story after story—and she'd told Jack, too—she'd slept with my husband. She'd spent time with my son, without me even knowing it.

But for tonight, at least, Jack was mine.

I helped Jack with my jeans, tugged at his belt, my body practically pulsing at the feel of him, hard and solid beneath.

If Willa could see me now, about to screw the man she'd screwed over.

She never would have guessed it, and I never would have, either.

I hadn't been with anyone since George, and it had been so many years, and it wasn't right—it wasn't respectable or smart or dutiful—to sleep with someone else only days after your husband had been murdered.

I should be going straight to bed, trying to get as much sleep as possible before my new life began tomorrow. But I didn't want to.

Jack tugged at my top, pulling it over my head, and I felt the alcohol swimming, grabbed onto his arm to steady myself, pulled his mouth to mine and sucked on his bottom lip.

In the background, I heard ringing—my phone—

For a second, I thought about going to it, in case it was Ruth, in case it was Detective Morales.

It was too late for any of that.

Besides, Jack's hands were already beneath my underwear now, searching. Finding.

Screw it, I thought, and leaned right in.

48

MARY

THURSDAY, AUGUST 19
WOODSTOCK, NEW YORK

Rain on the rental's metal roof. *Pitter-patter, pitter-patter.*

My eyes opened, and through the window, I saw that it was still dark—middle of the night—and I felt, along with the fuzziness in my mouth, the peeling ache along the inside of my skull, the heft, the warmth of another person beside me.

In those first seconds, I thought it was George, I really did.

But the reality of his death hit me before I even made out the figure beside me.

George was dead. I would never wake up next to him again.

Jack was in bed beside me. Wild.

I looked at him, sleeping next to me in the dark. At the subtle rise and fall of his chest, skin taut and glowing in the moonlight. I felt it again, that pull of desire, almost like I could wake him right now, sleep with him all over again.

For a moment, I imagined a life where this was more than a mutual trauma response, more than a one-night stand. Where Jack Junior and Alex still played together, getting along so well, like they always had. I imagined falling in love with this man. Dinners at the nicest restaurants. Last-minute vacations to far-flung islands. Benefits and galas, museums and film premieres and art openings. A life I'd had once, one Henry thought I'd always want.

It wasn't about the money with George, I'd always claimed that, I'd always reminded myself that I was nothing like Cassandra, I wasn't buying flashy jewelry, I wasn't showing off all that I had—only was it, in the end? Did I even know how to really be a mother to Alex without near-constant help? Even since I'd left George, I'd only had my son from Monday afternoons to Friday afternoons. And Genevieve came a couple days a week, to help me with that. I'd spent so long intent on getting away from George, intent on returning to my home, that I hadn't even really considered what would happen when I did.

The dream of being with Jack, of returning to that life, only with someone kinder, more understanding, of building a new future—maybe even having another baby—was so tempting. I mean, why not?

God, I must be still half-drunk. This was all ridiculous. I didn't care for this man. I didn't even *know* him—hell, I didn't know his last name, now that I knew Eric Walton was just another guy Willa had duped, had nothing to do with Jack at all.

I pushed myself up with two hands, and Jack's breathing caught, before slipping into a light snore. I climbed out of bed, pulled on a T-shirt and pair of soft shorts. I needed water and

Advil. I walked into the living room, checked the front door first, no way to shake Henry's visit last night, even if he no longer had a key. The door was secured, the deadbolt just as I'd left it.

I walked to the kitchen, turning on the light. Wanting to check the back door. It, too, was locked, deadbolt just as it should be, but the door itself gave me the creeps. It was windowed on top, six even squares of black. I stepped closer, peering out, but it was too dark, too rainy to see. I could barely make out the curve of a tree trunk.

Someone could see in, but I couldn't see out.

I stepped back, shaking my head. I was being ridiculous, doing nothing more than giving myself the creeps. Willa was in police custody. That was what mattered, above all.

I looked at the clock on the oven. It was after two a.m.

I pulled a glass down from the cupboard, flicked on the tap. In the basin sat the champagne flutes George and I had drunk from. A coffee mug and an errant water glass. Willa must have loaded up the sink when she came back here to make tea. How strange to look at it all now.

I drank down one glass, was about to head to the bathroom to grab some Advil, when I heard it. A sound outside, a *clomp-clomp-clomp*, like feet in wet earth, as if someone was walking around the perimeter.

My pulse picked up, and the water glass in my hand began to shake. I walked back to the front door, flicked on the exterior lights, bulbs that lit up both the front and back, then went back to the kitchen, turned off the interior light, stepped up to the windowed door, peered out.

The lights weren't that strong, but there was enough to see a hazy yellow glow, illuminating the falling rain.

The sound I'd heard could have been anything. A raccoon or a deer, maybe a black bear. Not unheard of, even in town. Up in Old Forge, we saw them constantly.

Still, I didn't spot anything, and my heart relaxed a bit. I was being paranoid, and why wouldn't I be? I had been through hell. I'd seen more this last week than I had in a lifetime.

A sound in the woods was nothing more than that—a sound in the woods.

I turned, once again, making for the bathroom, but then I heard it—

A thump. Clear and strong. As if someone had tripped, the full weight of their body heaving against the side of the house.

I looked to the window just in time to see, on the edge of the light, a shadow.

A shadow making its way across the backyard.

49

MARY

Jack," I said, rushing to his side of the bed. He was snoring lightly, and I reached down, shook him.

"*Jack.*"

It took a moment, but then his eyes were open.

"Mary," he said. "Are you okay?"

"Someone's outside," I said, my voice raising pitch, almost frantic.

"What?" he asked, pushing himself up with his hands.

"I heard a noise," I said. "A thumping, against the side of the house. And then I turned on the outside lights and I saw . . . *someone*."

"You sure it wasn't an animal?"

"I don't think so," I said. "But . . . Henry, my brother-in-law, he broke in here last night."

Jack's eyebrows shot up. "He *what*? You didn't say anything."

"I know," I said. "I should have, I just thought he was done harassing me. But someone is out there. I know what I saw—"

"All right," he said, sitting up. "Let me go check, then. Make sure it's not just an animal. Okay?"

I bit my lip, which was quivering now. "Okay."

I averted my eyes as Jack got out of bed and scrambled into boxers, jeans, and a T-shirt. He went to the main room, and I followed.

"Do you need a flashlight?" I asked.

"No," he said, digging in his jeans, tossing a mess onto the coffee table—receipts, wallet, a phone, which he grabbed. "I'll use my phone." I watched as he opened the door and stepped out, rain falling against the walkway. He turned back, hand on the doorknob. "And stay right here. Don't come outside, whatever you do."

I stood there, heart racing, unsure what to do.

I went into the bedroom, put on my own jeans, grabbed my phone from the nightstand, wanting it close.

It was nearing two thirty now, and my screen was lit up with a flurry of texts, a missed call from Rachel, but another one, too, a call made near midnight, and a voicemail from the same number, too. I reverse searched the number.

Woodstock police. Christ.

I lifted the phone to my ear, hit play.

"Mary, this is Detective Morales. Still have Ms. Williams in custody, but there has been a new development. We have received footage from the Haywoods' security cameras. I suspected this might be the case, as I told you, but the person we've identified from the camera is your sister-in-law, Cassandra

Haywood. *We believe she may have been working in tandem with Ms. Williams. We are still trying to locate her, without any luck. Please be careful. And if you see her or hear from her, call me right away."*

A brief pause.

"Cassandra Haywood may be dangerous."

50

MARY

Heart racing, I set the phone on the coffee table, forced myself to sit down on the sofa, to try to think straight. Morales had said that she suspected Cassandra of the break-ins. The detective's words had been so matter-of-fact.

Cassandra Haywood was at odds with the family. Of course *we're looking at her.*

But I hadn't really ever believed it, had I? Even once Willa had told me that Cassandra had asked her for help, the break-ins had still felt so far-fetched. I could hardly imagine her scrawling graffiti across walls. Cassandra had never had any issues with wealth. She'd always seemed to want it, much more than I did. You didn't cover yourself with Cartier and Harry Winston and then scrawl *Eat the Rich* and *Fuck the One Percent* in paint—did you?

Morales's last words rang in my head.

Cassandra Haywood may be dangerous.

Could Cassandra and Willa have killed George together?

Then I heard it, another thump outside.

My body jolted, instantly in fight-or-flight. I was too scared to go to the back window, too scared to even look. I was playing with fire here, and it felt suddenly too dangerous.

I opened the front door, stepped onto the porch. "Jack!"

I wanted him back inside, next to me. It felt wild that I'd sent him out there in the dark, nothing but his iPhone flashlight to guide the way.

"Jack!" I called again, but the rain was coming faster now, and my words were swallowed up by the wind.

I stepped back inside, my heart racing furiously as the words from Morales's voicemail flashed again through my head.

If you see her or hear from her, call me right away.

Enough waiting. Enough of all of this. I grabbed my phone and returned to my call log, tapped the number of the call I'd missed. It rang and rang but no one answered, and then I got a recorded message, Woodstock police. The station had to be open all night, didn't it? But the staff was probably a skeleton crew this late. Someone could have stepped away from the desk.

I couldn't wait.

I hung up, keyed in 911.

Then I took a deep breath, focused on what I had to do.

Make the call, tell the dispatcher someone was out here, prowling around my property, that I was sure the person was connected to a murder investigation, that they were wanted by the Woodstock police.

My fingers quivered, hovering over the button to start

the call, and I was about to push it when something else caught my eye.

Jack's wallet, the one he'd set on the table when he'd gotten his phone from his pocket.

The wallet had been embossed, words stamped onto it like a cattle brand.

Wright Holdings

Wright Holdings, I thought. Why were the words so familiar to me?

Wright Holdings. *Wright* Holdings.

It hit me like a flash. It was the name Morales had shown to me, the same day I'd seen Willa's full name, Charlotte Anne Williams.

Wright Holdings was the other name on the call log.

51

MARY

Why had Jack called George the night before he died? Was it a terrible coincidence?

Had I slept with a liar?

Worse . . . a murderer?

It can't be, I thought. Willa is in custody. Willa is the one who did it.

Willa Willa Willa.

I set my phone down, grabbed the wallet, flicked it open, looked at his ID—John A. Wright. An AmEx Black credit card and a few business cards:

Wright Holdings LLC

Jack Wright, Owner and President

The door opened then, sending my shoulders jumping.

Jack stepped into the room, shut the door behind him. His hair was wet, raindrops cascading down his cheeks, but his face was calm. "I walked the whole perimeter. There's no one out there."

He looked down to what was in my hand. "What is all this? Why are you going through my things?"

"I wasn't," I said. "I just saw the name on the front of the wallet. And I—" I stood, took a step forward, away from the table, my hands shaking, not understanding. "You knew my husband. You knew George?"

Jack tilted his head to the side, as if confused.

"The company name. The one on your wallet. The company you—" I gestured to the business cards, still spread out on the table. "The company you own."

Jack stared at me.

"Wright Holdings made a call the night before George died. The detective showed the log to me. She asked me to help identify who it was. But I told her I didn't know, that I didn't recognize the name."

Jack didn't look concerned—or guilty, even—only tired. He sighed heavily, and then his eyes connected with mine. "I'm sorry, Mary, I really should have said something. I didn't know."

"Know what?" I said, taking a careful step back.

"When I met you, that first time in the park with Willa, I had no idea you were George's wife."

"So you *did* know him, then?" I asked. "And you knew he had a wife. But he must have said my name at some point?"

Jack shrugged. "Maybe he did, maybe he didn't, I don't really remember. To be honest, we mostly talked about my situation. How much I loved Willa, and then, when we broke up, how much I missed her."

"But how did you even *know* George?" I asked.

"Oh, sorry," Jack said, and smiled. "I guess I skipped that

part. George was my climbing buddy, at the gym in Gowanus. We used to go a couple times a week. I called him the other night to try and arrange something for this week, but he told me he was out of town."

"Oh," I said, and then I remembered that Morales had said the same thing, when she was tying up all the loose ends around the investigation. That they had gotten in touch with the last name on the call log. It was me, after all, who'd confirmed that a call from a climbing friend made sense.

"Remember something?" Jack asked.

"Yes," I said. "The detective told me it was someone from his gym."

"Exactly," Jack said. "Unfortunate timing, on my part, I'm sure. But I really did want to see when we'd be climbing next. I had no idea that all this was about to go down."

I tried to take it all in. "But did you know that George and Willa . . ."

"No," he said. "I mean, yes, I put it together, today, once I realized it was George who'd been murdered. It wasn't until the officer called me that I understood it was him, that we were all connected. See, Willa and I haven't been together in months. I came up here, like I said, because I wanted to report Willa for using my credit card."

"So when did you know?" I asked, heat rising in my chest. "When did you figure it out?"

Jack sighed. "Just this evening, when the officer called me on my business number—those calls route through to my cell when I'm out of the office. They were asking why I'd been calling a murder victim, and I was able to figure it out."

"Did you explain it to the police?"

Jack shrugged. "I spoke to a different officer each time.

I'm sure they'll figure it all out should they think it's important."

"You didn't think you should tell me you knew him?" I asked.

"Well, when I saw you at the police station, I didn't know. It was only later, when the officer called me."

"But you said you had to go back down to the station."

"I did," Jack said. "To give a statement on Willa. That was separate from the phone call about the call log."

My eyes narrowed, but Jack pressed on. "I know, Mary, I know how it sounds. And okay, you caught me, I didn't explain to the police that the guy who'd come in about the stolen credit card was also the same one on George's call log. It felt like it would complicate things. Just give Willa's defense something to hold on to. And if she doesn't actually get convicted for this, I don't know how I'll ever feel safe. Not when she knows so much about Jack Junior."

"Okay," I said. "Okay." There were things I'd held back from the police, too, at first, afraid of turning the spotlight on me. I got that, I did. Especially when you felt like your kid could be in danger. I cleared my throat. "But what about me? Fine, you didn't want to tell the cops, but you could have said something to me."

Jack cocked his head to the side. "I wasn't planning on seeing you, Mary. And then you were in the bar, and you asked me to sit next to you . . . and then . . . this just kind of happened."

He stepped closer, and I didn't move away. "But I was happy it did, and not just because we were both drinking. I feel like you understand what happened to me more than anyone else. And I didn't know how to explain it to you last night, but I told myself that if this was something—if it was more to you than just a drunken hookup—that I *would* tell you. As soon as I got the chance." He smiled. "I *want* it to be something more. I really do."

He leaned in then, and his face was so close, I could almost taste him.

Then his lips were on mine again, and all I felt, in the midst of everything, was this strong and powerful wanting.

Wanting to believe him.

Wanting to trust.

Wanting all the bad feelings to sink beneath the surface, where I didn't have to feel them anymore.

I pulled back, breath in my throat, fingers pulsing with energy, desire laced with fear.

For a moment, I thought maybe I did believe him.

Then he tilted his head to the side, and in the light, in the glistening wetness of his rain-soaked hair, I saw it. It had been too dark there in the bar, and then I'd been too drunk, but under the lights in here, it was impossible to miss.

Spatters of red.

I thought of blood first, but I reached up, running my hand along his scalp, and I felt it, the plasticky feeling of latex remnants.

It wasn't blood.

It was paint.

Like the paint that I'd used on our brownstone's door in Brooklyn.

Like the paint that George had brought up here, to patch test on Henry's door in Woodstock.

Like the can I'd seen there at the crime scene, a paintbrush bobbing within, so close to the mess of George's bloodied body. Bright red paint.

Paint that had been used to scrawl words against the wall.

DIE RICH PIG

Farrow & Ball Lake Red.

52

MARY

Oh my god," I said, backing away. "You were with George that morning."

"What?" Jack asked, eyebrows scrunching up. "I wasn't. I came up to speak to the police about Willa."

"The paint," I said. "How did the paint . . . how did it get in your hair?"

"Paint?" he asked. "What are you talking about?"

I remembered when I had painted that stupid door I'd loved so much, when I'd dripped some on my ponytail, how some of it still clung, even after several showers. "Wear a shower cap or hat when you paint next time," Rachel had told me, when I'd complained. "Mom and her DIY ways really should have taught you better."

Jack hadn't had time to protect his hair. He'd been too busy . . .

"The words—on the wall—it was, it was—"

"Mary, are you okay? You've been through a lot, I know, but you sound a bit paranoid right now."

Morales had agreed with me, that the graffiti might have been nothing more than a diversion. I'd thought it was Willa's diversion, but it was Jack's.

"I think you should go," I said.

"Mary," he said firmly. In a flash, something passed across his face, and his whole demeanor changed, and for the first time, I saw it in his eyes: raw, vicious anger. "It's the middle of the night. It's pouring. You can't just throw me out."

I stepped farther back, my legs bumping into the coffee table. My eyes scanned the room for my car keys, but I couldn't see them. Everything had been tossed down in a drunken mess. Jack was in front of me, blocking my only exit to the door.

"What's got you so scared?" Jack asked. "Willa is in custody. There's no one out there. I walked around the whole place."

I took another step back, but the leg of the table caught me. I fell, my hands landing against the cups of tea Willa had spilled earlier. An awful clattering, and Jack looked down, towering above me.

"I'm not scared," I lied. "I'm just . . . I'm tired."

"Come now, Mary," Jack said. "You're being silly."

He reached for my hand, grabbed it, then leaned over, practically pinned me against the coffee table.

"Why?" I asked. "Why were you there that morning? Why did you write that on the wall?"

"Write *what*, Mary?" And then he cocked his head to the side, eyes widening as if he'd only just remembered. "'Die rich pig,' pretty clever, don't you think? George always going on and on and on about the damn break-ins, how they were driving his family crazy."

My breaths came short, but Jack only leaned forward now, pressing me even harder into the coffee table. Something solid dug into my back. It took me a minute to realize it—my phone—was 911 still keyed in?

Jack stared at me, nothing but rage there in his eyes. I'd ruined everything, I realized. I never should have said a word. Never should have asked. Should have pretended I never saw the wallet. Never saw the paint in his hair. I thought of Alex, Alex who I was supposed to get in only a matter of hours. I had to get back to my son.

"Please," I said, my voice begging. "I won't say anything, I swear. There's nothing to say, anyway. Willa killed George. Willa's in custody."

"Willa." Jack spat the word, droplets landing in my face. "You know I loved her, was getting ready to propose and everything. Thought she was a perfect mother to little Jack. And she was, for a while. Until I found out she was fucking around on me."

Desperately, I tried to give him what he wanted. "She was a bad person," I said. "She did that to everyone. Not just you. But she's arrested now. She'll be locked up for a long time. This is over, if we want it to be."

"George brought this on himself, you know. He *invited me*, Mary," Jack said, his hands squeezing so hard I winced. "He asked me to come when I called him Sunday night, when I got the alert that Willa had used my credit card up here. Told me he was going to be with you all day anyway, that his brother had already met with the contractors and left. Told me he was on his way to winning you back. That the place would practically be mine."

I tried to wriggle from him, but he only pressed harder, squeezing me against the table.

"But George didn't expect me to get in early, did he? Didn't expect me to see Willa walking out of his place, hair a mess, clothes barely on. He knew I loved her. He knew she was everything to me. He knew I was heartbroken when she cheated on me, when I threw her out. I told him everything, Mary, don't you see? I bared my soul. While he went on about stupid shit like the goddamn break-ins, some meaningless graffiti, and I'm telling him how the love of my life, the only person I ever felt even a tiny bit happy with since my wife's accident, how she's been fucking around on me. And the whole time it's with him. And when I confronted him, he didn't even have the decency to deny it. Calls Willa a filthy slut and says he did me a favor. A favor! Fucking the love of my life!" Jack's face was red with anger, his forehead sweating, his hands squeezing against my arms.

"Please," I said. "Let me go. I have a child. He needs me. I won't tell anyone."

Jack's mouth morphed into a cruel grin. "Oh, now you want to be the good mother," he said. "Even though you knew what Willa did to me and you still were running around with her up here. You're as bad as she is. But joke's on all of you," he spat. "George fucked Willa, but now he's dead, and she'll go down for it. And now I'm in *your* bed. The one thing he really wanted was to have you back. But I got mine instead. How's that for karma?"

I stared at him, and it was suddenly so clear. All of this. Jack showing up at the bar tonight, being nice to me, when he could have gone back to Brooklyn, when he'd already gotten away with it all. No, he wanted to have his cake and eat it, too. Take something of George's. Because Willa and I, we were no more than possessions to these men.

I realized something awful then—I was no different than Willa, was I? She said herself she fit herself into boxes, into the spaces men needed filled. But didn't I do it, too? Wasn't I contorting myself to be what they all wanted? George or Cassandra, Willa or Jack? I was afraid to be on my own. Only moments ago, I'd been looking at Jack, at a monster, wondering if something could happen between us, if I could twist myself to fit the hole left by his wife, then left by Willa, so we could build something together, so I wouldn't have to figure it all out on my own.

Fuck that.

Alex, I thought. Alex, I love you. More than anything.

And if I make it out of this, I'm going to stop trying to find someone else to complete me.

It's going to be you and me, buddy, and we're going to figure it all out.

I looked at Jack then, and I saw murder in his eyes. And I had to get out of this. I *had* to. For Alex. For the life I could live on my own.

I sent my knee right to his crotch, and he unclenched my hand, keeled over.

I flipped around, saw the phone still there, 911 waiting, tapped to make the call.

A wrench in my shoulder, and Jack spun me around, the phone clattering to the ground. "Why the fuck did you do that?" he asked, both hands on my shoulders now, shaking. "You think you're going to beat me?"

I shook my head, tears in my eyes now. "You won't get away with it."

Jack tilted his head to the side and again pinned me back against the coffee table. "Don't you see? I already have. I'm the one who killed him. I'm the one who grabbed that stupid paperweight on his bookshelf, slammed it against his skull. Proved to him that you can't take something that belongs to someone else, turn another man into a fucking cuck. And when Willa came back, probably begging for more, I'm glad she found him dead. Glad that whoring around finally caught up to her."

His elbow came up then, his forearm squeezing my neck, pressing, cutting off air, as he hefted the whole weight of his body against mine.

The edges of my vision went blurry, and I scrambled to kick, to fight back, but I could barely move. He was so strong, and I was nothing beneath his power, his anger.

The room began to spin, and for a second, I imagined George doing the same thing to Willa, pressing his hands to her neck. And in that moment, it seemed like all the men in the world only existed to overpower us. Henry, George, Jack. Maybe Willa had only been surviving, all this time.

It was time for me to survive, too.

Jack's body pressed harder against mine, but I managed to wiggle my arm away, scramble for anything still left on the table. And then there it was, ceramic and hard, the last drops of cold tea spilling from it as I grabbed a handle.

I took every bit of energy I had left, and I lifted it, and then . . .

Smack!

Suddenly, Jack was falling away from me, and I was gasping, choking, desperate for air, Jack prone on the floor near the table.

"Holy shit," I heard.

I looked up, and she was there, a shovel in her hand.

She rushed forward and lifted it above her, bringing it down on Jack, again and again and again, until he wasn't moving.

Then she stopped, looked down at me, still holding the shovel in her hand, straight out of *American Gothic*. "We need to get the fuck out of here."

I nodded, pushing myself up, and let her take my hand.

My old friend. Who I hadn't come through for, when she needed me. Maybe if I had, we could have avoided all of this.

But she'd come through for *me* in the end.

Cassandra.

53

MARY

s he dead?" I asked, looking at Jack, lying beneath us, disarray all around him.

"I don't think so," Cassandra said. "Just out."

She helped me to my feet, and as she did, Jack stirred, let out a light groan.

She lifted the shovel and popped him again.

"Oh my god," I said. "Don't kill him."

"He'd deserve it. I saw what he did to you. But don't worry. I didn't."

She tugged at me and I followed, only stopping to slip on my sandals, then out through the doorway, onto the porch. She tossed the shovel into a corner, and it clattered against the railing. We rushed down the street, my hand in hers, rain pelting us now, to an old Honda on the corner. Cassandra tugged at the handle, and I ran around the side. "My phone," I said. "My things."

"There will be time for that later," Cassandra said. "We have to get out of here. *Now*."

Inside the car, I took her in properly. She was wearing all black, her hair pulled back into a messy ponytail, and there were scratches up and down both arms. She shifted gears and stepped on the gas, the car jerking forward.

"I need to talk to the detective," I said. "It wasn't Willa. I think she was in the wrong place at the wrong time. It was him. I need to go to the police station. I have to tell them."

"Don't worry," Cassandra said. "I'll take you there. But I can't stay."

I nodded, told her the way, and it was only as we approached Tinker Street that I saw it there, looped around her left hand, the velvet bag, drawstring cinched.

"The jewelry," I said.

"*My* jewelry," Cassandra clarified, making the turn.

"You came here to get it?"

"Yeah," Cassandra said. "Willa used her phone call to talk to me. She told me where she hid it, right behind a prickly-ass rosebush. I was in Pennsylvania. I drove as fast as I could. I'm sorry, I know I freaked you out making noise back there. But I had to get it—without it, I have no money. And lucky I did come when I did. Christ. That man would have killed you."

"The police told me you were behind the break-ins, the graffiti. That they saw you on one of the camera's footage. I was worried you and Willa somehow worked together . . ."

Cassandra sighed. "We did work together, to get back my jewelry. But nothing else. I hate Henry, and yeah, I hated George, too—I'm sorry—and for a while I even hated you, but I wouldn't have killed anyone. And if I would have, it would have been Henry," she said with a scoff. "Not George."

I looked at my old friend, and for a moment, it felt like we were two girls at the gala again. There had always been that underlying sense that neither of us quite fit in, even if Cassandra played the part better than I did, and now, here we were, outside it all—both of us. "Ruth said that you slapped Henry once, that she saw you."

Cassandra pulled onto the road, her eyes locked straight ahead. "I did, once. I was drunk, and he said something so cruel to me . . . it just happened. I know that's what abusers say, that it's not an excuse, but—" She shrugged. "It never happened again. Though I guess that's what abusers say, too."

It was a shock to hear her admit it, and yet there was something, too, a fairness in it, knowing who Henry had become.

"But why all the break-ins?" I prodded.

"Because at first I didn't think of Henry going to George. My first guess was that he hid the jewelry in one of the properties. I mainly knew where the security cameras were, and I was careful to plan my entrances and exits around them, but I guess not quite careful enough, if something turned up. Although I don't know quite what they're going to do about that. I was still technically married to Henry when they all happened. I had every right to go into one of my own houses. And there's no way a camera saw the vandalism."

"That part was you, too, then?" I asked. "The detective asked me if I thought you could have been responsible for the break-ins, a couple of days ago, but I didn't believe it, not until she said she had you on video. I couldn't see you writing that."

Cassandra turned to me, smirked, and for a moment, it

felt like we'd picked up our friendship exactly where we left off. "I knew it would totally piss him off."

"But you don't really believe all that stuff, right? I mean, when you were wearing Cartier every day?"

Cassandra raised an eyebrow. "Total hypocrite, right? Like, who the hell am I to talk? But, you know, I didn't always want all of this, not at first. So much of it was Henry. The perfect hair, face, clothing, jewelry. And yeah, I did embrace it. And there were years when I know I was just as insufferable as I looked. But—" She took a deep breath, and tears came to her eyes, running down her cheeks like the water rushing down the windshield. She wiped the tears away and turned the wipers up higher. "I really saw, being on the other side of them, that no one should have that much money. Because when you have so much, so much that no one else can ever, ever match you, then you have power, too. Power to hurt people, just because you want to. Just because you think it's some game. I mean, do you think Henry needed my jewelry? Of course not. He only wanted it to deprive me of the gifts he'd given, of the money he knew I needed. So—" She shrugged. "Maybe it's not all that crazy to say the things I scrawled against their perfect walls. Maybe it actually, I don't know, makes sense."

I took a deep breath, taking all of this in. She was right, wasn't she? The Haywoods had tried to do the same thing to me, and if George hadn't been murdered, maybe they would have won, taken everything from me, Alex included. The thought was chilling.

The police station came into view, and I pointed it out, but Cassandra drove past the turnoff. "I can't go inside with you," she said. "Not when I finally have what's mine."

She veered off the road, slowly, onto the shoulder, put the car in park. Then she turned to me. "Charlotte Anne isn't a bad person, you know. She was just trying to help me, through all of this."

I shook my head, not ready to just brush it all way. "She conned me," I said, tears once again in my eyes. "She slept with George, she let Alex see her and George together. Do you know how confusing that must be for him? All the while she was pretending to be my friend."

"I know," Cassandra said, and she reached a hand across the console, taking mine in hers. "But girl, I loved you, but you chose him. You chose them. And when I asked for your help, you said no. Charlotte Anne said yes."

"I know," I said. "I'm sorry for that. I'm sorry I was too scared to help."

"Charlotte is actually a really caring person, you know. She was the only one who had the guts to tell me what she really thought of Henry. Because she loved me, she really did. And I bet, in some way, she loved you, too, even while she was doing things that hurt you. Because that's what she feels for her friends. That she would do anything for them."

"Still," I said. "She could have found another way."

"Maybe, but this was her way. And I know, deep down, she wanted to do the right thing. And anyway, she certainly doesn't deserve to go down for a murder she didn't even commit. I know there's the evidence you found, but Charlotte told me it was just from her trying to cover her tracks, once she unexpectedly found him dead. And I believe her."

I hesitated only a moment. "After tonight, I believe her, too. And don't worry. I'm going to tell them everything."

Cassandra nodded. "Tell the police what happened. Tell them about that horrible man. Protect yourself. But please, I'm begging you. Leave me out of it—leave the jewelry out of it. I could have left, you know? I had what I came for. I didn't have to help you. But I couldn't let you fight him alone. I love you, I still do, even with all the shit that's gone down between us."

Tears ran down my cheeks, and I struggled to brush them away. "I love you, too."

"Then do this for me," Cassandra said. "Please."

I hesitated only a moment.

"Of course," I said. "I would do anything to help you now. I hope you know that."

It was still pouring by the time my wet sandals tracked across the hard linoleum of the police station.

In the fluorescent lights, my shirt was practically see-through, my hair hanging, dripping, at my sides.

"Oh my god," the officer behind the desk said. She stood up, rushing around the desk and over to me. "What's happened? Are you okay?"

"No, I'm not," I said. "I was attacked."

I took a deep breath, and the weight of everything seemed to fall off me then, like raindrops cascading onto the floor.

"I was attacked by the man who killed my husband."

54

MARY

I love you, Mama," Alex said.

I leaned over, tucking the covers tight around him—he was in his big-boy bed, shaped like a race car, for only the third night, but so far, it was going fairly well. "I love you, too, sweetheart. It's sleepy time now. Big day tomorrow."

I hugged him, holding him close, feeling his soft locks of hair on my cheeks and taking in the scent of him—laundry detergent and grass and baby sweetness—then stood, made for the door.

"One more song, Mama?"

"Of course, baby. Of course."

"Twinkle, twinkle, little star . . . like a dinosaur in the sky . . ."

I had to sing the song three more times to be exact, but soon enough, Alex was in his sleeping position, hunched over, legs tucked beneath him like a frog, covers pushed all about, and the door was shut. I had a few hours to myself before I'd be crashing into bed.

I knew I indulged Alex—maybe a little too much—but it was hard not to. I had come so close to never being able to hug him again. An extra song, another sip of water—it was nothing, and I gave it happily.

I walked down the staircase, hand on the banister, the gorgeous original wood, one of the few things, along with the wide-planked floors, that I would not be updating when the renovations on the old Victorian started next month, the thing I'd fallen in love with the moment the agent had opened the door—and Alex, too: "Big stairs, Mama, wanna climb big stairs."

I walked into the kitchen, still littered with moving boxes, and popped a dinosaur-shaped chicken nugget into my mouth, the rest into a Ziploc, then put the tray into the deep sink. Grabbing a wineglass, one of the first things I'd managed to unpack, and filling it with pinot noir, I stared at the boxes. There was so much to do, and my sister was taking Alex tomorrow, had a full schedule planned—zoo, ice cream, and maybe even a pumpkin patch—but still, I really should get ahead of it.

In one of the few open boxes, I found Alex's journal, which had surfaced when the brownstone was cleared out. I grabbed it and one of my favorite pens, then made my way over to the massive leather couch, one of the few holdouts from my Brooklyn life, and sank against the cushions. I checked Alex on my phone—he was squirming around in his bed but looked close to sleep—then opened the journal, flipped to a new page.

My hand hovered over the blank lines, wondering how I could possibly sum up today.

Sometimes it was hard to believe that this life was really mine. I would wake up with that pinch-me feeling, that after thinking I'd lost everything, I was here, living in a home only miles from where I'd grown up, near my mom and my sister. Back exactly where I'd wanted to be.

It had been a wild couple of months.

The police had found Jack still passed out in my rental— alive, but only barely conscious. He'd been taken to the hospital, then into police custody. I'd been worried—terrified, really—that no one would believe us, given all the evidence stacking so easily against Willa, but the 911 call I'd attempted had actually gone through. My whole conversation with Jack had been recorded. It was irrefutable. Cassandra's voice had been on there, too, of course. But I'd told Morales that a neighbor had found me, helped me, driven me to the station. I got the sense that maybe she didn't believe me fully, but I'd stood firm in my statement. I'd done my best to protect my friend, this time, at least.

Morales explained to me that per Willa's own statements, she'd gone to George's that morning to discuss him threatening her, had arrived to find him already dead. Had slipped in the blood and used the only thing she had in her purse—the diaper—to clean herself up. Just like Cassandra had said. Willa was released after twenty-four hours, though I didn't see her again before I left to get Alex, to start my new life.

On my phone, I watched Alex's breathing settle into a rhythm and took another sip of wine.

My transition into single motherhood had been easier than I expected. Between George's life insurance and the stipend Ruth and Frank had set up so their grandson would be well taken care of, I had more than I needed. Enough to buy a three-bedroom Victorian. To pay for a good preschool. To provide a cushion while I tried to get back on my feet as a journalist. I had managed to interview the CEO for *Forbes*, and the piece had been published and made its rounds on the internet. I was starting to get more and more assignments, but still, journalism checks took forever to come in. I couldn't have done it without my safety net.

I knew I was lucky, so much more privileged than most. And I'd made two promises to myself. First, that I would use this freedom, this security, to be entirely me, to stop looking for someone else to complete me, to make me whole. The second promise was to never forget just how lucky I was.

I tapped out of the video monitor app and returned to the journal.

Was it a perfect existence? No. Was I lonely sometimes? For friends, for affection, for sex, for the excitement of the city, even if I always felt I had to be "on" there? The ability to meet someone new and fun, seemingly at random?

Of course, but I had learned something powerful. Loneliness couldn't destroy me, not as long as I stayed true to myself.

I began to write, detailing how Alex had turned the moving boxes into gigantic blocks that were perfect for climbing on and making a fort.

I knew I was in the right place now.

. . .

I'd written a few pages when I heard a knock at the door. I jolted, checking my phone. It was nearly nine o'clock. A friendly new neighbor wouldn't come by this late, and my mom or sister surely would have called.

My heart ticked up a notch as I stood, made my way for the door, peered out the peephole.

There she was. Her hair blond again, like it used to be, her eyes bright and eager, her sapphire necklace catching the light against an orange fall sweater.

The person who'd lied to me over and over and over again.

The person who, despite my promises to myself, I sometimes still missed.

55

MARY

Willa," I said, opening the door.

She smiled, cocking her head to the side. "I'm back."

"What are you doing here?"

We hadn't spoken—not so much as a text—since everything had gone down. Part of me felt bad for believing the worst of her, but the other part knew I had nothing to feel bad about—there had been so many lies, it had been impossible for me to separate reality from fiction.

"Right," she said. "I kept going back and forth about whether I should call first, but in the end, it seemed best to just show up. Plus, I lost my nerve on the drive over."

"How did you even know I was—"

"I have my ways," she smirked. And when I didn't smile back: "Nothing illegal, promise. I guess you bought this place, right? You pay one of those companies fifty bucks and they'll give you all the public records. It's nice, by the way."

I nodded. "Thank you."

She bit her lip, shifted her weight from foot to foot. She wore stylish but comfortable sneakers, jeans cropped at the ankle, a chunky sweater, and a leather moto jacket on top. No more Balmain, Moncler, or Chloé, but she looked fantastic, still. More than that, she looked happy. Almost . . . at peace.

"I'm leaving the country tomorrow," she said. "Starting fresh." She reached into her handbag, pulled out a small navy pouch. "But I really wanted you to have this."

She pressed it into my hands, and I took it, feeling its weight, lifted the flap of the pouch, and pulled it out.

A Cartier Love bracelet, in warm rose gold. No diamonds. No frills. Just the circle motif that felt so clean, so timeless. I had wanted it, this exact one, but George had always thought it was too flashy.

"Cassandra said this was your favorite. It's the only one we didn't sell. Thank you for covering for us."

I ran my finger along the smooth, hard edges of the bracelet. "Thank you," I said. "Of course, I'm not sure a country girl in Old Forge can pull off Cartier."

"You can pull off *anything*," Willa said with a smile. "Trust me, Mary. After what I put you through, you've earned it."

I laughed, then slipped the bracelet onto my wrist, taking a moment to admire it. "I guess I have."

"Well, I should be going," Willa said, shifting her weight once again. "I just wanted to give you that . . . and to say I'm sorry. For everything."

I nodded, then stared at her, standing on my front porch. "Unless you want to come in?"

Willa eyed me a moment, as if to see if I really meant it, and then finally: "Okay," she said. "I'd love that."

I poured her wine, grabbed us a couple of waters, and we set up in the empty living room amid the boxes, a single reading lamp illuminating us. We talked about Alex and how he was adjusting, and we talked about where she'd been these last two months—back in the city, but on her own this time, on her own for the first time—and when I was on my second glass of wine, I finally got the nerve to ask her.

"What happened that morning, with George?"

Willa pressed her lips together, then took another sip of wine.

"You didn't sleep with him again, did you?" I asked hesitantly, knowing it would hurt me if she did. "Because Jack thought you did."

Willa shook her head. "George saw me in town and followed me home to Rich's that last night, the one before he died. He threatened to call the police if I didn't give him back the jewelry." She shrugged. "I knew I couldn't, but I'd just seen you that night, and you'd told me that you slept with him. I figured he thought he actually had a chance to win you back. And I don't know." She eyed me. "Maybe he did."

"Go on," I said, not wanting to answer. It was something I hardly understood myself. I hadn't wanted to go back to George, but would he have worn me down, had all of this never happened? I honestly didn't know.

"When I went over that morning, I told George I'd tell you everything if he bothered me anymore. He seemed to accept it, and it all would have been fine, but then I couldn't help myself. I taunted him. Said what I really thought of him, how pathetic he was."

My eyes widened. "And he . . . hurt you?"

"Yes," she said, the sinews of her muscles tightening. "He lunged at me, hands on my throat. He squeezed so hard I passed out. He might have killed me, but then finally I came to, and I could tell he was as freaked out as I was . . . I would never have gone back, if not for my necklace. See, when I moved to the city, I'd left this stupid controlling prick behind, and when I got my first real set of tips at the restaurant, even though I owed Cass money, she said I should treat myself. It was totally irresponsible, but it was like a personal fuck-you to my ex, a celebration of leaving. Something mine, just mine, that a man didn't give me. The jeweler let me finance it through some program. I paid a hundred a month for it for a couple of years. I couldn't let George have it." She sighed. "I grabbed a rock on the way over, for protection. For a moment, I thought maybe I could do it—kill him—I was so angry, at what he'd done to you, to Cass, at the way he'd nearly killed me. But when I got there, he was already dead." She laughed. "I can't imagine what you thought when you overturned my bag and saw the bloody diaper. You must have been so sure."

"I was," I said as I took it all in. "But I know now I was wrong."

She fingered the necklace. "Thank god Morales let me have it back when I was cleared. All of that and to still lose it in the end—would have been tragic."

I laughed briefly, then looked at Willa. For the first time in our entire friendship, I felt like we were on equal footing, messy as it was. "Why didn't you tell me that you were over there that morning?" I asked. "Before, I mean. We could have gotten ahead of it."

"You never would have believed I didn't kill him. And I don't blame you, after everything I did to you."

"You know, Jack said you almost hurt Jack Junior," I said. "That he thought you might have actually hurt other kids."

"Never," she said solemnly. "I hope you know that about me."

I nodded. "I do."

I was quiet for a moment, then felt moisture in my eyes. I brushed away a tear. "You know, Jack choked me, too," I said. "That last night."

"I'm sorry, Mary. I'm so sorry that happened to you. I'm sorry I didn't warn you about him. I never thought in a million years he would kill George, but I knew he wasn't a good person." She paused, as if considering. "You know, the police in the city have reopened the investigation into the death of Jack's wife."

"What?"

"He told me she died in a car accident, but it wasn't that at all. She fell down the stairs. And you know, when someone falls down stairs, it's almost never an accident."

"Wow," I said. "Christ."

"Right?" she said. "I hope he rots. I hope they all do. They're all the same, all of them."

"You don't really think that," I said.

Willa took another sip of wine. "Sometimes I do. You know, I read somewhere that of the one in four women who experience domestic violence, something like sixty percent of them will be strangled. Can you believe that? It's like some kind of instinct, in these men. Push the right buttons and their hands find your throat. Rich was the only nice one. I suppose we should all go for Marxists!" She laughed. "And even he was still shit at splitting the mental load."

I laughed, too, but then I pressed my lips together, serious again. "Alex won't be like that," I said.

"No," Willa said. "But only because you'll raise him right." She set the glass down, looked at me, eyes wide, earnest. "Because you are good, Mary. Real and good."

She smiled.

"And in my new life, I hope to be, too. I hope to make up for everything I've done."

56

MARY

Willa stayed too late to drive back to wherever she was staying and crashed on the couch, but when I went downstairs, just after seven a.m., she was already gone, a note left behind on the hall table.

Thanks for everything, Mary. Enjoy your new life. You've earned it. Xx

Rachel wasn't due to get Alex until eleven a.m., and he was bouncing off the walls by eight thirty, so I filled a bag with Goldfish and juice boxes, and we packed into the car, headed to the closest playground, one with cedar play structures, that was nestled in the woods and entirely empty, apart from us.

Alex was careening across one of the bridges and toward a ladder, perfect for climbing, when a woman and another toddler approached. Her kid looked to be about Alex's age, and he rushed up to join him, not missing a beat. Alex smiled at the company, and the two chased each other back and forth across the wooden bridge.

"Talk about an instant connection," the woman said. She wore a Patagonia fleece jacket and yoga pants, her hair pulled into a neat bun.

I smiled. "Alex has been spending too much time with me. He's desperate for another toddler."

The woman laughed. "How old?"

"Turned two in July."

"Reese in August. No wonder they're on the same wavelength."

We turned back to watching our kids, running from one bridge to the next, taking turns on the massive slide, climbing and tripping and just being kids, one of us rushing in if they needed water or a snack or to be held after a boo-boo.

At ten thirty, I told Alex it was time to head back and as we packed up our things, the woman came up to me. "I'm Sarah," she said. "If you want to trade numbers, we could do a playdate sometime? The boys are getting along so great."

I hesitated only a moment. But then I smiled, feeling brave. "I'd love that."

She handed me her phone, and I punched my number in, and Alex gave Reese a hug before we headed to the parking lot, the two of us mothers promising to arrange something for next week.

When we were back in the car, Alex strapped in tight, the speaker playing Disney songs on a loop, the sun beaming through the windshield, making the rose gold glow around my wrist, I realized something.

For the first time in a long time, I wasn't scared to be alone.

But for the first time in a long time, I wasn't scared to give a person a shot, either.

After all, I thought, laughing to myself, everyone is trustworthy when you compare them to Willa.

EPILOGUE

WILLA

SATURDAY, DECEMBER 25
ST. MARTIN, THE CARIBBEAN

The sun was warm on my skin, nut-brown after these last two months, and the piña colada was cool in my hand. From the beach bar, the sound of "Mele Kaliki-maka" drifted across the golden sand.

I took a sip of my drink, savored the sweetness of the pineapple, the rich crème de coconut. It was shaping up to be the best Christmas I'd had in years. Maybe ever.

I thought of Cass, who had spent the last week bouncing around the island with me, whose plane had touched down in Santa Fe just yesterday—she'd insisted that Christmas Eve in her new home was something not to be missed. Art and paper lanterns on every street.

Santa Fe, I thought. What a choice! But there was something lovely about it, too. Very Georgia O'Keeffe escapes to the desert. And she'd actually found a cool job running PR for one of the museums there. Not to mention, the place had the most gorgeous silver and turquoise jewelry, things that Cass could actually afford on her own. She'd been practically jingling with bangles when I'd picked her up from the airport a week ago.

I took another sip, thinking about Mary, probably opening piles of gifts with her mom and sister, Alex screeching with delight. I wondered if they'd gotten to the little one I'd slipped in the mail before Cass came. A stuffed sea turtle I thought the boy would adore, signed with love from Aunt W.

Dear, sweet Mary. She'd been through hell, but she'd gotten what she'd wanted in the end: freedom.

Course, I'd gotten freedom, too.

And now, here I was. Sunning on a beach, not a care in the world. I'd spent months now not answering to anyone but me. I didn't have to worry about someone kicking me out of their fabulous home. Or taking care of their kids. Or keeping another man waiting in the wings if things went south.

I didn't have to worry about anything, really.

Nothing to do but lie in the sunshine, drink piña coladas, and read Agatha Christie.

I picked up the paperback balancing on my stomach, maybe the twentieth I'd read since arriving here. The woman at the used bookstore on the Dutch side had already come to know me by name.

I read for a good hour, was nearing the end, when Hercule Poirot was about to break down the whole thing—murderer, motive, the works—when I felt a splash of water against my foot.

I looked up. A little girl—three, maybe four—in a teal swimsuit, who was dripping with water from head to toe, was pointing at my toenails. "Purple is my favorite color. Daddy said Santa would bring me a purple teddy bear, and he did."

"Oh, did he?" I asked, wiggling my toes back and forth. I rested my book back on my stomach and sat up a little straighter in my lounge chair. "And what else did he bring you?"

"Chloe!" A man emerged from the water, shook his hair, and ran up behind her. "We don't bother people when they're relaxing."

The little girl ignored him, detailing this morning's haul. "A guitar, three bracelets, and a new Lego set." She beamed.

Sorry, the guy mouthed, but I smiled, mouthed *It's okay* right back. I couldn't help but notice the ripped, gym-five-days-a-week body, the expensive waterproof watch—Panerai—the distinct lack of a wedding band.

"And I'm getting more when I get back home," Chloe pressed on. "Mommy said Santa brought gifts to her house, too."

The man shifted his weight from foot to foot, sheepish. "First Christmas since the divorce. I may have gone a little overboard." He gestured around to the magic of the island. "Now, come on, Chloe, we don't want to bother this nice lady."

"Oh, it's okay," I said. "I love kids."

"Well, you're certainly good with them," the man said with a grin.

I hesitated a moment, then pushed my sunglasses up on my head, let him get a real good look at me, delivered my most killer smile.

He didn't know the half of it.

ACKNOWLEDGMENTS

I can't express enough thanks to all the brilliant and talented people who worked so hard to turn my wild idea about a mom-friend who's actually a con artist into a book I can hold in my hands.

As always, none of this would have happened if not for my incredible agent, Elisabeth Weed, who remains my number one advocate, book after book, and has fought so hard to build a career for me that I could once only dream of. Thank you so much to the entire The Book Group family, and especially DJ Kim, who somehow keeps all of us meticulously organized (no easy feat!).

To Danielle Dieterich, I am so thankful that our paths crossed at just the right time for you to be able to work on my books. Your passion for feminist thrillers has truly helped shape my career, and I couldn't have plotted this book without your impeccable ideas and notes. To Kate Dresser, thank you for so graciously stepping in, reading, and giving me the kind of notes that scared me silly at first read and I soon learned I could not live without. This book was waiting for the brilliant Kate touch before we could call it done, and I'm so glad to have your perspective on all things Mary and Willa, not to mention Brooklyn parenting! To Sally Kim and the rest of the Putnam team, I can't thank you all enough for continuing to believe in my career from one book to the next, and I can't wait to publish loads more with you!

To Grace Long, Joel Richardson, and everyone at Michael Joseph, you continue to make my across-the-pond book dreams come true and give me all the twisted little plot ideas I never even knew I needed. Joel, I will never stop laughing that you got me to turn a Pull-Up into a key murder-scene clue. I'm so thrilled that we get to keep on working together and publishing alongside so many of my favorite British authors.

To Jenny Meyer and your incredible team, including Heidi Gall, I am always so thankful for the care you've taken in pitching this book around the globe. Thank you so much for helping get it into the hands of as many readers—and countries!—as possible.

To Michelle Weiner and everyone at CAA, thank you so much for always advocating for me and giving me pinch-me moments that I can still hardly believe. I can't wait to see what comes next!

It's usually hard to say where exactly book ideas come from, but for this one, the origin story is quite clear. Picture two friends, catching up over a spa day, sitting in a hot tub talking over their next projects. One tosses out a seed of an idea—what if a woman makes a mom friend at a playground and later runs into that same friend in another town with a whole new family?—and the other won't stop talking about how cool it is until you've suddenly got the bones of a whole thriller plot. Thank you, thank you to Julia Bartz for the silly conversation that turned into my favorite book yet. Willa will always be Dawn to you and me, I promise.

As always, I am forever grateful to my brilliant beta readers, Andrea Bartz, Danielle Rollins, and Kamala Nair. Andi, thanks for the many, many park walks and frantic phone calls it takes to write a mystery. Danielle, your eye for plot, pacing, and theme theme theme is unmatched. And Kamala, it has been so fun to reconnect as beta readers and to bring characters to life with your wonderful notes.

This book is, in part, inspired by my own journey diving into the parenting social scene with a toddler in tow. I am so thankful, first, to my Sweeties, Beth, Chrissy, and Kate, for having my back in all things motherhood. And second, to the wonderful women and families who are doing the daily grind of parenting in Park Slope with me. Alex, Marie, Michelle, and Natalya, thank you for becoming the community I didn't know I couldn't live without! This book could not have been written without our frequent trips to Harmony Playground and Daytime Coffee! And a big thanks to all of my mom friends for not being con artists!

I've been surrounded by a team of writer cheerleaders my whole life, and I want to thank my parents and my sister for always believing in me, reading and buying my books, and never doubting whether this little writing thing could be a real career path.

Finally, to my wonderful little family, thank you for being there with me through every word and respecting when "Mommy is working," so I never have to choose between being a mother and being a writer. I'm lucky to have all of you.

KEEP YOUR FRIENDS CLOSE
DISCUSSION GUIDE

1. *Keep Your Friends Close* opens with a startling moment. What was your immediate reaction to the scene, and how effective was it in grabbing your attention?

2. *Keep Your Friends Close* is narrated in first person, allowing us to become intertwined with Mary's and Willa's inner thoughts, observations, and judgments. How did this affect your reading of each character? To what extent can you trust Mary or Willa?

3. When Mary first befriends Willa at the playground, Willa says, "It can be hard to connect with other women—for me, at least." In what ways did this statement make Willa more appealing to Mary? What did that statement tell you about Willa, and what did Mary's response tell you about Mary?

4. The story alternates between past and present, each section picking up a detail from the previous chapter. How did this structure maintain the story's mystery? Did you have a preferred timeline and narrator?

5. *Keep Your Friends Close* speaks to female friendship, but author Leah Konen's depictions of Mary's relationships with Cassandra and Willa also hold sinister qualities. How does Konen achieve this? Which friendship were you most intrigued by, and why?

6. Early in the novel, Mary encounters Willa after not seeing her for months, and Willa pretends to be someone else. How would you have reacted to a friend in the same situation? Do you agree with Mary's reaction?

7. In various forms, the women mention their desire for freedom—both financially and socially. How does motherhood exacerbate or reconcile their feelings of entrapment with their desire to be free?

8. *Keep Your Friends Close* is set in Brooklyn and Woodstock, New York. How do the settings impact the characters' ability to play "hide-and-seek" with each other? Which location was the most claustrophobic to you— the big city or the small town?

9. We see a glimpse of both Mary and Willa after the action of the novel has ended. What was your reaction to the ending? Were you satisfied by the resolution to the mystery of who killed George? What do you think is next for Mary and Willa?

LEAH
KONEN

**"Nobody writes twists like Leah Konen—
this woman puts Hitchcock to shame."**
—Andrea Bartz, author of *We Were Never Here*

For a complete list of titles and to sign up for
our newsletter, scan the QR code

or visit
prh.com/leahkonen

ABOUT THE AUTHOR

© Kate Lord 2019

Leah Konen is the author of the thrillers *You Should Have Told Me*, *The Perfect Escape*, and *All the Broken People*, as well as several young adult novels, including *Love and Other Train Wrecks* and *The Romantics*. Her books have been published in nearly a dozen countries, and her essays and articles have appeared in *Marie Claire*, *Vogue*, and more. She lives in Brooklyn and Saugerties, New York, with her husband; their daughters, Eleanor and Mary Joyce; and their dog, Farley.

LeahKonen.com
🐦 LeahKonen
📷 LeahKonen